ONE

Colden sank down onto a log. Its spongy decay gave way slightly, like a firm pillow, under her weight. She shifted from side to side a bit, searching for comfort. She was tired—not from the several hours of hiking, but from looking, trying to find those things that survived by remaining invisible. Her tiredness was the sort that comes from long concentration with little reward for the effort. There were things she was supposed to be looking for that she hadn't found—the elusive moose and beaver that made these woods and mountains their home and were the basis of her research, the cornerstone of her current scientific life. Then there were the creatures she hoped to find, members of a ghost species that might not exist at all.

On the search, she thought. *I am always on the search for something that doesn't want me to find it.*

The world around her was stripped of color, the many deciduous trees denuded of their recent riot of death-throe hues. A harsh, upstate New York winter was on its way. Bark, branches, sky, and ground were all slight variations of the same dirty-dishwater brown. There was an expanse of similarly colored water, stretching the length of about two flooded football fields in front of her. It was less than a pond, more than a marsh, with edges defined not by banks, but by cattails and wild irises, reeds, and low shrubs. Colden released a plastic bottle from the side pocket of her pack and squirted a stream of lukewarm liquid into her mouth. A breeze puffed up and subsided, chilling the sweat on her skin and corrugating the surface of the wetland. She shrugged her well-used backpack off her shoulders, yanked her binoculars over her head, and rubbed her face in her hands. A few leaves drifted down from the limbs overhead, tacking back and forth on the still air before settling among the dense layer already covering the forest floor.

She sighed, propped her elbows on her knees, and put her chin in her palms. She stared into the middle distance, resting her eyes and her mind. For many moments, the world seemed empty and silent. Then, small sounds reemerged. A rustling in the dry leaves. A chipmunk, probably. A crow *grocked* somewhere over the far ridge, its call unanswered and yet un-lonely. Wingbeats in the underbrush. The smallest possible wake appeared in the middle of the flat surface of the wetland, and the eerie cry of a loon crossed the open air. She watched, waiting for the bird's distinct silhouette to come into focus at the point of the *V* trailing out behind what appeared as no more than a black spot on the pond. But the shape did not form. Because while it was certainly a loon she heard, it was not a loon she was seeing. She squinted. The dot on the pond came into focus. It was the large nose of a beaver, cresting just above the water's surface, pushing a small branch as it paddled purposely forward. She turned her gaze in the direction the critter was headed. Ah yes, there on the far bank was a dense thicket of horizontal saplings, all woven into a mound that created a cozy den with an underwater entrance by blocking some small stream pouring its watery self into the pond.

BENEATH *the* TREES

Laurel Saville

ISBN: 1548831948
ISBN 13: 9781548831943

Cover design: Meghan Pruitt
Author photo: Brooke McConnell

She stared, watching the beaver approach. Then, right next to the lodge, a substantial tree with what appeared to be a wide span of dense branches came to life, its limbs shaking and dripping with water. But in this, too, her initial impression was wrong. Not a tree, but a magnificent bull moose lifting his heavily antlered head out of the muck, wet aquatic plants swaying from his mouth.

This was what she'd been looking for all day. This was what, she admitted to herself in times of exhaustion and vulnerability, she was tired of looking for. Yet, as so often happened, just when she'd given up, there it was, right in front of her.

Colden watched the moose move its jaw from side to side. She watched the beaver continue its homecoming, undisturbed. Her binoculars were at her feet. Her notebook was just an arm's length away, in the side pocket of her backpack. Her camera was there as well, alongside her digital data recorder. She should reach forward, release the tools of her trade, and put them to work. This was what she was there for: to study, record, and analyze the relationship between beaver and moose; to try to understand how the marshlands created by the semiaquatic rodent and favored by the large ungulate were affecting the health of each; to ascertain why the population of beaver, once hunted almost to extinction in these Adirondack forests, was growing, but the population of moose, after years of crashing, had barely recovered. Her academic credentials, granting sources, and eventual career depended upon what she found, figured out, and published.

But in that moment, all her scientific training, all the frustrations and boredoms of her research, all the striving and yearning to discover something, completely left her. In that instant of seeing nature manifest its quiet, unassuming routine right in front of her, she was no longer a grad student, a PhD candidate, or a wildlife biologist. She was once again what she had been so many times before: just a young woman in a remote area of dense woods, tucked between a couple of mountains, on a damp day in late fall, sitting silently, absorbing the mystery and beauty that surrounded her.

TWO

A week later, Colden was as close to a moose as she'd been in more than a year. This one was female, young, likely born the spring before. A local cop had called her about it. She, in turn, had called her dad. He met her on a small gravel turnout at the side of a narrow road hemmed in by trees, in the interior curve of a tight S-turn.

Colden paced around the animal.

"Sad," her father, Dix, said.

"Yes," Colden replied. "This girl was in her prime. She likely had plenty of years of productive breeding ahead of her."

Dix sucked his teeth. His hands were stuffed in his pockets. She knew he was waiting for her—not just to finish her examination, but also to calm down. She was angry. Frustrated. It was one thing to lose an animal to a predator. All creatures killed other things to stay alive. Plants were as alive and as complex and interesting as the deer that munched their fresh growth into oblivion. Black bear had as much right to live and provide for their cubs by taking a fawn as a mother deer had a right to protect her baby from bear predation. Sometimes the hard hooves and powerful legs of the mother deer won. Sometimes the curved claws and sharp teeth of the bear did. She and her father hunted deer, and many of her neighbors hunted and trapped to eat and make a few bucks so they could stay alive themselves. For Colden, all of this was neither politics nor philosophy—it was science. But this moose had not died as part of the normal course of living. This one was taken out by a tourist from New Jersey driving too fast on a back road. The car was damaged and towed. The driver was fine and taken to a hotel. The moose was killed and dragged to the side of the road.

Colden retrieved her sample kit from her truck. She took photos of the moose, cut some hair samples, pulled some blood, and made notes on the animal's overall condition and low parasite load. Then she nodded at her father. He went to his truck and unloaded four large coolers from the back. He then fetched a leather sheaf from the passenger seat and unrolled it in the dirt, revealing several gleaming knives, two of them almost as long as his forearm. He handed one to Colden. He took the other. They began cutting the animal apart.

This was familiar work for them; together, they had hunted, field dressed, and butchered a dozen deer in her life. This project was different, as the animal had been sitting for a few hours, and even though the day was cool, they wouldn't be eating the meat themselves. They didn't hang, skin, or gut the animal. They just hacked off the back legs, rump, and shoulders and jammed the coolers with messy hunks of fur and meat. They worked in silence. When the coolers were full, they opened bags of ice into the remaining spaces and dragged the remainder of the animal off the roadside and into the scrub. The local scavengers would make quick work of what was left. They rinsed their hands and forearms in a nearby stream. They stood side by side, drying their hands with rough towels. Dix used the corner of a towel to wipe a smudge of blood off Colden's cheek. She let him.

"I was supposed to be in Albany by now," she said.

"Why don't you wait until tomorrow?" Dix replied.

"I shouldn't."

Dix eyed her. Colden knew he knew that there was no reason she had to make the two-and-a-half-hour drive this afternoon. She also knew that he knew she would be glad to delay her return. She was not fond of all the people and sidewalks, cars and horns, conversation to be made, and traffic to manage. Nor the walls and hallways, buildings and elevators, cubicles and computers. She was used to stillness. She had spent countless hours hiking in the shadows underneath the heavy canopy of evergreens and deciduous trees that carpeted the mountain landscape where she had grown up and had canoed across silent ponds with nothing but the loons for company. Backpacking and camping for days on end made her forgetful about personal grooming and used to eating food made tasteless by dehydration. She'd rather be in her little cottage nestled into a far corner of her parents' property than in her bland condo on the outskirts of the state capital. She liked being someplace where her home and truck didn't need to be locked. But Albany was where the university was, where her department, colleagues, undergraduates, meetings, and reports were. She had to spend time in the city so she could get back to the country so she could work to protect all of this, for herself and everyone she knew or cared for and for plenty of people she didn't.

"OK. You're right," she relented. "No need to drive this evening."

"Why don't you take a couple of these coolers over to . . ."

"Yeah, I had the same thought."

"OK, we'll see you for dinner."

"What's it going to be?"

"Lasagna. Salad."

"Yum. My favorite."

"I know. Sally's, too."

They loaded the coolers into their trucks and parted ways, driving off in different directions. The sweet and bitter scents of dried mud from her boots and sweat from her body tickled her nose. She'd be back to clean clothes and regular showers soon enough. She'd get her hair trimmed. She'd buy new underwear. She'd get some good Mexican food. She'd see a movie. Small compensations. She'd also spend hours curled on the sofa of her apartment grading undergraduate papers and critiquing research reports. She didn't have any friends in Albany—it was impossible to maintain connections when she was there so infrequently. And she didn't have much need of friends. She hated hanging out in cafés and restaurants, chitchatting and gossiping. Her parents were her friends. Together, they formed a tight trio with few needs beyond one another and their various distinct but overlapping interests. Colden regularly gave herself internal pep talks about the efforts she should put into widening her circle. It had been a long time since she'd had a gal pal, a date, a boyfriend. Yet she rarely took her own advice.

She kept driving into the bright, dry, late-fall day. Snow and frigid temperatures would be here soon enough. She rolled down the window and let air, as crisp as a fresh apple, fill the cab of her truck. She shook off her dread of returning to classes and city life, her foul mood over the death of the young moose, and found the driveway she was looking for. At the end of it, there was someone whom she could call a friend. Not friends in the way of the city, where connection was made by sharing conversation and meals, but a friend in the rural way. Here, connection came from a nod and a beep as you passed on the road, from small snippets of conversation tossed back and forth as you pumped gas at the local Stewarts convenience shop, from gossip, handed over like illicit currency, and from whispers about someone in need, which was invariably followed by the unannounced appearance of a man with just the tool required for the necessary repair, the driveway anonymously plowed, a bag of groceries or load of firewood dropped off with no more than a wave of a hand expected or required by way of thanks.

Colden made her way up the quarter-mile drive and stopped her truck in front of a small cabin made of rough-sawn timbers and siding. She gave her horn a light tap to announce her presence, even though her truck's tires on the gravel had already done so. Killer, a compact and furious ball of terrier muscle and indignant barks, shot out from a small gap in the barn door. His attack quickly subsided into happy yips and dancing on his back legs. Jake, sixty pounds of indeterminate breeds, roused himself from under the porch, stretched back from his long front legs, moseyed over, and leaned his yellow body against her. Buck, the wolfdog rescued from a zoo that had closed down several years ago, bought with $200 quickly scrabbled together from the sale of some marijuana plants, watched her, unmoving, from his perch near the front door. His serene yellow eyes were neither wild nor domesticated, but he allowed his tail a few perfunctory thumps against the well-worn floorboards. Lucy, the now three-legged pittie who had been found, broken, bruised, scarred, and scrawny, by the side of the road after someone threw her from their truck and sped off, wobbled around from the back of the woodpile, wiggling her whole body so hard that she toppled over before she quite got to Colden.

Colden squatted in the patch of old gravel, dry weeds, and dirt that served as a parking spot and submitted to being licked, pawed, and muddied. She listened for the familiar clump, clump of crutches. The front door of the cabin swung open, banging itself on the wall, and a twisted, shrunken gnome of a man waddled out.

"Well, ain't you a sight for sore eyes," Gene said in mild reproach. "Where you been keeping yourself?"

Colden smiled and said, "Oh, the usual. Out in the woods."

"Collecting moose poop?"

"It's a tough job," Colden replied. "But someone has to do it."

"I see the welcoming committee has assembled," Gene said, smiling at his dogs.

Colden smiled back, and as she did, she also took in the man's weight and pallor. She looked for redness in the eyes, deeper twists in the body, any sign of gauntness or disease. He seemed no worse than the last time she had been there, a couple of months earlier. She stood and shook off the dogs.

"Brought you something," she said as she walked to the back of her truck and lowered the tailgate, revealing the stark white, blood-stained coolers.

Gene tipped his head back and howled like a wolf. Buck joined in, his voice more plaintive and musical. Killer yipped. Jake let fly a few low barks. Lucy looked from dog to dog to human to dog and then back again. This circus dissipated any remnants of Colden's bad mood.

"We love roadkill!" Gene hollered and then clapped his crutches together. "What did you get this time? Flatlander? Downstater? Some preppy from Connecticut?"

Colden laughed. "No, Gene. Just a local moose."

"Guess whoever hit him lived?" Gene asked, pouting.

"Yes. A tourist from New Jersey. And his girlfriend."

"Little late for leaf peepers to be cruising around up here," Gene said as he shambled down the two tilting steps off the porch.

"Maybe his disappointment that the leaves are all down was why he was speeding south," Colden said as she shoved the coolers down the truck bed. "Drove their little sports car right underneath the moose. Lucky for them, she flipped up, over the top of their car, and broke her neck in the fall onto the pavement."

"Driver hurt?"

"Nah. Car totaled, though, I guess."

Gene let loose a long cackle, like someone crumpling stiff paper for a fire.

"Serves him right."

"Yeah, she was a beauty and a young one. Real shame."

"Get any data off her?"

"Little bit. Fortunately, she wasn't one of the moose we radio-collared last winter. They're all still out there, wandering around."

"Gonna attract aliens with those things if you're not careful."

Colden shook her head and jumped down from the truck.

"Gene, it's hard enough for us to find the moose we put them on. No one from outer space is interested in moose."

"Set aside any meat from uninteresting moose for your dad and his dogs?"

"Oh yeah. He got plenty. There will be lots of happy canines at Ragtag Farm."

"How many he have up there now?"

"It varies. He does try to get most of them adopted. There are a few that aren't likely to go anywhere anytime soon."

"Good use of that property."

Colden felt her stomach tighten in on itself for a moment. It passed quickly. She knew people thought the property her father had turned into an animal sanctuary was cursed. Plenty of tragedy had transpired there. But Colden was not one for curses or conspiracy theories. Yet, she was also not one to spend time correcting other people's closely held misconceptions and badly supported beliefs. She was aware that sometimes these were all they had between themselves and complete, soul-sucking despair.

Gene's dogs were hovering and sniffing around the tailgate of her truck. She reached into a cooler and tossed each dog a hunk of moose. Then she went into the dark barn and found a hand truck. She off-loaded the coolers and wheeled them into a nearby shed, with Gene hobbling along behind her. There were two freezers there, wrapped with chains and a lock. Gene removed the chains, and they transferred the meat, hosed off the coolers, and returned them to the truck.

"Sit a minute?" he asked.

It was rare for Gene to ask for company. He lived off the grid in a variety of ways, and he didn't like people nosing around his patch of property or asking questions about how he acquired enough money to keep himself in dry gas for his vehicles and twelve-packs for his spirits. If he was asking her to stay, this meant there was something he needed or wanted to discuss, and it was likely he'd take a circuitous route to get to whatever it was. Colden nodded and joined him on the porch. Gene sat in a battered rocker, and Colden sat on the edge, swinging her legs in the emptiness. They stared up at the blue sky, swept with streaks of wispy clouds.

"Won't have many more days like this," Gene observed.

"Nope. Sure won't," Colden said.

They listened to the dogs cracking bones.

"How's things going out there?" Gene waved his arm vaguely toward the wall of woods that was no more than fifty feet away from any of the walls of his home. "Find your Sasquatch yet?"

"Nope, not yet," Colden said. "He break into your shed lately?"

"Nope. Last time I got a good shot off. Scared him a bit, I 'spect."

"Scared Lucy pretty good, too, it seems." Colden had noticed that the dog would not follow her into the shed like the other dogs did.

"Something spooked her good, that's for sure. Weren't me."

"Steal more gas?"

"Nope," Gene answered. "Not this time."

Last time she'd been here, Gene had claimed that a half-full gas can had gone missing, but she didn't see how he could possibly keep track of what he did and didn't have in the chaos of machinery parts, broken-down snowmobiles and ATVs, miscellaneous power tools, and other detritus that littered his outbuildings.

They sat in the long, low light of early evening, listening to the dogs licking their paws. Colden tried to surreptitiously look around the yard. The woodpile seemed big enough to get Gene through most of the winter. The freezers had plenty of game, even before she added the moose meat. The dogs seemed healthy and well fed. She'd learned to make these discreet observations from watching her father do it. Anytime she visited people with him, she'd noticed his eyes flitting over this and that, assessing what might need fixing, how prepared the people and place were for whatever season was coming next. Then, as they'd leave, she'd listened to him muttering his little concerns: hope they have enough oil because there's not enough firewood to get them through the season; that dog was scratching an awful lot, needs some flea treatment; corner of the barn going to need a jack . . . These were not complaints or criticisms coming from her father but more of a to-do list. Things he'd keep an eye on and fix if whomever they were visiting didn't or couldn't do it themselves. Colden glanced over at Gene's scrap pile. There were fewer old cars and appliances in it than he'd had in the past. It was getting harder for him to do that kind of repair work. There was also less need for it. Fewer and fewer things could be fixed with a wrench or screwdriver these days. Everything contained and required a computer to run. Gene didn't even have a phone.

"How's the scrap business?" she asked.

"Good enough."

"How are your other business interests?"

"None of your business interest," Gene answered. "What I grow is only for personal and medicinal consumption."

"OK. Well then, how are you feeling these days?"

"Also none of your business."

Colden glanced over at the band of skin showing between the bottom of Gene's pants and the flattened heel of his shoes. No swelling. Normal color. Just some reddening from broken veins.

"Stop it, Colden," Gene said.

"Just checking."

"I'm fine."

"You weren't this spring."

She'd found him stuck in a corner of the barn, one of his legs twisted beneath him, unable to get up, with no one near to call for help. She'd come because Buck was running on the main road, barking frantically at every passing car. Of which there were only a few. Finally, someone stopped and called the local police. Who called her father. Who knew the dog and came over with Colden. Because Gene had broken his back when he fell from a roof years ago, he hadn't even felt the sprain in his leg that had happened when he stumbled off a rickety stool he was using to reach for something on a high shelf that day. He also had diabetes. He wasn't exactly what the doctors referred to as "compliant" in his treatment.

"I'm too ornery to die," Gene said. "God don't want me."

Colden sighed.

"Chemtrails," Gene said, gesturing upward with his chin toward a dissipating white line bisecting the sky.

"Vapor trails," Colden said, shaking her head.

"That's what they want you to believe, girl.

"They, Gene? Who's this 'they' you're always referring to?"

"You know who they are. You go down to Albany. It's full of politicians and lawyers and executives. Those dudes. They're seeding the sky with chemicals that thin the atmosphere. They're doing it bit by bit, and eventually, it will destabilize things so much that those guys in the Middle East can take over."

"Where'd you hear that, Gene? Some late-night cable TV guy?"

Gene shook his head. "I don't have TV."

He used to.

"Got rid of the damn thing," Gene continued. "Didn't want the government spying on me. Radio is good enough. Better."

Colden didn't know if he actually believed these conspiracy theories or just spouted off to try to get a rise out of her. He didn't get much company. There were a few old coots who stopped by from time to time. Most, or maybe all, of his family was long gone. Generations of them had lived and died out here, scattered in many small towns throughout the Adirondacks. He was the last of a dying breed of mountain man.

Colden had been inside his cabin only once. She'd poked her face in through the door, looking for him. She was surprised to see the walls lined with shelving and stacked milk crates full of books and journals. She'd asked her dad about it. He'd told her that Gene had gone to college. A good one. Somewhere Ivy League or almost Ivy League. Had gotten a scholarship. Then an internship. People had stepped up to help him because he was smart and capable. But something happened out there. Meaning away from the mountains. Heartbreak or disillusionment or some sort of setback. Maybe he just didn't want to assimilate to the way the rest of the world worked. He was not a nine-to-five, much less an eight-to-seven, sort of guy. He'd quit whatever job he'd had and taken off, hitchhiking and train jumping. Had a bunch of adventures he used to talk about and several he never discussed. Ended up in Canada, got arrested on a small drug charge, and was sent home.

Some relative gave him this dank piece of land with nothing but an old hunting camp on it. He kept adding to it, using mostly duct tape and bailing wire, until he got it to basically the shape and size it was now, about eight hundred square feet, with no right angles in the whole place. He was a handyman, hunting guide, scrap dealer, taxidermist. Sold so-called antiques on the roadside. Had a hot-dog stand for a bit. Almost died a couple of times, like in the fall from the roof that broke his back. Just about froze to death in a snowmobile accident that took the tips of a couple of fingers and toes. People dropped off stuff for him to sell, old pallets for him to cut up for his woodstove, an extra deer haunch. He had a big garden. He made moonshine. Grew and sold a little pot. Painkillers, he called the rotgut and weed. People took care of him as he allowed them to, and no one needed to make much mention of it any further.

Sometimes, Colden wanted to know what he had studied, what his earlier life had been like, what words were on the spines and inside the books piled up indoors. But she would never ask him. There would be embarrassment, maybe even pain in those stories. He had enough physical aches as it was. She would not add others to his burden. It was enough to know that people were not often what they seemed. Or at least had not always been what they were now. She had learned from her parents to accept people for who they were and never underestimate who they might have been.

"Sasquatch. Chemtrails. Spies. You have an incredible imagination, Gene," she said fondly. "You should write a damn book. You'd make big money."

"What would I want big money for? What when I've got paradise right here," he said, gesturing with an outstretched hand.

"Impossible to argue that point, Gene," she conceded.

"You're a scientist," Gene said.

Colden nodded.

"You're getting your Post Hole Digger degree."

"Working on it."

"Point being, Miss Almost-Got-Three-Letters-after-Her-Last-Name, point being, as you know, as you're staking your career on, there is much out there yet to be discovered. There are many things we don't know or understand. Many things yet to be explained."

"It's true."

"I like to wonder about things," Gene said. "I like to think there are still plenty of surprises out there."

"Me too," she said. "Me too."

Gene shuffled to his feet, signaling the end of the visit.

"Tell your father to get his sorry ass out here to see me one of these days," he said, grabbing for his crutches.

Colden resisted the urge to stand and get them for him. He'd just wave her away. He'd said what he needed to say, and this was as close as he'd ever get to a direct request for assistance. If he needed a visit from her father, he needed something fixed. He was asking her for help and dismissing her at the same time. The latter took the sting out of the former, for him. She stood, stretched her back, and patted every furry head as she made her way back to her truck. She gave a little wave as she left and looked into her rear-view mirror just in time to see the back of his hand pop up over his shoulder before he disappeared inside his book-strewn cabin.

THREE

Brayden ran. Not to get anywhere, but to get away. To get into the deep quiet of the woods, away from people. Away from mirrors. He hated seeing his own face. The shadows that hung around his eyes, the hangdog set of his jaw. He hated how defeated he'd come to appear. How people's eyes slid away from him. He felt marked. Like that woman in the book they'd read last year, his junior year, the woman with the A *emblazoned on her chest. His mark was nothing so obvious. Nothing with that sort of clarity. Which made it worse. Teachers, people at church—he was convinced they knew something was wrong. They just didn't know what. And didn't want to find out, either. They didn't want to get caught up in something. Or find themselves knowing something they couldn't do anything about. Didn't want to do anything about. So he ran until his lungs screamed at him to stop. Like that year he ran track. Then he collapsed and waited for the wilderness to close in around him. For the small sounds of the tiny birds skittering in the leaf litter, the distant call of a loon echoing over a hidden body of water, the harsh hack of a raven splitting the still sky to take up residence inside his own head, and in their improbably insistent way, drown out the other noises that were there, the grunts and coughs, the sighs and moans, the shuffling feet and mumbled apologies.*

FOUR

Colden drove into an Albany that was gritty and gray. She had an indistinct and reluctant fondness for this old city, with its odd mash-up of architectural styles, where leafy, tree-lined blocks of Victorian row houses and an ornate, hand-carved stone capitol edifice butted up against a large plaza of brutalist buildings projecting into the empty skies. The highway and its multilayered collection of curving overpasses ran along one side of the Hudson River, brown and stagnant in this in-between season; decrepit factories lined the other shore.

Colden's university and nondescript condo were in the vague outskirts of not-quite-suburbia, a few miles from downtown. She didn't go there. She went directly to the heart of the city, to the State Archives. There was some research she wanted to do. It was not about moose and beaver, her officially sanctioned work—she had a side project, a personal interest, something she had many reasons to keep to herself. She walked down the long, sterile hallway, grateful that she didn't by chance run into some research colleague who might ask questions about what she was doing there, until she found the room she wanted. It was quiet, the tables and equipment impersonal, the fluorescent lights stark and somehow not particularly illuminating. What she was doing felt illicit, like she was at a cheap motel cheating on a boyfriend. Still, she found and slowly opened the drawers: there they were, canid bones. She carefully removed the skulls of a wolf and a coyote. She spent an hour taking measurements and photos, comparing jaw structure, head shape, teeth patterns. She spent another hour just staring at them, tilting her head and moving around the table to take in every detail, every nuance. She made a mental map of each specimen and tried to sear the image into her brain so that she could call it up later, at will. She was hoping that staring at these skulls would help create concrete connective tissue between the hazy bunch of impressions and inchoate ideas that had nestled in various parts of her brain, like small animals waiting for a warm day to come out and play. She imagined the coyote skull covered in flesh and fur; she did the same for the wolf skull. Then she tried to imagine an in-between creature, something that had some of the raw power of the wolf, along with the lithe adaptability of the coyote. She'd never seen such a hybrid, but she'd heard they might exist, way up north, over the border in Canada. She was wondering—in truth, hoping—they might be migrating south.

She couldn't confer with anyone she worked with about her suspicions. If other, more prominent scientists, who were better at getting grants and publications than she was, scented on this trail she was exploring and thought it might lead to interesting places, it could be overrun and thereby destroyed. At least for her.

The spell of the bones was suddenly broken. They'd given her no answers but plenty of interesting questions. It was thrilling to think about something other than the beaver and moose, which had occupied her mind for the last year or so. It was also thrilling, in a world of collaboration, detailed reporting, and lots of checks and balances, to have a secret line of inquiry all her own. She carefully replaced the materials she'd borrowed, packed up her personal belongings, and wandered her way down the anonymous corridors until she found herself back on the street.

It was late afternoon, in the middle of an early November week, in the midst of a lull before the holiday storm. It was too early for dinner. Ungraded papers from the online course she was teaching awaited her at the office, as did an empty refrigerator at the condo. She wasn't expected at the department until tomorrow. She felt restless and unsure of what to do with herself, like a bored teenager with a list of chores from Mom.

Her enthusiasm for her research was starting to feel drowned in the minutiae of data. She'd hoped for big discoveries, but everything she was finding seemed only incremental, like another small layer of stone on top of a wall already built by others. Another beaver moved from its natal home and dammed another stream a few miles away, then was shot by an irate guy from downstate who didn't want the back field of his summer home flooded. Another moose was plagued by parasites that compromised his health and biting insects that made him run himself ragged in the summer so he couldn't put on the necessary weight to get through the winter. There was nothing she could do about any of it, except keep collecting more repetitive information. She had to keep going, see the project through, and hope for more, for something sexy and exciting that could eventually influence policy, something she increasingly thought would never happen. City people didn't care about beaver or moose—they were nuisances to be harassed into moving off your own property and something to be avoided on the road. Long hours in the field left her feeling estranged from her department, but she had no desire to spend more time in the office than was absolutely necessary.

And there was this new guy. Larry. Ick. A full professor who worked long hours and had a creepy vibe. Being around him left her feeling like there was a film of oil on her hands that she couldn't wash away. Unfortunately, he'd taken an interest in her work—it was well funded and relatively high profile in the department if nowhere else—and she'd need his support to defend her thesis. He was unavoidable. It all felt oppressive.

But today, he could be dodged. Today, she'd take a walk instead of getting back in her car. She headed up the hill toward the stretch of blocks that held a cluster of boutiques, restaurants, and galleries. She felt a bit clumsy, as if her shoes, accustomed to dirt, were protesting the concrete underfoot. Everything around her seemed a bit shabby. Which was just how she felt—as if she'd forgotten to brush her teeth this morning. She thought back to those dark, predawn hours in her cottage. No, yes, of course, she'd brushed them. Her hair? Probably not, but her teeth, certainly. Colden tried to focus on the Victorian architecture, the intricate details, the wrought-iron gates and fences. But the early commuting cars, the belching buses, the bumping of shoulders when she passed people, the heaved pieces of concrete on the sidewalk, all made her feel awkward and distracted. She thought she'd duck into a gift shop and leave the street behind, but there were two people sitting on the stoop out front, scowling and smoking, and she didn't want to squeeze past them. Just ahead, at the next corner, was a very busy intersection, with clusters of people padded and invisible behind layers of winter clothing, hanging around the bus shelter, bodega, Indian food restaurant, and ATMs. It seemed vaguely sinister, full of dark potential. She didn't want to navigate all that, either. Then she saw a sandwich board advertising a coffee shop. That would work. She could use a caffeine hit.

The shop was shoe-horned into the lowest level of a brick row house. The windows were half below grade, and there were a few small chairs and tables padlocked to a black iron fence that ran along the sidewalk. She took a few steps down, past the corkboard layered with band posters, "For Rent" flyers, and event announcements, dodged the listing pile of alternative weekly newspapers, and stepped to the counter. The floor of the place was made of bright squares of colored laminate. Small acrylic paintings, in a style she thought of as so self-consciously abstract it must be the work of undergraduates at the nearby art school, hung on the walls. She was relieved to see no other people sitting in any of the mismatched chairs at the half dozen small, tile-topped tables. She and the person working there, a man about her age, with a scruff of facial hair, discs in his ears, and a few tattoos clawing their way up his neck, stared at each other for a moment. She realized with a sense of confused embarrassment that she was waiting for him to ask for her order, and he was waiting for her to just give it to him. She was accustomed to getting her coffee by pumping it from a thermos at the same place she pumped her gas. She asked for a medium latte.

"Grande," he said, annoyed.

Seriously, she thought, *he's correcting my coffee order?*

He punched a few buttons on the cash register.

"Anything else?" he asked, avoiding eye contact.

"And, um, one of those," she said, pointing at a black, moist piece of cake looking lonely and bereft in the mostly empty bakery case.

He gave her the total. She asked him to repeat it. It normally didn't take more than a palmful of coins gathered from the tray in between the seats of her truck for a cup of coffee back home. She paid and dropped some coins into the counter jar that said, "If you fear change, leave it here." Then she stood there.

"I'll bring it to you," the barista said, annoyed, as he spun on his heel and started futzing with the espresso machine.

God, Colden thought as she moved away from the counter, pulled out a chair, and shrugged off her coat. *Why is this all so awkward?*

But in fact, she knew why it was awkward. She knew she had not come completely out of the woods. Literally and figuratively.

When she was in the mountains, she regularly went days at a time speaking no more than a few sentences. Sometimes less than that, for longer than that. Unused, unnecessary, her social skills would atrophy and wither away. It had happened before. It happened regularly. Yet, it always surprised her. She didn't miss the parts of herself that knew how to banter and chitchat with strangers and colleagues, but others clearly did.

Colden opened the pages of the tabloid newspaper someone had left on the table. More band advertising. She wondered if she should try to see something while she was in town. But it was impossible to tell what kind of music any of them played. Their attitude seemed to be, "If you are not cool enough to know who we are, don't bother coming to our show." When was the last time she'd seen live music? The fiddle players in the farmer's market didn't count. She tried to conjure an image of herself standing in a darkened venue in front of a real band. Must have been in college. Five or six years ago. She couldn't recall the group's name now. They'd briefly been almost a big deal but had flamed out. She remembered the feel of the large, plastic cup in her hand, the flat, room-temperature beer on her tongue, and the sticky, slippery floor beneath her feet. The dry, raspy sensation in her throat from hollering over the noise of the music into the warm, moist ear of the guy who brought her.

Even back then, she had preferred silence. And now? Now she wouldn't last ten minutes at a loud concert. The sounds would overwhelm her.

She reached the last pages of the newspaper. Personals. She was surprised to find they still did personals this way, in the paper, with box office numbers. She read through a few. They all sounded the same. As did the ads for online sex talk and men's clubs that appeared on the same spread. In college, her friends had told hair-raising and funny stories of online dates gone bad. A few had worked out. She knew of one woman already married to and pregnant by a guy she'd met online. Yet recently, there'd been a news story of a woman, a mother of three, found cut into pieces in a recycling bin after having had a date with a guy she met online. He seemed so nice, her friends said. She was so careful, they insisted. Turns out, the guy had a long rap sheet and an ex-girlfriend full of regret that she hadn't filed charges when he'd choked her. The murdered woman left behind three daughters. The murderer claimed he'd had an alcohol blackout and didn't remember a thing.

The world is full of dangers, Colden thought. *Most people down here in this city would be terrified up in the mountains of my native habitat. Yet here, I'm the awkward, out-of-place, nervous creature.*

Scared. She didn't think that word. But it hovered on the edges of her consciousness when she was in the city.

Hands covered in tattoos and chunky silver jewelry set a large mug of foamy coffee and a small plate with a slab of cake in front of her. Colden folded the paper, set it aside, and sipped her drink. From her semi-subterranean perch, she could look out the windows but see only the feet and lower legs of people going by on the sidewalk. Wing tips and high heels. Canvas sneakers and sandals. Pointed toes and platforms. Sweatpants and saggy jeans with unlaced high-top court shoes. Stockinged legs beneath pencil skirts and pinstripes with a peek of argyle at the ankles. This was a city of lobbyists and lawyers, students and yuppies, hipsters and ghetto kids. She saw no canvas pants and water-stained or mud-caked boots.

She took a bite of the cake. The sweetness exploded on her tongue and made her teeth ache. She washed it down with coffee so bitter and strong it bordered on acrid, even with the softening effect of the milk. She wiped her mouth. She didn't think she could finish either. It was all just too much, too dense, too rich.

She sighed. And then a dark blue suit, pale yellow shirt, and pastel-colored paisley tie appeared in front of her, as if conjured by her exhalation.

Nice touch, she thought. A bit of fancy to offset the otherwise conservative look.

The suit surprised her by pulling out a chair and sitting down. A stranger was now a mere eighteen inches away. There was a slight smile on his lips. He was enjoying confounding her in this way. She saw black hair gelled back from his forehead, a jaw shadowed with a day's growth of beard, and a tie yanked back from the unbuttoned shirt collar. He was handsome—an observation she resisted but that came on anyway, like an uncontrolled reflex. Colden swung her eyes around the room. One other woman, hair short and severe, with black roots and platinum tips, a barbell through her nose and a scowl on her face, had come in and was tapping on a silver computer in the far corner. The other four tables were still empty.

"Hi," the man across from her said cheerfully.

"Hi," she replied cautiously.

His lips were dark and full, his teeth white, his eyes dark brown. She tried not to smile back at him. Neither said anything for a moment.

"I'm sorry," she finally said, even though she wasn't. "Do I know you?" she asked, even though she knew she didn't.

She was trying to do something she'd watched her father do: give a stranger the benefit of the doubt by asking a question before offering any information. It was a way of being polite but also circumspect.

The man across from her casually shook his head.

"Not yet," he said.

He ran his palm over his hair and then extended it across the table. Colden wondered if it would be slick with hair gel.

"I'm Andrew. Most people call me Drew," he said.

Colden kept her hands in her lap. He pulled his back.

"Sorry. Look. Don't mean to bother you," he said. "Want me to leave? I'll leave."

He pushed back his chair and lifted his body slightly, but he did not leave. Colden remained quiet. He sat back down.

"I'm just in town on business, been dealing with assholes all day, came in here. I promise I'm harmless. Just wanted to say hi, be friendly, have a little conversation. Public place—I'm safe; you're safe. Guy behind the counter knows me." He waved to him. The waiter waved back. "If I'm bugging you, I'll leave."

Colden shrugged. Drew folded his hands on the table.

"You a local? Here on biz? Student, maybe a student?" he quizzed her.

"Grad student," she said.

"Cool. Me, I'm a lawyer."

"Lobbyist?" Colden suggested, as if correcting him.

Many lawyers around here were but didn't want to admit it. Drew wagged his finger at her.

"Ah, you're sharp, aren't you?" he said. "Not technically. Just have one client. An association whose interests I represent, but I am not a suit for hire, in the way of a traditional lobbyist."

Colden nodded. This performance was entertaining. She hadn't decided if he knew he was performing or not. She'd never met anyone quite this brash before. Maybe this was truly his personality.

"Colden," she said.

Drew looked at her, his eyebrows drawn together in confusion by the word she'd spoken.

"That's my name. Colden," she explained.

Drew cocked his head and stared off into the distance. His lips worked over her name several times.

"Colden. Colden. Unusual name, but sounds familiar. Why? Wait, wait. Oh yes, like that book. That famous book. About the phonies. The guy who hates phonies. Had to read it in high school. Little red thing . . ."

"That's Holden," she said. "Not Colden. Holden Caulfield. *Catcher in the Rye*."

"Right, right, right," Drew said, drumming his fingers on the table. The waiter brought him something very dark, in a tiny cup. "Thanks, man," Drew said with easy familiarity.

Colden sat still, watching him. This was something she knew how to do, to wait and see what happened, without giving herself away. It was a professional skill required when working with wildlife. Humans, on the other hand, often found this behavior of hers a tad disconcerting. The man in front of her took a small sip of his drink.

"So, you've got brains and beauty," he eventually said, without looking up.

Colden couldn't tell if he was joking or serious. She felt herself blush but with annoyance, not embarrassment. She did not like remarks about her appearance, especially compliments.

"I mean it," he said.

Colden thought this might be true but didn't know why it mattered.

"Don't like your cake?" he asked, gesturing with his cup toward her plate.

"It's a little sweet."

"And you're sweet enough."

Colden rolled her eyes. She was no good at flirting. Also, no good at being flirted with. Drew grinned, undaunted, unembarrassed.

"Lame, huh?" he teased.

Colden nodded.

"I'm being an idiot."

"You're actually being rather amusing."

"That's generous of you." Drew looked ever-so-slightly deflated. He shifted in his seat. "So, grad student. What are you studying? Art? History? Literature? Tell me something about yourself. I've been with boring business dudes in the paper industry all day, and honestly, I just need a break. I don't live here. Don't have friends here. Usually this coffee shop is a great place to come make conversation with whoever is around. Tends toward the political. Which I get enough of. You seem like a nice person. Just say the word, and I'll leave. Or, better, tell me about yourself. I've got no good stories to share today, so why don't you tell me one? How'd you get that name? It's unusual. Never heard it before."

"It's a mountain. And a lake."

"A mountain. A lake. And a woman."

Colden shrugged again.

"Where?" he asked. "Where is this mysterious mountain and lake? And woman?"

"The Adirondacks."

He gave her that questioning look again.

"North of here."

"Oh. Local girl?" He sounded slightly disappointed.

"Not exactly. It's a couple of hours north of here."

"Isn't that, like, Canada?"

"Not quite. You'd have to drive a few more hours."

His questions and his accent had alerted her to the fact that he was likely from the New York City area. Most people from there thought that New York State ended on the far side of Albany and were unaware of the six-million-acre swath of wilderness that stretched between the capital and the Canadian border.

"Actually, I'm just teasing," he said. "I know about the Adirondacks. A tiny bit, anyway. My client. Paper company. Has operations up there, I guess. I'm new to the job."

Colden sipped her latte and said, "Wildlife biology and conservation."

"Excuse me?"

"You asked what I was studying."

"Conservation? Oh jeez. You probably hate guys like me."

Colden took another bite of her cake.

"Not necessarily," she said. "There are some paper companies that have done really good things. Public–private partnerships that help conservation efforts and provide jobs. Sometimes they plant more trees than they actually remove."

"See," Drew said, smacking his hand on the table. "That's what I'm talking about. I should have you come testify on my client's behalf."

"Yet, you don't even know where Lake Colden is," she chastised.

"Nope, guilty as charged, ma'am," he said. "I live in the city. Well, Hoboken, actually. But that's basically the city, these days. Costs almost as much, anyway. I just started. January will be my first legislative session."

"Well," she said, "you might, you know, want to head north and see the raw material that's funding your role, don't you think?" Colden said.

"Absolutely. It's on the calendar." He grinned at her. "If I promise to go, will you promise to show me around?"

Colden shook her head, smiled indulgently, told him it was nice to meet him, and collected her things. This time, she did shake his hand when it was offered. It was smooth, soft, and dry. She waved good-bye and left without answering his invitation or leaving him any way to contact her. The offer was not something she took seriously. Neither was he. When she looked back through the window, he was eating what was left of her cake.

The next day, Colden was at her desk early. She powered up her desktop computer and logged into the university's scientific archives. She checked every scientific journal she could think of and did a variety of online searches to see if anyone was publishing work or looking for grants to fund work on anything related to interactions between coyotes and wolves in the lower forty-eight states. After more than an hour of scanning, she found nothing other than a few efforts to discover how wolf kills impacted the scavenging habits of lower-level predators, like coyotes and foxes. Good. There seemed to be nothing that might threaten to preempt her simmering ideas. The scientific gap she hoped to fill one day remained. It was time for more coffee. She was just about to push her chair back when a reflection appeared on her monitor. Large glasses, loose jowls, thinning, steel-wool hair.

"Decided to come in from the cold?"

Larry. His voice like a rasp over wood.

Colden stiffened and resisted the temptation to start closing the still-open tabs and windows visible on her screen. Instead, she turned her chair and hoped her body would block his view of her computer.

"Hey, Larry. What's up?"

She tried to sound casual. It was difficult to keep the defensive note from her voice. Larry was the type of guy who stood too close, didn't keep his eyes on your face, was cagey when queried about his professional background, and interrupted midsentence, even when you were answering a question he had asked. He was a mansplainer. But there was more than that. It was worse than that. She just couldn't pin down exactly what made it worse.

"You here for the rest of the term?" he asked.

"In and out."

"No classes to teach?"

These queries were none of his business. He acted like he was her superior or a department head. He was neither. A professor, yes; senior to her, yes. Not the boss of her, though.

"Just an online class this term and nothing next term."

"All research, then? Going home for the Thanksgiving break?"

Colden wanted to get him to stop grilling her, but she didn't know how. She was trapped in her cubicle, with him blocking her escape.

"That's a couple of weeks away yet. We'll see how the weather is," she replied.

"You don't seem like the type of woman who would be daunted by a few snowflakes," he said, his eyes narrowing.

"Not a few, no," she replied. "But if it's two feet, on a holiday weekend, with tons of people on the highways? It's the other drivers that concern me most."

"Yeah," he said. "I'll be here alone over the long weekend, myself. Just get some work done while everyone else is gone."

Colden reached for her coffee mug, making a motion to get up. He didn't take the hint and stayed where he was. His eyes moved away from her face, over her shoulder, to her monitor.

"Coyotes?" he said suspiciously. "Thought you were into beaver and moose."

"Well, they're all sharing the same environment and habitat," Colden blurted out. She didn't want him questioning why she was looking into canid behavior. "Just looking for some overlaps with my beaver and moose research," she dissembled.

Having little use for anything other than the truth, she knew she wasn't a credible liar.

"I'd like to know more about your moose research," he said. "And coyotes are an area of interest for me, too."

Colden doubted either of these statements was true. Larry seemed interested only in whatever was getting attention or money. He was also strangely vague about his own research projects. Nothing was ever definite with him. Colden had looked him up once. He had very few articles in his name, and where he was listed, he was never the lead researcher. She couldn't figure out how or why he'd gotten hired. No matter how off-putting and unimpressive he was, she had to find a way to accommodate him because she would likely require his support for her thesis. She hated this need and hated that he was so clearly aware of it.

"Yeah. Well, we'll keep you in the loop as we move forward," she said, brusque and noncommittal.

She moved as if to get up from her chair. He widened his stance and crossed his arms over his ample stomach.

There's no way he's doing much fieldwork with a gut like that, she thought.

"Fascinating creatures, coyotes are," he said. "Amazingly adaptable. Able to exploit any environment, from the center of New York City to the remote wilds of Montana."

"Yup."

This was information accessible to anyone who'd ever watched a PBS nature show, she noted to herself.

"We should collaborate," he said. "Work together more closely."

Colden said nothing.

He stared at her. His eyes drifted down from her face, over her shoulders, then stopped. Colden flushed, hot and claustrophobic, and then stood up abruptly, bumping him with her chair.

"Sorry."

But she wasn't.

He finally took a step backward and pivoted so that there was just enough room for her to pass. As she pushed through the opening between him and her cubicle wall, she was forced to brush up against his shoulder. His breath, moist and slightly rancid, filled her nose as she fled.

Storms were promised, but they never came. The day before Thanksgiving, Colden closed the door on her echoing condo and drove through an atmosphere of monotone gray, back to the mountains. Her truck smelled of the stale oil staining the wrapper of the sandwich she'd eaten as the highway signs ticked past. It was late afternoon when she pulled off the highway. She passed the long-decrepit signs for a once-vibrant amusement park that had closed before she was born. She stopped to fill up the truck and buy a six-pack at the one-pump gas station near the exit ramp, putting her beer on the small square of open space on a counter cluttered with

Slim Jims, a jar of pickled eggs, energy shots, smoking paraphernalia, and a display of dry gas. An hour later, she pulled into the driveway of her parents' home and saw, through the lowering light and the uncurtained windows, the silhouetted heads of her father and his wife, Sally, sitting on the sofa. She filled in the rest of the details she knew she'd find when she walked inside: the local paper littering the expansive sectional; the small side table with two mugs holding a few damp dregs and collapsed tea bags; the wood stove with a compact fire crackling within its iron confines; the two cats, either curled in a lap or draped over the back of a chair; the smells of something nose-tickling and hunger-inducing, chili or stew, a casserole or hunk of meat, simmering or roasting on the stove or in the oven. This was home. She knew she took it for granted, even as she felt a deep-seated appreciation for her good fortune seep upward from her gut and fill her face with warmth.

She was pleased to be there. She was relieved to know that she had no classroom teaching obligations for a full year. She was glad to put Albany behind her.

She stepped from her truck and went into the house through the back door. She levered off her boots, shrugged off her coat, put her six-pack in the fridge, liberated one for herself, and wandered over the worn-to-a-patina wood floors and compressed oriental carpet to the large living room, where she collapsed into one corner of the sofa. Her father and Sally smiled at her. A gray cat extricated itself from a small rocking chair and padded over to her, imposing itself onto her lap with a deep purr. Sally set down the stack of papers she was reading.

"I don't need to interrupt," Colden said.

"No, no," Sally replied. "Happy to stop reading yet another report about the sorry state of our juvenile justice system."

Colden wanted to complain and whine about her trip to Albany, about the annoyances of being in the city, the drudgery of academic committees and departments, Larry. But her concerns always seemed so petty compared to what Sally dealt with in her life as a social worker—every day she managed a steady onslaught of people who had very little and then made the worst of even that.

"How was Albany?" her father asked.

Colden lifted and dropped her shoulders, took a swig of beer.

"Irritating, as always. But necessary. And I don't have to go back for a few months. So it's in my rearview mirror."

Sally reached forward for Colden's beer, took a long swallow, then handed it back.

"Did you do anything fun?" Sally asked.

Sally was forever trying to nudge Colden away from work and into a social life. Colden was forever resisting her efforts. She rolled her eyes dramatically in response to the question. Sally shook her head in return. Colden asked if her father had been out to see Gene.

"Yes. There was a small leak in his roof."

"Glad to know his days of ladder climbing are finally behind him," Colden said.

"And a few repairs to the doors of his outbuildings so that he can actually close and secure them."

"Working doors? What a concept," Colden teased.

"Any more thefts?" Sally asked.

"Nothing recently, it seems," Dix replied. "We got things tightened up for winter, so hopefully, it will stay that way."

"I heard of a few other incidents recently," Sally said. "Small stuff. A few cans of food. Some camping supplies."

"Not the normal stuff of meth heads or drunk teenagers," Colden noted.

"Whoever this is leaves the shotgun and booze but makes a light raid on the pantry," Dix observed.

"Sounds like someone in need," Sally said.

"Speaking of need," Colden interjected. "I'm starving, and something smells delicious."

This remark broke the spell of their conversation and lightened the mood. They lifted themselves from the sofa, gathered in the kitchen, and filled plates with her father's venison chili, cornbread, and salad. After the dishes were washed, Colden hugged Dix and Sally, shoved her feet back into her boots without lacing them, and clomped through the dark, down the familiar path to the cottage that she had made her home within a home.

The cottage had been built by her father's parents, whom Colden had never met, in the style of a classic Adirondack lean-to. Constructed in traditional style, with logs milled from their own property, notched and sealed with oakum, it had been decorated simply, with tab-top linen curtains, a Mission-style rocker, birch-twig-style bed and small desk, an iron lamp, and pegs for clothes. Colden had added only an electronic tea kettle and a Wi-Fi booster so she could work. Her father, as he always did, had turned on the heat and the single bulb porch light, to ensure it was comfortable when she arrived.

The cottage was a place both full of and free from memories. She had begun staying there during her trips home as an undergraduate at Cornell. There was no decision, just a sort of slow migration away from the room she'd grown up in, down the hall from her parents, with her martial arts and archery trophies, schoolbooks and science manuals, the toy moose her father had given her as a baby, now missing an eye and with one antler bent at an oblique angle, resting against the pillows on her bed. As a child, she visited the cottage from time to time with her father to help him with maintenance and repairs. She'd help him replace the oakum that mice had tried to pull free and sweep the droppings they left behind. They'd wipe down the cobwebs that formed in the corners where the ceiling met the wall, replace pillows that had become mouse nurseries, patch the roof when a blown-down tree branch raked a few shingles free, wash the linens on the bed that no one ever used. Sometimes they'd fish or swim in the shallow, gravel-bedded stream that was a mere fifteen steps away. In high school, the cottage became the place she occasionally took friends to hang out by the fire pit. It was the first place she'd made out with a boy, an awkward experience due to his inexperienced clumsiness and the braces that covered her teeth. It was the first—and last—place she'd smoked a joint and discovered how much she hated the blurry feeling the weed induced. It was where she started to get used to the idea that her peers didn't think she was cool. It was also where she discovered she didn't care about being cool.

And it was where she first started to ask questions about her mother, her "real" mother, as much as she hated the word. Her birth mother. Colden still struggled with how to think about, how to place the woman she had never met. Entering the cottage on this unseasonably mild late-November night, she recalled the day she found the barrette. They were stripping the bed of linens. She must have been about eleven or twelve. No one stayed down there, but Dix always kept the place cleaned and ready, as if it was a guest room, even though they never had guests. While sweeping her hand between the mattress and box spring, her fingers found something hard and plastic. She liberated it and showed it to her father.

"That was your mother's," he said without affect.

Colden remembered how the phrase gave her pause. Sally was her mother. But Sally didn't use tortoiseshell hair ornaments. Dix had sat down on the bed and taken the barrette from his daughter's hand, turning it this way and that, each movement seeming to shake free a memory.

"Miranda had thick, honey-colored hair," he'd said. Then he paused and added, "Like yours."

The comparison had made Colden uncomfortable, a feeling that she came to associate with her mother.

"She kept it long. We always joked about finding strands of hair everywhere. On the pillows. In the sink. In our food."

Colden had wondered where all these strands had gone. She'd never found one herself.

"She lived down here," Dix continued. "For a little bit. Before we became a couple."

"Why?" Colden had asked.

"Why what?" her father had countered.

Colden remembered being unable to get more specific in her query. At that time, she knew so little. Only that her mother had experienced some sort of tragedy or tragedies, she and Dix became a couple, never married, and then she moved out for some reason, to some sort of hippie commune or something, found out she was pregnant, died soon after giving birth. Sally had been involved in some way. She'd met Dix when she came to tell him about the daughter he never knew he'd had. That was how they'd met and fell in love. Trying to get Colden back from the commune. It was too big of a story for a little girl. Now, even as an adult, her mother's tale—because it was something she'd been told but had not experienced—felt more burden than legacy.

"Why did she live here?" Colden had finally asked, those many years ago.

Her father was always careful and measured when he spoke. Even more so, whenever, as rarely as it was, the topic of Miranda came up.

"She'd lost her family and her home. She needed a place to live. To feel better. To start over."

"Did it work?" Colden had asked. "Did the cottage fix everything?"

She remembered that it took her father a very long time to answer.

"For a time, it did," he'd said. "For a bit, yes, the cottage did fix everything."

This evening, some fifteen years later, with each step she took closer to the low, dimly lit front door, she felt as she imagined her mother must have: that for a time, at least, this little dollhouse tucked into the edge of the woods by a stream could—would—fix many things, indeed.

FIVE

"Are you excited?" Sally asked when Colden came into the house the next morning.

"Excited about what?" Colden asked in return as she poured herself a mug of coffee.

She knew what Sally was referring to; she just didn't want to give in to her nudging and prodding.

"About getting out on the moose-tagging project?" Sally insisted.

Over dinner the previous evening, Colden had told them that after the holidays were over, sometime in January, she was going to join a moose-tagging team that included biologists from the Department of Natural Resources and a private contractor. They would be heading out in helicopters, looking for moose, then dropping in, subduing the animals, taking samples, checking their condition, and fitting them with radio collars for tracking and monitoring. The collars would help them understand how far the animals had to range in search of scant forage during the harsh winters. They also wanted to overlay moose movements with beaver pond locations and see how and if the two overlapped. Data like this would help determine both land use and hunting policy, as well as, hopefully, determine some of what was causing the moose population to stagnate. The team, without Colden, had been doing this for a couple of years. Colden had been helping organize and analyze the data. But this was the first time she was going along for the actual collaring.

"Oh you know, Sally," Colden said with practiced nonchalance. "All in a day's work."

"C'mon, Colden," Sally said. "Helicopter rides and netting moose. Sounds really wild."

Colden gave her a tight smile and bobbed her head. Sally crossed her arms over her chest.

"What is wrong with you, Colden?" Sally said. "Why aren't you more, you know, enthusiastic? I mean this is cool. Don't go all science-y and Spock-like on me."

Dix, who was cracking eggs, one-handed, into a pan at the stove, snickered. Sally was often exasperated at both his and Colden's temperate, laconic personalities. Yet, it was true that Colden was holding back her enthusiasm. She wasn't sure exactly why. She didn't know if she was just playing with Sally or if her attitude had something to do with her flagging and frustrated interest in the project overall. In fact, she had been hoping the excitement of helicopter rides and radio collars would reignite her passion for the work.

"Nothing is wrong, Sally, dear," Colden said. "It's just, you know, work. It's just my job. Yours involves paperwork and juvenile delinquents. Dad's involves trucks and tools and vacation homes. Mine, well, some days, my job involves moose and helicopters."

"And hot guys in pilot uniforms?" Sally said, raising her eyebrows hopefully.

Colden shook her head indulgently at her stepmother's teasing. Sally often made it clear she thought Colden didn't get out enough. Which was certainly true. Colden often countered that there was lots of time for a social life and there was less time to establish herself as a scientist. There were plenty of men out there and always would be. There were far fewer grants and research opportunities.

Colden took the plate her father handed her. Two fried eggs, a slab of toast, thick cuts of bacon. The plate he gave to Sally had exactly half the portions. Sally was smaller in stature and frame than Colden, naturally wiry and lean, hated exercise, and looked at food as no more than an occasional necessity to the pesky task of staying alive. Dix's plate was piled with an extra egg and more bacon, as if he'd taken what should have been Sally's. They sat at the table, ate together, and discussed their plans for the coming weeks. Dix would be busy—many people gathered their families at their Adirondack "cabins" for the holidays. As caretaker for the wealthiest and fussiest of those in their area, he had to lay in firewood, scare off mice, seal up cracks, repair furniture, and in general, make these often-enormous homes feel both comfortable and rustic for their owners. It was a busy time for Sally, too. The holidays were stressful for even healthy families. The people she worked with, who lived on the margins in the best of times, often blew up or broke down around the holidays.

In contrast, Colden had little to do. She was up-to-date on all her reports and grants. It was a quiet time in academia. She was winding up her online course with just another easy-to-grade test ahead. She and Dix and Sally were not much for celebrating the holidays, the three of them. They usually opted to spend Thanksgiving serving at a soup kitchen and eating grilled-cheese sandwiches, themselves, and spending Christmas visiting a homeless shelter, senior home, or hospital, dragging along one or more of the rescue dogs Dix collected, in the hopes that a wiggling canine would cheer up the residents. This year, Colden hadn't even made these sorts of plans. It didn't seem like Dix or Sally had, either. Colden spent most of her time in the ensuing weeks, as the year wound down, sprawled across the living room sofa, reading books and articles, snacking on crackers and handfuls of nuts, and making cup after cup of tea. When Dix and Sally weren't working, they joined her.

Meanwhile, snow fell steadily outside their windows, big flakes piling up fast, coating the bare maples, the stark birches, and the lush evergreens with a thick layer of white. Many evenings, after dinner, Colden didn't even return to the cottage but instead crawled, contented, into the single bed of her youth, her knees pulled high up, her hands pressed together beneath her cheek, a cat tucked against the small of her back. She slept darkly, deeply, dreamlessly for ten hours a night. It was as if she was recovering from something. Or maybe readying herself for something.

January came on bland and dry. The snows that had softened the landscape were whipped away by aggressive winds, leaving the denuded trees, flinty boulders, and brown earth looking raw and abraded. Evergreens offered the only relief of almost-color, their dark branches swaying and scraping, storm-tossed in the cold gusts.

The day the collaring project was to begin, Colden left the house before dawn. She drove along black, twisting, two-lane roads with dense trees growing right up to the pavement. When she got to the small airport where she was to meet the rest of the team, they were already there, sitting in the small lounge area, sipping coffee from Styrofoam cups. She waved at Jack, the only person she knew, as he was a colleague from the Department of Natural Resources who also taught the occasional class at the university. He stood up, pulled a chair out for her, and introduced her to Liam, the pilot, and Darryl, the animal wrangler. She'd worked with Jack many times. He'd been a guest speaker in several of her classes. They shared information and experiences. He was what she thought of as a solid, north-country guy. Married to a schoolteacher, three kids, hunted, fished, boated, liked country music. Had no interest in pop culture or foreign cars. Not intellectual, but super-smart in a resourceful, practical, useful way. The kind of guy you'd want around if you were stranded on a desert island. Colden was fond of him in the way she would be toward a friend of her father's or an uncle. Not that she'd had experience with either of those sorts of relationships.

The other two men nodded at her as Jack said their names. Darryl was burly, somewhat scowling, with a ball cap pulled down over his forehead. Liam was tall and leggy, stretched out casually in the too-small chair. He had almost comically chiseled good looks, his square jaw covered with a few days of dark-blond stubble, his hair a thick brush growing above the severe cliffs of his cheekbones.

Colden wanted to get going. She looked at her watch. Nobody was moving.

"Are we waiting for something?" she asked.

Jack nodded reluctantly, then pointed his chin toward the door. "Yeah, that guy."

Colden turned and tried, unsuccessfully, to hide her surprise. Larry was ambling across the room. She furrowed her eyebrows and turned her hands up at Jack, asking for an explanation. He shrugged, rolled his eyes, and looked away. Larry came to the table, introduced himself, shook hands, and said her name once by way of a greeting. Again, no one moved. She looked from man to man and saw that all their eyes were lowered to the floor. Finally, Liam lifted his head and began scrutinizing Larry.

"Don't I know you, mate? Haven't we met before?" he asked, the slight accusation in his voice softened by an Australian accent.

Larry shook his head. "Nope, don't think so." He remained standing, stamping his feet and blowing on his hands. "Well, shall we get going?" he asked.

There was a moment of uncomfortable silence. Colden saw the problem immediately. There were now four men. One woman. The helicopter would have only four seats. She was angry that he was here. Yes, she found him creepy and annoying, but this was more important and potentially damaging: he was now jeopardizing her place on the expedition. He didn't belong here. He was an academic, not a field biologist. He wasn't part of this team, and he wasn't part of the plan. Plus, he was overweight. He was soft. He was wearing sneakers. She waited for someone else to deal with the situation. Again, it was Liam who spoke up.

"Well, we shan't get going until we figure out who the 'we' is going to be," he said cheerfully.

Colden figured Liam was in his late thirties, although his face was deeply lined in the way that comes from years of outdoor work. He stood up. He was well over six feet tall, broad-shouldered, with a vaguely military bearing. Not someone to be messed with.

Larry looked up at Liam with a furrowed brow.

"What's the problem?" he asked.

"Only four seats, mate," Liam said. "We hadn't planned on you."

Colden tried to catch Jack's eye. He stared into his coffee cup.

Larry shrugged. "You'll be making several runs. Bring me on a couple and her on a couple."

Colden fumed. Of course, he'd pick her, not Jack, to be the expendable one. Jack was senior to her, more experienced, and from the organization that was funding this work, but still. Colden also knew that there was a more fundamental and embarrassing hurdle to Larry's participation. She was not going to be the one to bring it up. Liam sucked his teeth.

"Well, my friend, there's a weight restriction, too," he said.

Larry stared at him, uncomprehending.

"We've got quite a lot of gear," Liam added. He paused and then said, "Necessary gear. And then three other men. Also necessary."

Colden suppressed a smile. Liam had quite a way of stating things. Larry wasn't getting it.

"And her," Liam said, nodding in her direction. "She knows the terrain and the targets. She will be telling us where to go. So, she is also quite essential."

Larry rolled his eyes. "Not for every run, she isn't."

Liam kept talking. His tone was breezy and matter-of-fact.

"Well, even if that's true, there is another problem. Not sure what you're carrying, lad, but I'd guess pushing past two hundred and seventy-five? That puts us over the weight limit. No matter who else is on board with you."

Larry looked from one person to another, and Colden watched as comprehension slowly started to sink in. She wondered why he was pretending to care about this project that was so out of his comfort, academic, and research zones.

"Fine," Larry said, lowering himself to a chair. "You guys go as planned. Take me out later." No one moved. "I just need to get a sense of the landscape," Larry said. "That's what I'm here for. To get the big picture and bring that information back to the department."

Colden doubted this was true. She suspected he had simply elbowed his way into this somehow simply because it was high profile. Larry carried on, undaunted.

"I'll go on one of the surveys. When you don't have as much equipment. When you're not netting. When you don't need Darryl. Or her."

He glared at Colden. She didn't care. She was going, and that was all that mattered.

"Go," Larry said, shooing them out, trying to take control. "I've got stuff to do, anyway."

Larry shrugged off his coat and set down his briefcase. The other four stood, shouldered their packs, and pushed in their chairs.

Let him have his moment of pretend-being-in-charge, Colden thought. *I've got a job to do.*

They did helicopter runs for four days. Colden saw the mountains she knew so well from a totally new perspective. The naked trees reaching up like penitents toward the severe skies. The alabaster expanses and icy ribbons of frozen ponds and lakes. The blankets of somber hemlock and firs interrupting the snow-covered hill-sides. The sudden adrenaline rush as a form took shape and began to move in the otherwise-still landscape, the long legs and shaggy brown head of a moose resolving itself against the white ground as they approached. Then the propulsive shot of the net, followed by the animal tripping up and falling to the ground. The 'copter's descent, with Darryl scrambling out before it was fully landed, rac-ing to embrace the animal's legs in ties and its face in a blindfold that rendered it immobile and quiet.

Jack was always the next out, assisting Darryl and then as-sembling the collar around the animal's massive neck. Colden ran with the equipment bag, her fingers stiffening in the cold as she grabbed syringes and bottles, snippers and labels, and took blood and hair samples, ran her fingers through the animal's thick fur, looking for ticks, feeling for bones where she hoped there would be a layer of fat instead, dodging Jack who, once the collar was set, used a stethoscope to listen to the heart and lungs, and stretched out a white tape measure. Colden was always shocked at just how big the moose were, their heads as large as her body, ears almost as long as her forearm, legs like saplings. Then, everything was quickly packed up, Jack and Colden stepped back toward the waiting 'copter, and Darryl gingerly released the moose and shooed it, stumbling, confused, but unharmed, away and back to its life.

Colden watched the moose grow small and distant as the he-licopter pulled away and felt her own heart thump boldly in her chest. Sally was right—this was exciting. This was exactly what she had been working toward with every class and test she took, every grant she wrote, and every hour she spent staring into the landscape, hoping for something interesting and mysterious to materialize. She would be back to staring at a computer screen and charting data soon enough, but for these days, the cold slapping at her cheeks, the 'copter wings thumping overhead, and the moose's hot, damp breath in her face made every hour she had to spend indoors seem worth it.

No wonder Larry wanted to be in on it. He was there every morning when they arrived at the airport. He didn't need to be, as Liam never took him out until the last run of the day. But there he was, in the lame little lounge, making himself appear busy with papers or his laptop. She asked him once if his hotel room wouldn't be more comfortable, but he just grumbled something about better Wi-Fi at the airport. She shrugged and reminded herself that she didn't need to care what Larry did, as long as he wasn't in her way. Liam took him up for a couple of brief outings. They came back looking like a couple who'd been on an awkward, uncommunicative first date. She lost track of how many runs the team did together, but by the end of it all, they'd collared and taken blood and other samples from fifteen moose. Nine more than they'd gotten last year.

One morning, Jack made the point in front of the whole team, including Larry, that Colden's vast and specific knowledge of the mountains had been an invaluable contribution. She blushed unexpectedly at the professional compliment. In addition, the condition of the animals had been generally good. The parasites were fewer than they expected. Only one moose gave them concern, but she was mature and had most of her reproductive years behind her. Even Larry's looming presence couldn't dampen her—or everyone else's—enthusiasm at the overall success of their mission.

It all ended late on a Thursday afternoon. They packed their gear and lingered, making small talk, unwilling to separate and break the spell and camaraderie of the last few days.

"Let's go get a pint," Liam said suddenly. "Anywhere near here decent? Maybe with a pool table?" He looked directly at Colden as he spoke. "You're local; you must have a favorite spot."

"Sure, I know a place," she said, holding his gaze.

"Lead the way," Liam said.

"Yes, let's go," Larry interjected. "My treat."

Liam slowly drew his eyes off Colden's face and looked at Larry as if trying to remember who he was. Colden turned her head and rolled her eyes. Larry was trying again to be one of the cool kids. When nothing else worked, use money.

"Good idea," Liam conceded, clapping Larry hard on the shoulder. "Your treat, eh? I like the sound of that."

The restaurant Colden chose had a few pickup trucks in the parking lot when they arrived. It was that almost-end-of-day hour, well after lunch had finished but before dinner had begun. The five of them gathered around a table, and Liam immediately took charge, ordering pitchers and appetizers for everyone to share.

After they'd clinked mugs, Larry started to say something. Some serious, academic question that he was prefacing with a dry dissertation designed to prove that he knew arcana about moose.

Jack lifted his hand to stop him, muttered something about everyone being off the clock, leaned back, and said, "Liam, tell us a story."

Larry lowered his drink and his eyes, his body stiffening and shrinking into itself slightly, a slug touched by a fingertip.

Liam began telling stories, and the awkward moment passed. All his tales involved various, often dangerous, frequently funny mishaps and malfunctions he'd experienced—bears coming out of sedation faster than expected, caribou running off with a net tangled in one leg, an enraged female moose charging them, an idiot jumping up from his seat at the sight of wolves below and unbalancing the 'copter so that it almost crashed. He was entertaining and self-deprecating. He had a deep and throaty laugh. Colden knew there were plenty of real calamities in his line of work. Large, confused, and scared animals are notoriously dangerous. Helicopters are fickle aircraft. Scientists and academics sometimes lack common sense and practical abilities. Liam made it all seem like a lark.

She noticed that Larry listened, distracted, snickered a bit, but seemed generally annoyed and put out somehow. She didn't care. She felt unusually buoyant and gregarious. They'd had great success, and she was ready to unwind. This was not something that came naturally to her. It was not something she generally felt she needed or wanted. The beer, the laughter, and their achievement loosened something in her that was more usually overshadowed by her drive to be on the move, looking, searching, and making things happen.

She allowed herself to register the fact that Liam had pulled out a chair for her and then placed himself in the one right next to it. He'd then slowly and casually closed the gap between their seats until she could feel the heat from his body. He topped off her beer and pointed at something on her menu, asking her if she'd tried it before. The fingers of his hand were muscled, well used, with large knuckles, and one was bent at a funny angle from what must have been a bad break. No wedding ring. As the light outside the windows dimmed and the lights inside came up, as the pitchers emptied and new ones arrived, as her cheeks began to ache from sustained laughter and her stomach filled with nachos and artichoke dip, fried foods, and pizza slices, she felt increasingly that she and Liam were contained in a small, clear bubble that only they could see or feel.

Then it popped. A waiter was unexpectedly at her side, tapping on her shoulder. Liam was leaning around her from the other side, protectively. Colden couldn't quite work out why the young man was standing there, so clearly uncomfortable and embarrassed.

"What's up?" Liam asked the waiter on her behalf.

"The gentleman at the bar asked me to bring this over to the lady."

The waiter set a martini glass in front of Colden. The brightly colored drink looked like an expensive and gaudy jewel next to her pint of piss-yellow beer. Colden turned in her seat, away from Liam, toward the bar. A dark-haired man in a pair of jeans, an oxford shirt, and lightly worn day hikers raised a glass, similar in shape but different, darker, in contents, at her. He had a tightly trimmed beard. She couldn't place him. It wasn't until he smiled, showing his bright, white teeth, that Colden was momentarily transported to that coffee shop in Albany. This was the guy who had sat across from her so unexpectedly. The lawyer. Or lobbyist. What was the guy's name? Allen? Aiden? No, Andrew. Drew. He'd told her to call him Drew. What was he doing way up here? It was disconcerting to have a piece of Albany appear in the Adirondacks. Colden gave him a desultory and unenthusiastic wave.

"Boyfriend?" Liam's breath was warm, moist, and gently teasing against her neck.

"Nah," she said, trying for lightness. "Just some guy I know from Albany. Have no idea what he's doing up here."

Of course, she did have an idea. She was the one who had chastised him about coming to see the raw materials of his employer's wealth.

"Nice drink," Liam grinned.

"Not really my cup of tea," Colden said.

"You mean the drink or the dude?"

Colden laughed.

"I should go over and say thanks."

"Don't be gone too long."

As she stood, Colden tried not to be irritated. She didn't want to leave Liam. She blamed Drew and his stupid pink drink.

"Hey," she said.

He was alone at the bar, several empty seats on either side of him, as if he was surrounded by a moat. Locals would have him instantly pegged as a city slicker and give him a wide berth. Hopefully, he didn't notice this self-protective, preemptive rudeness from her neighbors.

"What brings you up here?"

"Took your advice," he said. "Came for a visit."

Colden didn't really want to start a conversation. But she didn't want to be impolite, either.

"Well, hope it's going well. Not the best time of year to see the 'daks in all their glory," she said.

"Honestly, it's a biz trip."

"Oh. Yeah. That makes more sense."

Colden didn't know what else to say. She realized she was buzzed. It had been a long time since she drank more than a couple of beers. She didn't know if she should stay or turn away. Her thoughts were vaguely garbled and foggy.

"Well, thanks for the drink."

"Colden?" Drew asked, his voice low and grave. "I could use your help with something. Could I give you a call sometime?"

She blinked in confusion. The bold and provocative tone she remembered from their first meeting was no longer in evidence.

"It's work related," he said, unfolding his wallet where it lay on the bar. "Here, take my card. Call if you can. There's some . . . um . . . something I'd like to sort out, and I could use a local's perspective."

Local. In some people's mouths, that word had the whiff of insult. Colden reminded herself that he was just being descriptive. She found herself wondering why he wasn't flirting with her like he had in Albany. Which annoyed her—not so much that he wasn't flirting, but that she noticed. Which was a sign that she cared. She didn't want to care.

"Aren't your clients local?" she snipped.

Drew shook his head. "Not local in the way I mean," he said. "Not local in the way I need."

"Sounds serious."

Colden sounded more flippant than she meant to.

"It kinda is."

Drew was not joking.

She took the card. Slid it into the back pocket of her jeans.

"OK. I'll call you. I'll try to help." She fluttered her fingers at him. "I should get back. Good to see you, and thanks for the drink. Enjoy your visit."

As she turned to her table, she saw Larry on a direct path toward her.

"So many admirers," he hissed as he passed her on his way to the bathroom.

Ugh. Gross, she thought as she settled back into her seat.

She felt Liam draping his arm over the back of her chair. He tipped his head toward hers. She felt the tickle of his goatee against her ear.

"Keep me company tonight," he whispered.

His words caused her insides to flush in an unfamiliar way. He moved his arm closer to her back. She felt his bicep against one shoulder blade, his forearm against the other. She took a deep breath and let herself relax into his embrace. She allowed her head to brush his cheek and closed her eyes for a moment. She opened them and saw Larry lowering himself clumsily into a chair. He was still glaring at her. Or maybe that was just his habitual expression. Maybe she took everything he did too personally. Maybe she should just lighten up.

Liam wasn't really a professional colleague, she reminded herself. He was going back, somewhere out west, tomorrow. She'd probably never see him again. Anyway, her private life was none of anyone else's business. She felt Liam close his hand over her arm. Those gnarly, knotted, bent fingers. She imagined them moving against her bare skin. She moved closer to him. She breathed, "Yes," into his ear.

SIX

Brayden lay as still as possible. This was how he had been spending a lot of days, lately. The cold had enervated him. He'd piled a thick layer of evergreen branches and dead leaves under his ground tarp as a bulwark against the frozen earth. He was mummified in multiple layers of clothes, socks, face mask, gloves, and two fat, down sleeping bags he had taken from a poorly secured garage. Judging from the quantity and quality of the gear he'd left behind, he figured those people could afford to replace them. In any case, he was only borrowing the bags. He planned to return them. If he could remember exactly where he had found them. He had some canned food. Also pilfered from a couple of houses and hunting camps. He was too cold and stiff to raise himself to eat it. He had no fuel for his stove. He'd tried to find some in what he thought was the garage of an abandoned junkyard. But then someone in a little cabin he'd assumed was uninhabited let a few dogs loose, and he had to run. He'd thrown a fat stick at one of the dogs and heard it yelp. He was sorry about that.

The thick wool blanket his friend Bruce had given him, almost by way of apology, after telling him he had to leave, was between him and the tarp. His own, older sleeping bag, the one his father had given him years ago for achieving some level or another in scouting, was underneath him, as well. Scouting. Everyone thought his father was such a good dad. Tough, an old-school father, and this was a good thing. Just what a boy like him needed, given where he'd come from. Hah. If they only knew.

Brayden was pressed as far under the rock overhang as he could go. The tarp that formed the outside wall of his shelter, which was also shielded with a thick layer of evergreen boughs, lifted and fell slightly, as if it was breathing. He thought of himself as a hibernating bear. No, not hibernation. Torpor. That's what it was called. He'd learned that somewhere. He couldn't recall the context just now. It didn't matter.

He felt clear, cold, and still, like a fast-frozen lake, where you could see straight through the ice to the creatures still moving about below, out of reach. He didn't have the energy to build a fire. Maybe tonight. When there was no one to see the smoke. When the temperature dropped further. Maybe. Maybe he wouldn't even need it.

There was that sound again. The whump whump of the blades. He'd never heard a helicopter here before. Certainly not this close. He rarely even saw planes. And why had he heard it so many times over the last few days? Strange. They must be looking for something. Someone. Maybe convicts. An escapee from that prison north of here. It was a maximum-security place. They'd be after them, for sure, if someone had gotten out. It had happened before. Rarely. But still. They'd bring out the Staties. The dogs. He didn't care if the convicts found him, but he didn't want the cops anywhere near.

He'd lay low until it all blew over. Too cold to do anything else, anyway. He wondered briefly how the guys might have escaped. Him, he'd simply walked out of his personal prison. So easy, in the end. Made him wonder why he hadn't done it sooner. But unlike the convicts, no one would come looking for him. No one would even miss him. Of that, he was convinced.

SEVEN

Everyone dispersed. Larry and Jack went back to Albany, Liam and Darryl went back to wherever they were based, somewhere out west. Colorado or New Mexico, Colden thought. She couldn't remember. There was no reason to. She had no expectations and wanted no promises from Liam. Liam, thankfully, didn't burden her with any. Their night together stoked some embers within her that had almost died for lack of fuel, and that was enough for her. Liam, who was almost a caricature of a masculine presence, had reminded her that she was a woman and a scientist, not just a woman scientist. His naturally broad, six-foot-three frame had obviously been kept powerful and lean by outdoor work and regular trips to the gym. He had plenty of luxuriant body hair. He had a three-day beard around his goatee and a musky smell. He was about a dozen years older, clearly more experienced than she, and she appreciated his skilled, careful, and patient ministrations. He took his time, and he was interested in her pleasure. He was different, that way, from the boyfriends she'd had in college.

Being with him was a test to herself. It had been a while, many, many months, actually, more than she wanted to count, since she'd been with a man. She was glad to know she was still capable of physical intimacy, that her body was good for more than just carting her through the mountains and carrying around her brain. At one point in the evening, she had thought about asking him about Larry. But they didn't discuss work. They hardly spoke at all, turning themselves over to corporeal connection instead. She felt refreshed by the experience of being with Liam. She was happy it had happened—and also that it was over. It was time to get back to work.

She immediately began tracking data from the animals they'd collared. She made maps of their movements, puzzled over what they were doing, where they were going. She buried herself in the effort of trying to tease out patterns that could lead to conclusions, which could be used to create policies that would improve protection and conservation. The data were merely tiny blips. Some days, the moose barely moved at all. She began tracking weather data, as well. It would be years before patterns emerged that could be given scientific or behavioral meaning. But it was all still deeply consuming. She would sit down with her computer and a cup of coffee in the dim dawns of the short winter days and often not look up until the crepuscular gloom began to fall and her protesting stomach was the only indicator of how many hours had passed.

Then, the strange e-mail arrived. It was about a week after the collaring adventure. The return address was unknown, but the subject line referred to a well-known scientist, so she opened it. It was a picture of a Sasquatch. That was all. Just a blurry image of a large, hunched, and hairy form against a green, woodland backdrop. The quintessential Bigfoot shot. She deleted it without thinking about it. Just spam of some sort. She got back to her data. But a week or so later, another popped up. Then another.

There were a couple of goofy images, cartoon overlays of oversize, hirsute creatures. One GIF of an indistinct form suddenly coming to life and sticking its tongue out at the viewer. Some of the images were pseudo-scientific. Colden opened them, deleted them, and vaguely wondered how she'd gotten into this particular spam cycle. Maybe someone was playing a prank on her. Whatever. Easy enough to trash and move on.

That was, until the GIF arrived that showed a man in a hair suit, grinning maniacally, with a whip and a woman, naked, tied to a tree, her face turned back in a caricature of a damsel-in-distress posture. Colden wasn't a prude. Consenting adults, whatever turned you on, she didn't care or judge. But she didn't want unsolicited pornography popping up on her computer. It was distracting at the least and offensive at worst. If these sorts of images kept coming or got more pornographic or violent, she'd have to look into the sources. She'd recall the e-mails from her trash folder. Not what she wanted to be spending her time on.

Fortunately, they stopped. It took her a while to notice. Curious, she checked her spam folder. Nothing. The last one was two weeks prior. OK, so just some strange spam list. It was over, there was nothing to do, and she could move on. Which was good because she suddenly had a bigger issue to deal with. One of the transmitters was sending a "no-movement" signal from a very remote and difficult-to-reach area. The moose was either stuck, which was unlikely given how little snow they'd had, or more likely, dead. She and Jack were heading out together, very early, tomorrow. It was going to be a long and difficult day.

EIGHT

Brayden brought a can of chili under the covers with him overnight. By the morning, it was no longer frozen. He ate it, cold. Then he made himself get up, get dressed, and get moving. His blood felt congealed. He stepped into the open space just outside his lair and stamped his feet. He was too thickly bundled for proper calisthenics, the jumping jacks, push-ups, and burpees his father used to make him do before breakfast when he first adopted him and his sister. Before he lost interest in insisting on self-improvement schemes he thought would help Brayden gain the confidence and discipline needed for a boy who had been in and out of foster homes for so much of his life.

In the open space in front of his small cave, Brayden jumped up and down a few times, swung his arms in the bright, crisp air, shaking off stiffness and memories at the same time. He took a few deep breaths, like a thirsty man gulping water. His head began to clear. His blood began to move. He felt hungry, in spite of the belly full of beans and beef.

I don't want to keep stealing, *he told himself.* It's not right.

He had outdoors skills. His father and a few sessions of summer camp had taught him some useful things. He knew how to start a fire, how to make a snare and a pole, how to ice fish and butcher an animal. He had a good knife, a small shovel, and an ax. He didn't need much else. He knew the forest around him could supply the rest.

First step was to clean up. He had accumulated too many empty food containers. The freezing air was keeping them mostly free of smell, but he didn't want to attract hungry critters. He collected tools and garbage in his backpack and set off. It felt good to have a purpose in his mind and in his sights. He walked for more than an hour, at first intending merely to get away from his camp and find a place where he could bury or at least cache his empty cans. But he kept walking mostly for the sheer joy and simple pleasure of movement. There were few sounds in the winter woods. His mother always had the television on at home. He was relieved to be free of commercial background noise. There was little snow, just enough to leave tracks, so the going was easy, and he was confident he'd find his way back. He found a seep where some underground spring came up, thawing the ground. He dug a hole, flattened and buried his cans.

It was while resting on his heels, surveying his work, that he saw the large brown form at the edge of the wet area. He stared and stared. Whatever it was wasn't moving. It took a few moments, but finally, he realized he was looking at a moose. Brayden stayed very still—moose could be aggressive and dangerous. This one was resting, and he didn't want to wake it. He watched and watched and slowly realized that this moose was never waking from its sleep. The body had the caved-in quality of death, like a lightly deflated balloon. He slowly stood and waved his hands in the air. Nothing. He jumped up and down. Still nothing. So, he approached. It appeared to be an older cow, fallen down with her head in the muck, black mud splashed over her neck and body.

Meat.

Brayden realized this was no longer a living, breathing animal but was now a pile of meat. Probably not very tasty meat, certainly—an old animal, died instead of shot, left to wither instead of bled and butchered—but there were still calories and nutrition there. He would make smoked jerky, not grilled steaks. He knelt down. He got to work.

NINE

Colden arrived early at the trailhead where she was to meet Jack. It had snowed the night before, and everything was sugarcoated in a thick layer of white. Few cars were in the parking area, the usual array of battered Subarus and pickup trucks, with an old Saab thrown in for variety—the typical ride of the winter hiker and backcountry skier. There was one sedan. No sign of Jack's official DEC truck, yet. Colden dragged out her pack and strapped her snowshoes to either side. They were in the midst of a mild and dry spell, but conditions were likely to be different where they were headed, and the weather could, and often did, change quickly. She sat on the open tailgate of her truck and began putting on her gaiters. The door to the sedan across the lot opened. She expected to see a mom, someone here to pick up a kid or something, a woman who felt out of place and who would ask her a question in an effort to find reassurance.

Instead, Larry stepped out. Colden was too surprised at the sight of him to hide the feeling.

"Larry. What are you doing here?"

"Thought I'd join you."

The idea of him hiking into the winter wilderness with them was beyond improbable. It was absurd. She shook her head in annoyed disbelief.

"What? You can't be serious."

"Colden, this isn't your personal, private, pet project," Larry lectured. "There are other people and organizations interested in the results. There is money involved. I'm coming because I want to, and because I can, and because it's part of my responsibility to the department."

Colden looked him up and down. He was wearing an outdated outfit meant for lift service, downhill skiing, not backwoods hiking.

"Actually, Larry, I don't think you can. Not in that getup, at least."

Larry pointed his finger and opened his mouth to say something, but just then the DEC truck pulled up, and Jack hopped out. Larry turned his attention to Jack, instead. Jack looked at Larry, running his eyes up and down, just as Colden had. He shook his head. Colden read the expression on his face. It said two things: "amateur" and "dangerous." If you were the former, you were likely to be the latter to anyone else with you on a trip like this. She went back to adjusting her gaiters.

"That all you brought?" Jack asked.

Larry looked confused by the question.

"Dude," Jack said. "You're going to freeze your nuts off."

"I'll be fine," Larry said. "It's not that cold."

"It will be. And weather can change around here in a minute."

They stared at each other.

"Did you bring snowshoes?" Jack asked.

"I was told you had an extra pair that you'd be bringing for me."

"I was not told that," Jack said.

"You?" Larry said, looking at Colden. "Do you have an extra pair?"

Colden compressed her lips and shook her head.

"Nope. Even if I did, they're not your size. They wouldn't support your weight."

What she said was factual, but it came out as an insult. She didn't care. She actually enjoyed it.

"This is ridiculous," Larry said. "I don't need snowshoes. There isn't that much snow at all."

"There may be plenty where we're going," Jack said.

"There is an outfitter in town," Larry said. "I'll go rent a pair. I'll be right back."

"While you're there, rent a real pair of boots, gloves, and a face mask," Jack said.

"OK. I will," Larry said.

"Also, gaiters, hiking poles, extra socks, headlamp, flashlight, heat packs . . ." Jack ticked the items off his fingers.

Larry crossed his arms over his chest.

"Look," Jack said. "They don't rent that stuff. Snowshoes, yeah, but you need a lot more than snowshoes. I was told you would be prepared, but you're not equipped for this trip, and we can't wait for you. There's not enough hours of daylight. Right now, if we brought you, it'd be dangerous for you. And for us. We gotta get in there and get to this moose before the bears and coyotes spread bits of him or her over a multiple-mile radius." He grabbed his pack and locked his truck. "Sorry, man. Just not going to work this time. We'll try again next time. There will for sure be a next time. Go back to the lodge, put your feet up by the fire, take the day off."

Larry glared at the ground. Colden expected the heat of his gaze to melt a circle of snow and send up wisps of smoke. She wished she had the freedom to talk to her colleagues the way Jack did to Larry. Men accepted that kind of raw banter from each other. Not from a woman. Not ever. Jack cocked his head at her.

"Ready?"

She started moving toward the trail in answer. They left Larry standing in the frozen parking lot and never looked back. They hiked in silence for an hour, both working off their irritations. Then, it was time to go off trail. They stopped to coordinate location and route.

They were about to set off again when Jack said, "That guy. He can be such a tool. Feel sorry for him, but seriously."

"Did you know he was coming?"

"My boss tells me that according to his boss, Larry's coming. When I ask questions or express concerns, he tells me to just try and accommodate the guy. I don't know him very well; he's not a bad scientist, not even that bad of a guy, but man, is he annoying. He's also not from around here. He doesn't get it, that's for sure."

"You handled it well," Colden said, wishing she could have done the same.

"No, I didn't," Jack said, shrugging. "Maybe I'll be fired when I get back."

"Just think of him as the FNG."

"Fucking new guy. That's for damn sure. Keeps popping up. Like a cold sore."

"All I know is that he gives me the massive creeps," Colden said. "Puts my spidey sense on way-high alert."

"We better get going," Jack replied, looking up at the sky.

They did. The effort of slogging through the underbrush, the concentration required to not trip over a slippery rock or get an ankle caught between logs hidden by the mess of leaf litter and old snow, kept them quiet. They stopped once or twice to get their bearings, drink some water, eat a granola bar and apple slices slathered in peanut butter. They were careful to pick up every scrap and crumble of food. There were enough problems with bears associating the smell of humans with the presence of snacks. There was no sun, just a looming ceiling of gray skies that felt like it was coming closer to their heads inch by inch. It seemed like it was taking longer than it should to get where they needed to go, but there was nothing to be done about it. Besides, it often felt that way in the backcountry. They might be walking out in the dark. So be it. They had headlamps. They were getting closer. They paused to take out the portable antennae. At every stop, the clicks got louder and more regular. They seemed to be right where they needed to be, yet they didn't see the moose. They were trudging in lightly frozen mud—a spring underfoot was thawing the area. The moose might still be alive and just weak or injured, but it might also be dead and covered in fresh snow. They paused in frustration.

Colden tipped her head and began looking overhead instead of on the ground. She found them. Crows. There were two in a tree. Three more nearby. She moved toward them. They flapped away, protesting. She called to Jack. She pointed. There was the carcass, her head in the snow, a part of her flank ripped away by some large animal, opening the tough hide so the crows could gorge themselves.

Colden squatted and wiped the snow from the moose head. The animal's fur was matted with frozen mud. She must have collapsed here, trudging through the muck. Colden didn't need to read the ear tag and collar number to know which moose this was. She remembered the old gal. She'd been in poor condition when they had collared her. Too thin, worn-down teeth, drab coat. There were no marks on her face and neck that would suggest predation or injury.

Seems she'd simply gotten too tired and given up, and really, who could blame her, Colden thought. Life out there was damn hard.

Colden examined the wound on the cow's back leg. It was strangely tidy. No claw or tear marks. She tilted her head back and forth, her mind resisting what her eyes were telling her.

"Jack," she said, warning in her voice.

He was at the head of the animal, unscrewing the collar. He looked up, stopped what he was doing, and came to stand near her. They both stared.

"What the . . ." Jack finally whispered.

The flesh on the moose's back leg and flank had been butchered. No bones with teeth marks or strands of sinew hanging around. The hide cleanly cut and peeled back, the edges of the flesh squared off in a way that could only come from a knife. No sign of the animal having been killed or gutted the way a hunter would. This work must have happened after the moose had died.

Who would be way out here in the middle of winter, stumble upon the animal, have the skills and equipment to take away a good twenty pounds of meat, but leave the rest? All these questions hung, unspoken, in the air between them.

"Look," Jack said, his eyes going wide. "This is really freaking strange, but let's get what we need to get done and get out of here. We're going to lose the day, and we can talk about this later."

They hurriedly took samples and photos, packed up the radio collar and their gear, and headed back to the trail. They didn't talk much on their way. Talking took energy and concentration that was better used for hiking. It was dark by the time they got to their trucks.

"Come have dinner with me and my parents," Colden said suddenly.

It was an unprecedented invitation. She'd never asked a colleague to her house before.

"They'd love to meet you," she continued. "I've talked about you so many times when I've told them about our work. We're close by. My dad is a great cook and always makes too much."

"Well, OK, then," Jack said, smiling. "My wife and the kids happen to be away this week. In Florida with the grandparents, lucky them. So, it's either cold, leftover pizza at my empty house or a hot meal and good company at yours. Lead the way, lady."

Dix had a hearty turkey casserole waiting for them when they got there. They filled him and Sally in on the strange butchering of the moose.

"Are you sure it was a cut?" Dix asked as he served.

Colden and Jack both nodded, vigorously.

"I'll show you the pictures," Colden said.

"Something was there with a very sharp knife," Jack added.

"And opposable thumbs, apparently," Dix observed.

"So, this moose dies a natural death, no signs of hunting or trauma, and falls in the middle of a remote area, totally off trail, total backcountry, and yet someone finds it, and they either have in their possession or have the time to go get a knife strong enough to cut through hide and meat and joints, and they hack off a bunch of flesh, and they disappear with it?" Sally asked, incredulous.

Colden nodded. "Seems so."

"The question is, why? Why would someone be out there? And if they're good enough in the backcountry to be out there, at this time of year, why do they need to take part of a dead moose?" Dix asked.

"It's totally bizarre," Colden said.

"Would this person get in trouble if you reported them?" Sally asked.

"There's absolutely nothing to report," Jack said. "Even if we did know who did it. No law against scavenging a dead animal."

"No," Dix said. "No law. But there is common sense against it. Probably will taste awful."

They snickered around the table. Except for Sally.

"Someone is out there in an awful lot of need, then," Sally said quietly.

"Isn't there always someone out there in an awful lot of need?" Dix sighed. "Isn't there always?"

TEN

Colden had to go back to Albany for a few days. She had a couple of meetings. Needed to check her mail. She had some grants to discuss with the department chair. So much fieldwork depended upon office work.

She headed south on the highway, and as she pulled out of the mountains and into the foothills, Colden was surprised to see spring creeping in. By the time she got off the exit for Albany, lawns and trees were already bathed in a soft haze of green. The Adirondacks always seemed reluctant to let go of winter and held the cold and snow tight in the embrace of rocky arms. Colden knew it was not an easy place to live, and she liked that. She respected hardship. Some days she realized this was an attitude only someone with privilege and comfort could afford to hold. Other days, she thought there were plenty of stubborn folks, without even two nickels to rub together, who also seemed to relish the challenges of their mountain home. Rarely, it occurred to her that maybe they just didn't have any other options.

She exited the highway and went straight to her office. The condo could wait. There was nothing there for her anyway, not even a plant that required watering. It was late afternoon by the time she walked down the long corridors of her building. She said a few quick hellos to the people she passed; poured herself some end-of-the-day, dense, and lukewarm coffee; softened its harsh taste with plenty of milk and sugar; and went to her desk. She caught up on e-mails. She scanned the endless stream of departmental and administrative directives and policies and procedures sent out in elaborately worded and unnecessarily complex notes.

Lawyers, she thought, annoyed. All this crap is not for the benefit of students or scientists. It's just to reduce the chance of being sued.

The room darkened. She turned on her desk lamp. She heard doors open and close, footsteps in the corridor as everyone left. Slowly, she was surrounded by welcome silence. She logged on to the university system and began a search for research articles. She looked for anything new on moose. On beaver. It was important to keep up with the competition. Both creatures were common enough research subjects, but nothing came up that was particularly helpful or hurtful to her project. She did a quick scan of articles on wolves and coyotes, but there was nothing new to be found there, either. She thought about getting more coffee but imagined the dark ring of scalded brew she'd likely find in the bottom of the carafe and stayed in front of her computer. A door opened and closed. Must be the cleaning crew. She should quit soon. She should go get something to eat. Something decent. Take herself to a restaurant. Stop subsisting on a steady stream of snacks and eat a real meal. But she kept clicking and reading, her reflection ghostlike in the screen. She heard someone coming toward her. She listened for the rolling sound of a cleaning cart. Nothing. Just a few heavy, widely spaced footsteps. Colden got a fluttering rush of nerves, as if a small bird was caught inside her rib cage. She started to close tabs and shut down programs. An alert came on. Updates. Do not turn off your computer. A shadow darkened her monitor.

"Working late?" said a familiar voice.

"Larry," Colden shot back without turning around. "What brings you in at this hour?"

"Been here all along. Saw you come in."

Colden had missed him. She was annoyed at herself for not noticing.

"You decide to come for a little warm-up?" he asked.

"Oh, you know, gotta come in from the field from time to time. Meetings. Paperwork. The demands of the academy," Colden said, trying to keep her voice light, her answers meaningless.

She willed her computer to hurry up. Updating. Updating. Do not shut off your computer.

"Did you and Jack have fun out there in the wilderness?" Larry asked.

"Well, if you call trudging through the backcountry in the middle of winter looking for a dead moose, fun," Colden said.

"Didn't appreciate your blowing me off," Larry said. "Not very polite or collegial, now was it?"

"There was a job that needed to be done, Larry. I'm sorry, but you weren't up to the task at that moment. Maybe some other time."

"Did you find the moose?"

"Yes. An old cow. Died of natural causes."

"That's too bad," Larry said.

It seemed he was genuinely saddened by the news. Colden gave him that. She didn't respond. She hoped he'd take the hint and go away.

"You and Jack find anything else while you were out there?"

There was something suggestive in his question. Colden looked at him, not understanding. A sneer spread across his face.

"You and Jack. Such good friends," he said, making air quotes around the word *friends*.

Still Colden didn't understand. Then suddenly she did. Her stomach recoiled.

"Oh, please! Don't be ridiculous, Larry," she snapped. "Jack and I have worked together for years. He's a professional. And married."

"That didn't stop you before," Larry said, his voice low and mocking. "The being married thing, I mean."

Colden went cold. The feel of Liam's body under her hands came back in a rush. Suddenly, she was too warm. She was embarrassed that her face flushed in front of Larry.

"Ah," Larry said. "Guess your kiwi pal forgot to mention his wife. Sorry to be the bearer of bad news." He threw his hands up. "Don't shoot the messenger. Just thought you'd want to know what you were dealing with."

Colden set her teeth. *He doesn't know what he's talking about,* she thought. *He's a jerk. He's making this up. There's something wrong with this guy. He's out to get me for some reason. He's a misogynist. He's an overweight, unattractive, sparsely published, unknown scientist looking for a fight.*

Her computer screen finally went dark. She snapped it closed, slid it into her backpack, and pushed her chair back. One wheel bumped into Larry's foot. Larry didn't move.

"Please move," she said.

Each word seemed to fall from her mouth and clatter on the floor. Larry stayed where he was. Colden reminded herself that she knew how to fight. All those years of martial arts training. It had been a while, but she remembered. She tightened her fist and mentally rehearsed the act of pulling her arm forward, loading her shoulder muscles, then slamming her elbow backward. She'd never done this to a person. Only on large pads. Well, he was a large pad. He was so close, she could sense his fingers moving in his pants pockets. Only the thin chair back and a few inches of empty space between them. She wouldn't. But it was good to know she could.

Suddenly, the room was filled with light.

The cleaning crew. This time it really was them. Voices in some language unfamiliar to Colden bounced toward her. The words came fast, like little barks between two small dogs. Larry finally took a large step backward, out into the hallway, and walked away without another word. Colden waited, counting her breaths and his steps, imagining his retreat out of their area, down the corridors to the elevators. She sat very still, steadying her breath, something else she'd learned how to do in her training. Finally, she stood up and went to the window. There he was, his lumbering bulk moving down the path to the parking lot. He got into his car, the sedan she'd seen before. He backed out and drove away. Now, it was now safe for her to leave.

Colden passed his office on her way out. The lights were on, and he was gone. She paused and peered in. There were several pictures tacked to the wall above his monitor. One of Larry and some buddies in a boat on some lake. A total cliché shot, Colden thought, a bunch of dorky dudes with beer bellies holding fish aloft. Also, stock school photos of two different boys, both elementary school age. Both blond. One wore glasses and seemed slightly cross-eyed, with a loopy grin that made him look slightly drunk. Another photo showed the two boys together, one crouched forward, grinning widely, as he leaned over a wheelchair where the bespectacled boy sat. There were braces around the smaller, younger boy's legs. His head was cocked at an unnatural angle. There was someone, an adult, standing to the side of the chair. The photo showed only this person's legs and the lower half of an arm holding crutches. There were no photos that showed a woman, someone who might be a wife and mother to the boys.

Larry had a private life. Children. Had or once had a wife. Hobbies and friends, too. Colden had never bothered to imagine this. She looked around his office. It was bigger than hers. Of course. It had real walls and a real door. There was a mug on the desk. She couldn't read all the words on it, but saw something about "Dad." She saw a plastic storage container with the residue of some sort of food still in it and a baseball hat that said, "A bad day of fishing is better than a good day at work." Strange that she'd never heard Larry say things like, "Gotta cut out early today for a teacher conference," "Can't come in—one of the kids is sick," or "Spent the weekend at a birthday party," the phrases that routinely peppered other parents' conversations. Must be divorced. Maybe he never saw the kids anymore. Maybe the one in the wheelchair had died.

She realized that she'd always imagined Larry living alone in a sparsely furnished, soulless condo, watching television at night from a big lounge chair. In fact, that was the way she lived. At least when she was in town. Minus the television and lounge chair. Maybe, much to her surprise, Larry lived in a nice ranch house with a big yard and a sweet wife who made his lunch and felt her children were gifts—and tests—from God.

Colden went back to her condo. The only living thing that greeted her there was a large spider that had set up a web in a corner above the hook where she hung her coat. She stared at it and its empty web and wondered how it found anything to eat in her place. Certainly, she would not. She threw her backpack on the sofa and sat next to it. Then she twisted sideways and put her head on the pack and her feet on the cushions without bothering to remove her shoes. She didn't mean to fall asleep, just to rest and figure out what to do next, but she conked out and woke up many hours later, decidedly confused. She was stiff and ravenous, with deep creases in her cheek from where it had rested on the pack.

She rubbed her face and raked her hands through her hair. Serrated, predawn light came through the slats in her half-open mini-blinds. Albany, she told herself. Right. She was back in Albany. She extricated herself from her uncomfortable position on the sofa, stood, stretched, and looked around as if she had woken up in an unfamiliar place.

She'd had the condo for more than a year but had never gotten around to putting anything up on the off-white walls. She had a single stool at the kitchen counter, which also served as dining table and desk. The door to the bedroom was cracked open, but there was no point in looking there because she knew the room was empty, other than a few clothing items hanging, lonely, in the closet. The inexpensive, Euro-style sofa where she had fallen asleep clicked open and flat to double as a bed, but when she was here, she rarely bothered with even that little effort. The door to the bathroom was ajar; she caught a glimpse of the bare floor, clear plastic shower curtain, bottles of generic-brand shampoo and conditioner, and a cracked bar of soap on the sink. Colden knew there was nothing more than a half-empty can of Folgers, a wizened lemon, a bottle of club soda long gone flat, half a jar of peanut butter, and some stale English muffins in the fridge.

I live like a middle-aged bachelor, Colden thought.

The exchange with Larry came back to her, like a bad smell wafting in on stale air. Liam. Larry said he was married. It had never dawned on her that Liam would have a wife at home. Which was naïve, of course. Maybe Liam hooked up with plenty of grad students. Larry made it seem like he was trying to do her a favor by telling her. Maybe he was. Maybe it was better to know. The whole experience with Liam, which had been so lovely in her memory, was now dirtied and tawdry.

Her condo suddenly seemed oppressive in its emptiness. She had to grow up. She had to get a life. She went to the bathroom and quickly brushed her teeth and washed her face. She stared at herself in the mirror. She looked tired. There were shadows under her eyes; her cheeks seemed to sag. She yanked her hair into a ponytail and lightly slapped her cheeks—she wanted to raise the color in her face and in her life.

She fled the condo, drove to a nearby diner, and ate a hearty breakfast of eggs, hash browns, bacon, toast, and a fruit cup. She then drove to the local mall. It was still early, the doors just being unlocked. She stepped into the starkly lit, echoing space. It smelled of strong cleaners and hot grease from the food court. She passed few people as she wandered the cavernous halls. She watched teenagers and middle-aged women setting up cash registers and folding clothes—these were the sort of low-wage jobs she'd never had to have and would likely never need to have. She walked past oversize posters of savagely made-up and barely dressed women striking absurdly awkward poses. She winced with discomfort. She kept moving down the corridor, feeling like she was in school after hours, until she found a department store. She took the slow-moving escalator to the home section, where there was one clerk wrestling a plastic-wrapped, oversize duvet onto a shelf.

Colden stalled. Every surface around her was packed with shiny, colorful, decorative, useless things. She ran her hand over a comforter and was shocked by its cold, shiny, slick surface. The item was completely misnamed, she thought—there was no comfort in that sort of bed covering. Everything she touched or picked up seemed both new and artificial. She couldn't stop herself from making comparisons to her parents' home, where almost everything she used had a backstory. They ate with silver that had attained a lovely, soft patina from a hundred years of use, starting with Dix's grandmother. She read books and journals curled up on an oversize down sofa Dix's father had bought and Sally had reupholstered with a muted-jade linen. The heavy, handmade pottery plates that Dix filled at mealtimes had been handmade by a friend of his mother's. The Adirondack-style twig dining table and chairs had been made and gifted to Sally by a man who was once a kid she had helped through foster care. It occurred to her that almost everything at home was made or acquired by people she'd never met. The realization flooded her with sadness. She felt suddenly like the items that surrounded her in the store—new, callow, without substance or history.

She walked up and down a few more aisles. Such a cacophony of colors, prints, patterns, choices. Who knew bath mats came in so many varieties? How was a window treatment different from a curtain? Trash cans with hands-free sensors? Really? Were placemats actually necessary? And the pillows! Where to begin with the options in shape, size, color, and promises for sound sleep, design sophistication, and delighted friends. She grabbed at one. It was small and plump, with a sunny starburst print. Colden tossed it in her cart. She plucked a set of towels in the same color and grabbed a matching shower curtain. She knew her cupboards were bare. Everything in this store came packed in sets of a minimum of four. She never had guests. But she could be clumsy in the domestic sphere, she reminded herself. She'd probably break a dish or two over time. She put a box of plain white dishes in her cart and headed for the checkout. This was enough. More than enough. Probably too much. Certainly, more than she really required.

She left the mall feeling wrung out but made herself stop at a grocery store and pick up some fresh fruits and vegetables, a loaf of artisan bread, a wedge of expensive cheese. She thought she'd get some cereal, but when she got to the aisle, she was overwhelmed by the quantity and variety. There were seven kinds of raisin bran alone.

Colden went back to the condo; put the groceries away; hung the stiff, creased shower curtain and the vaguely plastic-smelling towels; and then set the pillow on the sofa, where it did not make the cheerful statement she had hoped, but looked merely lost and insubstantial.

"Why am I such a freak?" she wondered aloud.

Well, because, she reminded herself, she got most of her clothes at a place that sold guns, ammo, and camping gear. She picked up sandwiches, frozen food, and granola bars at the same place she gassed up her truck. She didn't cook or watch television or keep up on pop culture. She hadn't been to a movie theater in more than a year. Most of her meals were prepared by her dad from things he had grown or killed himself. She'd spent more nights in a tent or lean-to than in the condo.

I'm basically feral, she told herself.

Colden stripped out of her clothes, went to the bathroom, and took a scalding shower. She dried herself off with her thick but strangely nonabsorptive towels. She wrapped up her hair and again stared at her face in the mirror. A smattering of freckles was permanently printed over her nose and cheekbones. Her eyes were the color of faded denim. There were chapped flakes of skin on her lips. Creases were beginning to assert themselves at the corner of her eyes. She wondered if she saw this exact face on someone else, would she think the woman was pretty? Liam had told her she was lovely, right before he gripped her face in his work-roughened hands and opened his mouth against hers. That compliment didn't count for much, anymore. She saw herself as run-down and washed out, an oft-laundered shirt left out on the line in the sun and rain.

The image of a snapshot rose before her. Miranda, her mother, the woman who birthed her, in the garden, dirt on her cheek, gloves, and knees, smiling at the camera. She couldn't recall where she'd seen it. But looking at her own face now, she saw something from that photo asserting herself there. Her mother's life had been cut so short. Yet, her mother had experienced so much before she died. Most of it tragedy, but also a huge love and a baby. Things that seemed exotic and unknowable to Colden.

She shook off the uncomfortable feelings and found a pair of jeans she'd left in the apartment the last time she'd been here. She'd been wondering where this favorite, comfortable, full-of-memories pair had been. She stuffed her hands into the bunched-up pockets and found a wad of something. It was a business card.

Printed on high-quality stock, she saw the name but didn't recognize it. Andrew Accorsi, Esq. Ah yes, Drew. His face at the bar came back to her. He'd asked her to call him. That had been weeks ago. Actually, months. Months since that night with Liam, the night Drew had said he'd needed her help. She flushed with embarrassment. She'd been dismissive of him at the bar. She'd blown him off and forgotten him.

I drank too much that night, she chastised herself. *If I hadn't had all those beers, I might not have been with Liam, I might not have been embarrassed by Larry, I might not have forgotten Drew.*

Liam had been the one pouring. Now, she had another reason to be mad at him.

The card had no address, just the name, his credential, and a phone number with a New York City prefix. Maybe there was one thing about that night she could try to repair. She tapped the numbers into her phone.

"This is Drew."

His voice was firm, deep, warm, and open. Colden was surprised into silence. She hadn't remembered that. She'd also been sort of hoping for voice mail.

"Hello?" he said, his tone encouraging and more bemused than irritated.

"Drew. Sorry. It's Colden. Colden McComb. We met . . ."

"Colden!"

His voice was a blast of blatant enthusiasm. She was caught off guard.

"Um, yeah," she stammered. "Hi. Sorry it took me so long to call. I lost your card. Just rediscovered it."

"Where are you?"

Colden had forgotten how abrupt, how imperative, he was.

"Where am I? You mean right now? I'm in Albany."

"Great. Me too. Let's have dinner."

"Dinner?"

"Yes, Colden. Dinner. Tonight. Eat. It's what people do," he said.

Colden was silent. She didn't know how to respond. How she wanted to respond. She couldn't remember the last time she'd had dinner with a man, just the two of them. She wondered if she'd remember how it was done.

"Do you have other plans?" he asked.

Drew seemed to always be teasing and nudging her. Which always illuminated the otherwise opaque defenses she had for keeping people at a distance. Defenses she almost never otherwise realized she had.

"Just, you know, work," she hedged.

"Blow it off until tomorrow."

"I thought you were in the city. Don't you live down there?" Colden asked, stalling.

"Not anymore. I just bought a little row house in Albany. It's a wreck. I must have been out of my mind. Starting to fix it up."

Colden tried to imagine Drew in work boots and a tool belt. It seemed implausible.

"I've got no working kitchen," he said. "So, come downtown and have dinner with me. There's a great little Italian place just around the corner. Now that I have your number, I'll text you the address."

He hung up. A moment later, her phone pinged. A restaurant name, an address, a time. And a silly smiley face. Colden wasn't used to people being so definitive, so impossible to say "no" to. But there it was. She was going to dinner with Drew.

The restaurant was tucked into a heavily treed historic district, on the ground floor of a residential building, a few blocks away from the coffee shop where they first met. Stepping through the front door felt like entering someone's living room—because that is exactly what it once had been. She'd wanted to get there first, to get herself settled and watch Drew come in, but he was already there, waving at her from a small table in the far corner of the dining room. There were only seven or eight other, white-tableclothed tables, all full, crammed into a compact space, forcing Colden to thread her way awkwardly through the chairs, bumping and apologizing to people as she went, aware that Drew's eyes were on her the whole time. Most of the men she passed wore button-down shirts, still stiff from dry cleaning, with crisp creases where their arms bent. The women were wearing dresses and pumps or boots with heels, or pantsuits, with lipstick and hair that had been styled and colored. Colden was wearing jeans and a button-down shirt with a light sweater. It wasn't like she kept a dress-up outfit at the condo. She felt young and callow, underdressed and out of place. When she got to the table, Drew stood and pulled out a chair for her. There wasn't enough room for what he was doing, but he managed the cramped spaces gracefully.

Old-school manners, Colden thought.

A tuxedoed waiter instantly appeared, asking if he could get her a beverage. Drew asked if she'd ever had a particular brand of Italian beer. She shook her head, and he ordered one for her. The waiter bowed and backed away as Drew thanked him by name.

"Guess you're a regular here," Colden observed.

"This place is one of the main reasons I bought a house nearby," Drew said, smiling. "Best home-style, old-school Italian food there is. Other than my grandmother's. Totally authentic."

"You're Italian?" Colden asked, not bothering to hide her surprise.

"Hunnert percent," he said. "'Joisey Italian."

"Really?"

"Dad was a handyman, Mom a lunch lady," Drew said. "Grew up in Hoboken. Third generation. Grandparents came off the boat."

"Seriously?"

Colden didn't know at first why she was so surprised at these personal details. Then she did know. She'd assumed he came from privilege.

"Nope, not joking, I promise," Drew continued. "Parents scrimped and saved to help me get to law school. First in my family to go to college, much less grad school. Cliché, yes, but no joke. Of course, I am eternally grateful. And eternally guilty. I'm their pride and joy and also a disappointment because I'm not home enough and because I'm not married yet, for shame, in spite of every fix-up and all the meddling they've tried. My two younger sisters are hitched, living nearby, and giving them grandkids to fuss over already. Here I am, just turned thirty, didn't buy a place in the old neighborhood and not yet working on rug rats. You know."

"Actually, I don't know," Colden said, smiling. She was going to say she was an only child but stopped herself.

Drew started to say something else but was interrupted by the waiter's appearance with her beverage. He poured her drink and stood at the ready with a small pad of paper and a stub of a pencil. She'd not had a chance to read the menu. Drew hadn't even opened his.

"Will you allow me?" he asked, placing his hand briefly over hers.

Colden nodded, unsure what she was acquiescing to. Drew and the waiter conferred. Colden looked around at the small candles flickering on each table; the thick, cloth napkins; the reflections on the silverware. She was more accustomed to pubs, burger-and-beer-type places. She let herself be charmed by the setting and the courtly manner of her host and waiter. Something else she was unaccustomed to.

When the waiter left, she and Drew spoke of the mild winter, the early spring. He told her about his home, how it had once been a "house of ill repute," then a flophouse, and more recently, a duplex, which he was converting back to a single-family, two-story home. There was a tiny but sunny backyard, he said, where he hoped to grow tomatoes so that he could make fresh pasta sauce like his grandmother had.

"You'll have to talk to my dad about tomatoes," Colden said. "He's an expert at growing them in difficult conditions."

Drew raised his eyebrows at her. She was vaguely embarrassed by bringing up her father, suggesting they chat. It felt like a slip-up, as if she was being overly familiar.

"How's the beer?" he asked.

It was light and refreshing. She asked him more about his house, and he regaled her with comical stories of home-repair efforts gone wrong. He pointed to scraped knuckles and blistered palms as proof of his labors.

"Am I boring you?" Drew said suddenly, interrupting himself.

"Not at all," she said. "I actually grew up doing stuff like that with my father. He's a carpenter and caretaker."

"Weird that our fathers do the same thing," Drew said. "Both handymen."

They were not the same sort of handymen, Colden knew but didn't say. The issues that came along with the million-dollar vacation homes her father cared for had to be quite different from those Drew's father undoubtedly handled in the apartment complexes of Hoboken and Jersey City. Her father was also college educated. And wealthy. He held his wealth so quietly that few knew about it. Even Colden knew little beyond the fact that he had a lot of acreage, most of which he protected for conservation and recreation. There were many times in her youth that he'd taken her hiking in wild places, and when she'd asked where they were, he'd quietly said they were on their own land. Colden figured Drew pictured her dad as a rough-around-the-edges, backwoods sort of guy. Which he was and very much was not. The contradictions were too much to explain, and she didn't know Drew well enough to try.

"Well, I don't imagine splitting wood is often on your dad's to-do list," was all she said.

"No. But I bet they both deal with a lot of rats," Drew replied.

"Mice more than rats. But yes, plenty of rodents, nonetheless."

"So, you have the blue-collar-parent, high-expectations, over-educated-kid thing, too?" Drew asked.

The waiter appeared with their plates, giving Colden a reprieve from answering his question. There were three thin cutlets, swathed with linen-colored sauce dotted with sliced mushrooms. Colden took a bite and chewed slowly, savoring the delicate, buttery flavors.

"Wow," she said, not exactly intending to change the subject.

"Yeah, amazing, isn't it?"

"What is this?"

"Veal. Best I've ever had."

"First I've ever had," Colden admitted.

Colden was a bit perplexed and also intrigued by the unexpected contrasts between the two of them. Her family was apparently more wealthy and educated but seemingly less sophisticated and worldly than his. She felt both beyond Drew and behind him in unfamiliar ways.

"So, you were telling me about your family," he said. "The challenges of being the first to get some letters and titles after your name."

"That's not exactly my experience," she said cautiously. "My dad is actually college educated. Similar field to mine. More forestry and conservation than wildlife. But there was little work in the field when he graduated. And he's incredibly good at fixing things. All sorts of things. So, he fell into caretaking and kept at it."

"And your mom?"

Colden wiped her mouth. Her mom. Whom should she talk about, Sally or Miranda? Discussing both was too much. She struggled with what to say. She was so unused to being asked direct questions about her family. Everyone she'd grown up around already knew her history. Knew more of it than she did, in fact.

"That's a much longer, more complicated story," she said carefully.

Drew held up his hands.

"Say no more. Some other time."

Colden was both relieved and disappointed that he didn't push the issue further.

"You told me you needed help with something," Colden said, taking advantage of the break in conversation to change the subject. "Still a problem?"

She watched Drew and saw his expression change from open and friendly to thoughtful and serious. He cleared his throat, then leaned forward and put his elbows on the table. He lowered his voice and spoke as if everything he said was in confidence. As he began to explain that his employer, a large forest products and paper company, was in negotiations for a land deal that would give thousands of acres back to the state in exchange for all kinds of easements and conservation, recreation, and continued logging rights, she realized why he was being cautious. These situations were complex and controversial, with many competing demands, all of which were difficult to balance. They were surrounded, at every close table, by other lawyers, lobbyists, politicians. Drew said the goal was to maintain access to raw materials while protecting land for recreation, tourism, and jobs.

"Sounds like a win-win all around, right?" he said.

"Seems so," she replied. "But I can guess what the problem is."

Drew looked at her encouragingly.

"Gossip. Misinformation. Lack of community support," she ticked off.

"Exactly. And a few other things besides."

The waiter came and removed their plates. He brushed crumbs off the white tablecloth with a small metal scraper. He said an unfamiliar word in question to Drew, who nodded.

"What other things?" Colden asked.

"Vandalism."

"Of land or equipment?"

"Vehicles. Windows broken. Tires slashed. One of our guys was stranded for hours in a serious snowstorm with the weather blowing through the busted windshield."

"Expensive. Dangerous," Colden said.

She wondered how or if any of this was connected to the petty thefts she'd heard about. The moose-meat incident. The stuff taken from camps. The rustling around in Gene's outbuilding. Such different behaviors. Unlikely the same person or persons. But still. She didn't mention any of this to Drew.

"My employers want to crack down hard on whoever is doing this."

"And you don't?"

"I'm afraid that sort of response will only make things worse. Cause more problems. Ruin any goodwill we might have. The problems are pretty localized. Near an area where we are trying to gain easements or buy land outright. Someone doesn't want to give up. Can't seem to find out who even really owns the land. All tied up in complex trusts. Makes it even harder to determine who might be responsible."

"Sounds like maybe you want to make friends of your enemies."

"I do. And that's where I was hoping you could come in. Local girl. Maybe with local connections. Maybe could do some asking around. Quietly. In a nonthreatening, nonconfrontational way."

"That's not the way most downstaters approach problems within the boundaries of the Adirondack Park's blue line," Colden said.

"Right," Drew said. "Well, I guess I'm not your typical downstater. I'm looking for another way."

The waiter appeared and set a tiny glass in front of her. It was filled with three distinct bands of color, red, white, and green. He set another one in front of Drew.

"Italian flag," the waiter announced, quite formally, addressing Colden. "There are two rules with this drink. You can't ask what's in it, and you must drink it all at once."

He nodded to Drew and walked away. Drew lifted his glass and gestured to her to do the same.

"To the local girl and to the other way," Drew said, gently clinking his glass against hers.

Colden swallowed. The drink was like liquid jewels slipping down her throat. The meal was done. Drew rose and helped pull out her seat. She asked about the check, and he just shook his head. They danced their way past the other tables and stepped outside. Colden promised to look into things. She thanked him for the dinner. He asked her where her car was, took her elbow, and walked with her there. He didn't leave until she was seated in her truck. She watched his retreating back in the rearview mirror. She was both relieved and just a tad disappointed he hadn't tried to kiss her. On the cheek even. It was a signal that their relationship was that of friends. Perhaps colleagues. He was polite and professional. Probably that way with everyone. Probably had a girlfriend. Guy like that? Likely. He wasn't her type, but she could see he'd make a great catch for someone. Someone who had shiny pumps and an array of matching purses in her closet, not muddy hiking boots, well-worn Carhartts, and several backpacks.

ELEVEN

Brayden never made a clear or conscious decision to stay in the woods. He just never made the choice to leave. When he thought about it, about what was next, where he might go, he didn't see any clear path out, any destination that would give him a safe landing spot. It was so peaceful where he was. No trying to fall asleep as adults drank in the next room and then jerking suddenly awake to the sound of voices raised in anger, a glass crashing into a wall, someone slamming the thin metal door so hard when they fled that it rattled the entire trailer, as if an earthquake had just passed through. No other kids whispering, arguing, making out, sneaking around, trying to steal your stuff, and all the other things they did in his foster homes. No need to try to watch out for your little sister. Although he missed that part. He missed her. He just didn't miss any other humans he'd known.

He watched the moments pass. The sun was in the sky for so few hours and so often obscured by clouds, it was hard to tell where one day ended and the next began. He had his few chores, setting and checking his rabbit snares, setting and checking his ice-fishing poles, keeping food strung up, away from the bears, keeping his bedding aired out, keeping himself warm.

He slept when he could no longer see a few feet in front of his face and rose when the darkness lifted. He had no idea and little interest in how much time had passed. It was still winter. That much he knew.

When he ran from what had been his home for the last five years—that's what they'd called it, all those smiling adults from social services when they brought him to that imposing, complicated house, that he was now "home," "home forever"—he'd had no plan other than to try to find his sister. He'd gone first to the home of a mutual friend from high school. She was not there. They hadn't seen her. Then he went to another's. No sign of her.

Neither he nor she had many friends. They always felt like outsiders. Their swarthy skin and black hair set them apart from the other kids in school. People thought they might be French Canadian, but they had no accent, so people figured they were at least some part native. Which caused an immediate bias. He didn't know, and there was no one to ask. Their body types, too, set them apart. Both broad in the shoulders, which they carried slightly slumped. He always knew why he did that. Now he understood why his sister did, too. They wanted to curl in on themselves and show only a protected side to a hostile world. Like oversize pill bugs.

Their dad was not a popular man in town. This didn't help. And their mother didn't go out much. She tended to keep the shades drawn. Seemed to spend her days cleaning. Did she know? Was she trying to wash away what was going on in her own home? Maybe so, maybe not. He would not blame her. It was an unfathomable thing. The mind rebels against it. He was experiencing it himself and still didn't see the signs in his sister until it was too late.

He tried another house. A friend of his sister's, a nervous, skinny thing, with lank hair and gray teeth, who had told him Belinda knew someone in Montreal. Had mentioned a friend up there. No, she didn't know if it was a guy or a girl. Some French name, so she couldn't tell. Said Belinda had once talked about hitching up there someday. No, Brayden couldn't stay there. Her mom's boyfriend wouldn't allow it.

Brayden went to the house of a friend from back when he played football. He spent a few nights there. But this guy's parents started to question why he hadn't returned home for so long.

Brayden moved to his friend Zach's trailer. That's where he heard that his dad, Bruce, was in the hospital. Head injury. Coma. Something. All gossip passed over hand by hand, the original information getting worn and dirty in the process.

Bruce was a tough bastard, everyone said. He'd make it. He was a God-fearing, churchgoing, shrewd businessman who developed cheap, contractor-grade homes, ran a bunch of low-income, Section 8 apartments, was unembarrassed to be called a slumlord, and often said that he'd been sued more times than he could remember, but no one ever got a dime from him. He bragged that he gave out a lot of shit but didn't take any. There were plenty of stories about Bruce's exploits when angered or crossed. He'd filled a front loader with old bricks and dumped it over the new truck of a man he suspected of cheating him out of money on a job. He had shot rounds into the air when too much booze at a backyard picnic turned what had been a pleasant afternoon into an ugly shouting match. His knuckles were scarred with what he said was the results of fights but which Brayden knew were more likely the remnants of a fist slammed into the cabinets on more than one occasion as a means of stopping an argument with his wife. This was not a guy who would go down easy.

Zach's mother was a meth head. Her boyfriend had a grow operation in the garage. Zach didn't want Brayden's father, Bruce, looking for him at their trailer. Brayden had run out of couches. He had a lot of experience in the backcountry. His adoptive father had at least given him those skills, had taught him self-sufficiency. He'd said it was preparation for when the government fell and the "towel heads, Mexicans, and blacks took over the country." Brayden didn't buy that racist nonsense, but he was interested in knowing how to survive outdoors. He had taken those lessons from his father, greedily. When Zach finally told him it was time to leave, Brayden went into the woods. It was the safest place he knew. It was perhaps the only safe place he knew. It was also his only option.

Once he got there, he ran. As if something real and living, something breathing fire, was chasing him. Now, months later, he realized that creature was not something he could outrun because it lived within him.

TWELVE

Colden had another task to do while she was in Albany. The morning after her dinner with Drew, she put on the same button-down shirt and pulled a pair of khakis from the back of her closet. She felt like a guy going on a job interview. Too bad, she told herself, that this was the best she could do. She drove to an office park with a 1970s-ish building, introduced herself to the receptionist, sat in a cushioned chair, and flipped through a *People* magazine. She didn't recognize any of the celebrities. They almost all looked like high school students to her. Finally, the receptionist came from behind her desk and showed her to a conference room. The table was dark, slick wood, large enough to seat a dozen people. The chairs were high back and leather. She felt small and insignificant. The receptionist brought her a glass of water. The door opened, and a man entered the room. Middle-aged. Spreading out at the middle. Thinning hair. Getting jowly. A big smile showing crooked teeth.

"Bill Flannery," he said, sticking out his hand.

Colden had never met this man before. But ever since she was twenty-one years old, envelopes had begun arriving at the house with the return address of this building in the upper-left corner, and inside, a few pages of paper with numbers on them and his name in the top corner, right after the phrase, "investment advisor."

"Nice to finally meet you," he added as he sat down.

He offered coffee. She declined. A woman came in with a plate of cookies and a folder of papers, then backed out of the room. Bill smiled and pushed the plate toward Colden. She took one and set it down on a napkin in front of her. He twirled his pen. She didn't know how to begin.

"How can I help you, Colden?" Bill asked.

She cleared her throat.

"I'd like to take some funds from my trust," she said.

"OK," Bill replied, his voice going deeper and quieter. "I don't know how much you were hoping to withdraw today, but we can look at the figures. As I think you know, your father set up the trust so that once you turned twenty-one, you could have access to a percentage of the interest that has accrued since he opened the account, and then you can access the capital itself when you are thirty. If you want to."

Colden nodded.

"Do I have to tell you what the money is for?"

Bill smiled and lowered his eyes.

"No, Colden. It's your money, you're of age, and no one, not even your father, needs to know that you are taking out money or how much."

"OK. Thank you."

Colden felt childish. As if she was a nine-year-old asking for a raise in her allowance. The truth was, she had never had or handled money very much. Her needs were few, her expenses low. She'd been a student all of her adult life, making do with stipends, fellowships, and grants. Her computer and technology tools were owned by the university. Her truck and most of her outdoor gear were gifts from her parents. Her father owned her condo outright. He figured it was a good investment, and she lived there, and in the cottage, for free. She hardly knew what the raw stuff of life cost. But she had recently made a spreadsheet of several seemingly expensive items she wanted to buy. She knew her father would help her if she asked. She just didn't want to ask. She knew this money was hers, but she'd mostly tried to forget it was here, in an account somewhere in the ether. When the monthly statements came, she usually threw them away, unopened. The money felt compromised. As if it came from illegal activities. She wondered if some of it did.

"How much were you hoping to withdraw today?" Bill asked.

Colden swallowed. "Eight thousand dollars."

Bill stared at her for a moment as if unsure he was hearing her correctly. Colden flushed. She wondered if that was too much. She didn't know how much of what was in the account was interest and how much was capital. She wasn't sure she even understood those terms.

"That's all?" Bill asked.

Now, Colden stared back, equally confused.

"Yes," she said. "Is it too much? I thought I saw, when I opened the last statement, maybe I read it wrong, but . . ."

"No, Colden. It's not too much. Not too much at all." Bill leaned back in his chair. "I just thought, because you called a meeting, that there was something . . . that you wanted a bigger hunk for some reason. You know, like to buy a car or for a down payment on a house or something. Eight grand is really . . . well, of course, it's plenty of money, but you don't need to set up a meeting for that. You can transfer that amount to your checking account yourself."

Colden felt even more childish now. But why wouldn't she? she reminded herself. This money, after all, came from a mother she'd never known. Who got it from a father who'd ruined his family and lost much, much more than he'd left behind. It felt wrong to have it, even more wrong to use it.

"Dad?"

"Yes?"

"Can I talk to you about something I did?"

Dix set down the knife he was using to chop onions, wiped his hands on the dishtowel hanging from the waistband of his pants, and turned his back to the kitchen counter, to his work. It was a familiar thing for him to do. When someone asked something of him, he set down his tools, whether it was an ax or a wrench or a whisk, and gave whoever it was his full attention. Colden had witnessed this behavior chain countless times. But before that moment, she'd never fully realized what a considerate thing it was for him to do.

"I'm going to delay dinner," she said, waving her hand. "We'll talk later."

Dix crossed his arms and leaned against the counter. "There's no deadline on dinner," he said.

"Right." Colden knew she was stalling. "So."

Dix was still and silent.

"Um, when I was in Albany last week, I went and saw that banker. Bill whatever," Colden said.

She peeled the label off her damp beer bottle and rolled the paper remnants in her fingers. She waited for her father to comment. He didn't.

"I took some money out of that account. The one you set up for me. The one with, you know, Mom's money in it."

As if there was more than one account that she could possibly be referring to.

"I feel really bad about it. But there's something I want to do, and I need money to do it."

Dix regarded her for a moment. Colden couldn't read the expression on his face. She felt her lungs tighten with worry. It was an unfamiliar feeling. Especially around her father.

"Why do you feel bad about it?" Dix asked.

She was expecting him to ask what the money was for, and this was the answer she had prepared. The label from the beer bottle was now completely shredded into a small pile of detritus on the counter.

"I, I guess I don't really know why I feel bad," she said. "It just seems like that money was—is, should be—off-limits."

"Why?"

"I don't know, Dad," Colden said. "It all just feels kind of icky. Like dirty money. Money with a bad history."

Dix nodded. He seemed to be trying to collect his thoughts.

"Honey, how much do you know about that account, where it came from? I know we've talked about it from time to time, but I'm honestly not sure how much of the story, the details, you know. How much I've shared. How much you remember."

Colden sketched out the basics of what she'd pieced together over the years. She knew that the money was made by her grandfather from whatever work he did on Wall Street. No one had said exactly what he'd done there. The name of the street alone seemed to convey more than enough—something unsavory, vaguely illicit, and likely exploitative. The money was also all Colden's mother had left after her father had died, killed in a freak accident when a tree branch fell on him in a thunderstorm. Miranda had expected there would be a lot more. Apparently, they lived like there was a lot more. House in Connecticut, vacation home in the Adirondacks, private schools, country clubs, caretakers. But it turned out that Miranda's father had lied to his family. Miranda discovered he'd made a series of bad investments and was embroiled in more than one lawsuit over advice he'd given clients and illegal deals he'd made in constructing the summer home. After his death,

Miranda's mother went into a tailspin of depression, drinking, and a series of strokes that left her incapacitated, leaving her twenty-something daughter to figure things out alone. Well, with the help of Dix, who was their handyman. A situation that led, ultimately, to her, Colden.

Colden couldn't meet her father's eyes as she spoke, but she knew he was watching her; she could see, out of the corner of her eyes, his head bobbing up and down in encouragement and acknowledgment.

"I think she also gave a bunch of money to that commune guy, where she lived after she left you."

"I think she did, too," Dix said.

"This is all so damn embarrassing," Colden whispered.

"There's no reason for you to be embarrassed."

"Yes, there is. Look at what I come from. A bunch of shysters and whack jobs. And yet I'm using their money. It's all pretty gross."

"Your mother, Colden, was not a whack job or a shyster."

"Wasn't she? Spoiled little rich girl running off to some groovy commune—what was it called, the Source, of all things? Leaving you behind, giving birth in a dank hovel, not even telling you about your own damn kid, you having to find out from a stranger named Sally what happened?"

Then, as if in answer to Colden's little tirade, Sally herself walked in.

"Sorry I'm so late," she said. "There was a problem. Police called. Some tweakers camping out at my grandmother's old place set the trailer on fire. Again. Damn spot is cursed and doomed."

Dix and Colden stared, bug-eyed, at each other.

"What?" Sally said. "What's going on?"

"We were just talking about the Source," Dix said. "Doomed and cursed, indeed."

"Why were you guys talking about the Source?" Sally asked.

"Tell us what happened, first," Colden said.

Dix turned back to his chopping block and onions.

Sally shrugged. Said there was nothing much to tell. Cops said there was a report of some smoke; they went out to the falling-down homestead that had belonged to her grandmother and found a small fire and drug paraphernalia in an old trailer. Whoever had been hanging out there had skedaddled. They put out the fire, locked the door, and left the place to continue its slow decay back into the earth.

Colden asked Sally if she went out there herself. Sally shivered.

"No, not with all those bad memories. Pretty much wish someone would burn the whole thing down, finish the job, be done with it."

Colden looked away. Dix looked at Sally with raised eyebrows.

"Sorry," Sally said.

"Don't be," Colden replied.

"Colden, would you like to go out there? Would you like to see . . ." Sally left the thought unfinished.

Colden turned the question over in her mind. What would she see? An ancient, abandoned farmhouse, in a damp patch of ground, with a few falling-over outbuildings, just like so many others that dotted these hills. Only this one had history. Heavy, personal history. The property had been in Sally's family, belonged to her grandmother. After the old woman died out there, apparently while chopping firewood, with ax in hand, Sally couldn't sell it. That is, until the guy who eventually started the Source came along. He gave her some promise money, began fixing the place up, and started collecting his band of lost souls—all women, it seemed, including, eventually, her mother. His project didn't last for long. Maybe a year or so, from what Colden could tell. There were drug issues. Her mother died out there a few days after giving birth, prematurely, to Colden. They did some sort of home cremation and tried to keep the fact of Colden's birth a secret. They wanted to raise her in some back-to-nature, away-from-modern-society way. They wanted her to be a kind of new-age science experiment.

Sally had been living out there herself, not as part of the commune, but to keep an eye on things. She knew Miranda. They had talked about Dix. Sally had hoped Miranda would return to him. With the baby that he thought was the product of a relationship between Miranda and the commune leader. Then Sally went away to a conference, and when she returned, Miranda was dead. Sally found Dix. They alerted the authorities. The place was shut down; Colden went to foster care until paternity could be proved; and Darius, the self-styled cult leader, was sent back to his parents in Connecticut and ordered to complete a lot of community service.

All of this was Colden's personal backstory. But none of it felt like it had anything to do with her. Her life was here, with Sally and Dix, with her work. There was nothing more she wanted to understand about that place. She didn't believe it had anything to tell her that she didn't already know.

She shook her head. Sally nodded acknowledgment. Dix stirred onions and garlic. The air around them was filled with a damp and bitter fragrance.

Colden wanted to return the conversation to where it began. She also wanted to change the mood. Asking for her father's help was, she knew, a good way to achieve both.

"So, Dad. I wanted to ask your advice on something."

Dix looked up from the stove and smiled at her. Relief and anticipation lightly animated the typically serene composition of his features.

"The money I took from the account? The trust?" She looked at Sally here to include her and catch her up. "It's for a side project I want to do."

"Do tell!" Sally said.

"It's very speculative," Colden said. "And I want to keep it quiet. I don't want other scientists or my colleagues to know."

"Why all the cloak and daggers?" Sally asked. "Aren't scientists supposed to keep everything open?"

"Yes. But . . ." Colden struggled to explain. "It's just that. The moose and beaver project is great. Truly. But it's so conventional. It's so basic."

"Flying in helicopters with a bunch of dudes and shooting nets to capture moose is conventional?" Dix said.

"Ugh. No. Of course not. It's amazing. It's a great opportunity. It's important research. I know it sounds weird. Ungrateful even. But the helicopter stuff? That's just a tool. That's just a few days. The rest is the grind of collecting and analyzing data. Data. Data. Data."

"Much of which comes from poop, right?" Sally said, smirking.

"I want to actually *discover* something," Colden said quietly, embarrassed by her own ambition.

The room fell silent other than the sound of Dix's knife, methodically scraping against a chopping block as he sliced some green peppers. They sizzled as they hit the hot oil in the pan.

"Well," he said, "what do you propose to find?"

Colden went into a long disquisition that took them all the way through dinner and into cups of tea on the sofa following the meal. Everyone knew there were coyotes in the Adirondacks. Coyotes were everywhere. Even though the government had spent millions of dollars over decades trying to eradicate them, they continued to breed and spread into every nook and cranny of the United States and beyond, from downtown Manhattan to the desiccated deserts of the Southwest, from remote mountains to suburban golf courses. They were amazingly adaptable creatures that could hunt, scavenge, work in packs, or be perfectly successful as individuals. Wolves, in comparison, were much more fragile. Apex hunters, reliant on big game and strong pack structures, which were easily disrupted by human activity and indiscriminate killing. They had been long gone from the Adirondack Mountains and many other landscapes, as well.

Dix and Sally listened carefully. Colden knew none of this information was exactly news to them, but she was offering a great deal of detail and nuance. She wanted them to understand both her thoughts and hopes thoroughly.

She told them she'd been hearing stories from hunters, trappers, and farmers complaining a lot more about coyotes. Not just the normal coyote, but what they claimed were much larger, bolder, and yet even more elusive coyotes. Colden had mostly taken the gripes in stride. These people were always complaining about predators, and no amount of her explaining that the bulk of their diets consisted of rats and gophers and other small animals, which the farmers and hunters hated equally, would sway them to the benefits of having at least this one predator still in their midst.

But then she read some reports from eastern Canada that described the same sort of coyote. These were in the scientific literature. There had been scattered sightings of a canid that was larger than a coyote but smaller than a wolf. A creature that seemed comfortable in both wooded and open settings and that had the long legs and larger skull of a wolf but the litheness and elusiveness of a coyote. Some scientists wondered if wolves and coyotes were crossbreeding. Others scoffed at the notion. Wolves had a long-documented history of despising and killing their smaller cousins. Coyotes avoided wolves assiduously, scavenging their kills only after they'd been safely abandoned. Yet, the theory persisted. Some posited that severely depressed populations had driven some wolves to mate with coyotes simply because that was their only option.

"And you tend to agree?" Dix asked.

"I tend to not know," said Colden. "But I also tend to want to find out."

"Is this your way of telling us you are relocating to Canada?" Sally asked.

Colden shook her head. "No, I want to study them here. Well, I mean to say, I want to find them here. See if they're here. Then study them."

"Are you suggesting wolves have returned to the Adirondacks?" Dix asked.

"No, I doubt that," Colden said. "The terrain is not right for them. But maybe some of these hybrids, what they're calling a coywolf, came down from Canada. They could live comfortably in these dense woods. Maybe what these hunters and trappers are seeing is real, but it's just that it's not a coyote; it's a coyote hybrid."

Sally asked again why this needed to be kept quiet.

Colden squirmed and hesitated. She explained that she wanted to protect the animal from hunters. Dix looked at her quizzically. She knew he was thinking that the hunters didn't care what it was called or how it was made—to them it was just a big varmint. Colden withered under his scrutiny.

"And I want to keep it quiet because if it is out there, I want to be the one to discover it. That's all. It's selfish. It could be a career-making find, though."

"Making your own career isn't necessarily selfish if it does something very good for the environment, as well," Dix said.

Colden was embarrassed by his generosity.

"If I do find it, I won't keep the information to myself. It's too important not to share."

Dix and Sally nodded at her.

"So, that's what the money is for. I want to buy a bunch of game cameras and tracking equipment, a better computer of my own, not the one the university gave me, and maybe an ATV, so I can get deeper into the woods more quickly, and see if I can find them. I'd like your help, Dad. Picking out the equipment. Maybe finding spots to set the cameras."

Dix stared into his teacup. Sally and Colden stared at him. They were waiting for him, as if for a benediction.

"I don't think this is exactly what you want to hear, Colden," he said. "But your mother would be very happy to see the money used this way. She'd be very proud of you."

It wasn't what Colden wanted to hear. But she knew it was what her father needed to say. And that by offering her mother's blessing to the project, he was also offering his own.

Colden and her father went online and picked out equipment to create camera traps. He made a few calls, and one of his customers happily sold them an almost-new ATV that had been sitting in his garage, unused, for several years because his kids had grown into teenagers who now preferred city pursuits over spending vacations and weekends in the mountains. They laid out detailed topographical maps and tried to imagine the type of terrain this hybrid canid might prefer. They picked several areas that would be accessible to Colden yet inaccessible to most hunters, tourists, and hikers.

"There are a few locations I'd really like you to avoid," Dix said, somewhat ominously.

"With six million acres of Adirondack Park and only ten cameras at my disposal, I think I can cross off a few spots without jeopardizing my research," Colden replied. "But may I ask why?"

Dix pointed to several places on the map, without marking them. He didn't need to. Colden recognized them immediately as locations where there had been reports of vandalism and break-ins. Most were at deer camps. There had been a few at a set of vacation homes around a small lake. The one at Sally's grandmother's abandoned house. One was near Gene's home. Which reminded her that it had been a while since she'd seen him.

"Have you been over to Gene's recently?" she asked her father.

Dix nodded slowly.

"How is he?"

"Same as ever," he said. "Seems to be holding up OK."

Good, Colden thought. Her dad had covered this. Gene was now a line item in a mental checklist that could be ticked off. The suggestion of these petty crimes reminded Colden of her conversation with Drew. The damage he had described was different than the bulk of the thefts they'd heard about. Mostly it had been someone taking a bit of camping equipment or food from a poorly secured garage or pantry, the kind of stuff spoiled teenagers or people in deep need might be expected to do. The stuff Drew had mentioned was more intentional. She had promised to look into it.

"Dad, the stuff that happened here." Her finger hovered over the map at a spot not far from where Gene lived. "Do you know anything about all that?"

Dix shrugged.

"Seemed an attempt at some sort of sabotage," he said. "But then again, it could just be testosterone-poisoned boys or whacked-out tweakers. They seem to love destroying other people's property."

"Just seems different from the other stuff we've been hearing about."

"Agreed," he said. "Something more, more like someone was making a point, trying to send a message."

"I have a"—Colden hesitated, unsure what word to use—"I have a friend in Albany who was asking me about it."

"In Albany?"

Colden wasn't sure what aspect of her sentence Dix was surprised by: that she had a friend in Albany or that someone in Albany knew of the problem.

"Yes," she continued. "He works for the paper company whose equipment got destroyed. He asked me if I could ask around. Without making a fuss."

"And you're now asking me to do the asking around?"

Dix's ability to zero right in on the crux of a situation or request was sometimes discomfiting.

"Yes," Colden allowed. "I guess I am. You're better at it than I am."

"How would you know that if you don't try it yourself first?" he asked.

"Dad," she pleaded. "C'mon. You know everyone and everyone knows you, and they trust you. And you're a guy. Guys hate talking to women about stuff like this."

Dix gave her an indulgent smile.

"Of course, I will," he said. "Because you asked. Because it's for a friend of yours. And also because I'd be happy to help avoid some sort of confrontation or a lawsuit with the Park Authority or a paper company. We seem to have enough of those around here these days."

Spring was starting to creep into those few spots that were warmed by the reluctant sun. Maple trees were hazed with red buds. Lawns were giving way to green fuzz. Daybreak was marked by intermittent birdsong. Fat robins were beginning to appear, flitting in open areas, tilting their heads as they listened for the movement of insects tentatively exploring the new season. Then there was a cold snap, a wet snowfall, and the ground gripped in on itself again—the last gasp of a dying season.

Colden was glad for the change in temperature and conditions. The frozen ground would be easier to drive and hike through, while the fresh layer of white, which wouldn't last long, might reveal tracks. She quickly packed up for a few days of camping, loaded the ATV, and set out with her first set of wildlife cameras. She rode for about an hour, first on the shoulder of two-lane streets, then on gravel roads that turned and meandered into areas marked by the increasing absence of human habitation, then through several former farm fields that were reverting to scrub, and finally onto trails just wide enough for her vehicle to lurch and twist between tree trunks. She finally came to an impasse marked with a large outcropping of rock and a couple of old blowdowns.

She turned the ATV off, dismounted, and shoved the vehicle in under the granite overhang. She then took an ax from her pack, hacked at a few evergreen boughs, and placed them strategically to camouflage the machine. It was highly unlikely any other human would pass this way, but just in case, she saw no reason to draw attention to herself or her work. She tightened her boots, adjusted her gaiters, shouldered her pack, and headed north through dense, unmarked woods. Every step was an exercise in caution. One slight miscalculation and she might slip on a rock and end up with a twisted ankle, or catch her leg in between a couple of pieces of deadfall, and possibly break a bone. People had disappeared out here. Even experienced people. Even after weeks and months of being searched for. You could not be too careful. After two hours, she figured she had made it a little more than three miles.

The days were still short, and the light began to fail. Colden started scanning the land for a flat space that would fit her tent. There was plenty of leftover winter snow around. The whisper of spring warmth that had been in the air earlier in the day was quickly giving way before a distinct chill. The sweat against her skin began to feel clammy. She saw a likely location just beyond a small ridge. There was a rivulet that would give her water. A smooth area just big enough for her tent. A large erratic that would provide some protection from wind.

She dropped her pack and began to brush the snow away with an evergreen bough. The light, new snow dissipated quickly, like confectioners' sugar off a donut. Beneath was a thick layer of crystalline slush. Colden started to kick it out of the way. Her boot encountered some hard, icy spots. She stopped. The breaks in the old snow were regular in shape and spacing. They were familiar and unlikely, at the same time. The only explanation was improbable enough that her brain resisted understanding. But there it was: she was staring at the blurry edges of footprints. Well, hiking-boot prints. They must have passed this way a few days ago. Curious. Odd. Not necessarily alarming, but very unusual for anyone to be this deep in the backcountry.

Colden wondered who and why. Her immediate concern was that someone might be lost and in need of help. But there was nothing she could do for them now. She was losing the light and had a tent to set up, and she was, of course, not the only person who knew what they were doing in the backcountry.

That night, Colden slept deeply, as she always did when camping. The physical exhaustion of hiking and the almost total silence of the woods were an instant soporific. She became vaguely alert a few times in the night but never passed out of the liminal state between sleep and wakefulness. She woke to a haze of snow covering everything. She recalled vague dreams of creatures passing her tent, sniffing at the door, curious about this interloper, then moving on. She packed quickly, eating an apple and granola bar for breakfast instead of bothering with the camp stove. She drank her instant coffee cold. As she sipped, she followed some of the human footprints a bit, puzzling over what this person, a tall man, judging by the boot size, was doing out here and where he might have been headed. Some looked older, others fresh. But it was so difficult to tell. The spring thaw-and-freeze cycle, the heaving and settling of the ground, the mix of fresh and old snow, and her own movements as she had worked at the site muddied things. These were not the tracks she'd been hoping to find. In any case, they were quickly lost to the variable terrain. She packed her tent, checked her bearings, and set out to find the spots she and her father had marked on the map.

One by one, over the next two breezy, balmy days, Colden set up camera traps and bait scent over as wide an area as she could cover. She'd seen deer droppings. She expected fawns to drop soon, as well. There were potential denning sites for coyotes. Or coywolves. In a few weeks, she'd come back, pull the data cards, and find additional places to set up cameras. Even with as much care as she and Dix had put into selecting the sites, she was aware that luck would play the largest role in this project. She knew most science started with guesswork overlaid with a thin veneer of education and experience. She chose sites by intellect as well as instinct. She made notes about their distinguishing characteristics. She reminded herself that things would change fast from day to day as the spring thaws competed with the remnants of winter for supremacy over the landscape.

The third day dawned overcast and cool. Colden was out of cameras. It was time to go home. She allowed herself the indulgence of looking forward to the hot shower and cold beer on the horizon at the end of her day. But first, there was plenty of hiking and ATVing to get through. As she rolled up her sleeping pad and took down her tent, she felt a little giddy. She couldn't wait to get out of the woods, and she couldn't wait to get back. She allowed herself another brief imaginative indulgence: that her cameras might be capturing something interesting, something valuable.

Her pack was lighter and the hiking easier than a few days prior. The snow had dissipated, but the ground had not yet thawed into boot-sucking mud. She was refreshed by the concentrated work, the conversation-free solitude, and the long hours of sleep, so she kept up a fast pace and made good time getting back to the spot where she'd stashed her ATV. As she grabbed the first of the branches she'd placed to cover the machine, she felt clear and focused, as if she'd been scrubbed clean. Then the feeling vanished.

Something wasn't right. Her skin flushed warm and then cold with suspicion and alarm. The machine was right where she'd left it, but the branches were not. Had they just fallen away? No, there were the pieces with her own ax marks. Several had been tossed aside. By a good six feet. Not something an animal likely would have done. She looked for footprints. She found only indistinct depressions in the soft muck around the vehicle. The ground had thawed, refrozen, and thawed again in these last days, destroying whatever boot edge might once have been there. Colden pulled away the few remaining branches she'd used to obscure her ride.

A gust of wind came up, the just-beginning-to-bud tree branches overhead swayed, and a bright reflection of the sun briefly bounced on and off the ATV's now visible cargo carrier. Which was empty. It should not have been empty. It should have held a can of gas. Gas she needed to get out of here and all the way home. Colden traced her thoughts backward. She reimagined herself putting the red plastic extra gas can onto the back of the machine, double-checking the can itself for fullness and the seals and cap for tightness, using a bungee to strap it down, deciding to get an extra bungee because the terrain was full of bumps and because a bungee can always burst out of its clip. The can had been here. She had made sure of it. Now it was gone. One black bungee had been left behind, dangling there like something forgotten on a clothes line.

This was crazy. No one in their right mind would steal gas from an ATV this far into the woods. They'd know that doing so was likely damning someone to a long walk at best and possibly an unexpected and underprovisioned extra night in the woods at worst. Colden quickly checked the gas tank—whoever had stolen the can hadn't been desperate enough or mean enough to siphon out her tank.

She thought back to her dinner with Drew. The area where his client had experienced vandalism was miles and miles away. Maybe it was the same person or persons, or maybe it was just a random coincidence. There were plenty of people in these mountains who were decidedly antiestablishment. Not in the way her mother's groovy commune had been but in the conservative, keep your government out of my life, make sure you are well armed and stocked, prep for impending disaster sort of way. Of course, it could be anyone. So many folks around here were anti-something—against anything and everything they perceived as causing their own misfortune. Blame. Such an easy route to take. She thought back to the stories of petty thievery they'd been hearing about. Sleeping bags. Food. Gas. Essentials. Even magazines. People getting by by taking from. It wasn't a new story. Just new to her experience.

Colden shook off these thoughts. She had to get going. There was only a little bit of gas in her tank. She had plenty of unexpected hiking ahead. She didn't think she'd have to spend another night in the woods—only if the weather got bad—but it wouldn't be a problem. She always packed for a couple of extra nights as a precaution. She'd have a temporarily unexplained absence, but her parents wouldn't worry. They knew where she was and would think the extra night had been her choice, as it had been on many other occasions. Still, she wanted to make the most of the light and fuel she had left. It didn't take long before the ATV sputtered to a stop. It had taken her to the edge of the woods, where the trees and shrubs were beginning to encroach on an abandoned farm field. She dismounted and reached into her pack for her mostly useless cell phone. She turned it on and watched as it sputtered to an intermittent and single bar of signal. She sent a text, watched the wheel spin, and hoped the message would find a pocket of a signal to ride out on. She had no choice but to walk.

Colden trudged through sodden fields and thick mud. It was hard work and slow going. But when she made it to the thin gravel of a small road that had once led to a long-forsaken farmhouse, her father was there, sitting on the tailgate of his truck in the slanting afternoon light. He had two small cans of gas, a large thermos of hot coffee, an Italian-style submarine sandwich, and a box of chocolate chip cookies. She stumbled toward his crooked grin and gratefully allowed him to lift her pack off her back. Newly lightened, she felt unstable. Dix helped her to the tailgate. She sat, and he bent over to unlace and remove her boots. He pulled off her sweat-soaked socks and handed her a fresh, dry pair he'd brought with him. She was happy to be a child for the moment. She was also relieved that no words were required between them. Not yet. He'd wait for her to speak. He knew how hard it was to get used to human company and conversation after a few days free of it. He handed her half the sandwich and poured the coffee. They both ate and drank. Colden threw a few scraps of bread to a chipmunk darting in and out of a crevice in a stump nearby. She was comfortable, warm, dirty, sore, and now also sated, safe, and content. These were feelings she associated with her father, having had just this combination of sensations so many times in his presence. She finished her meal, crumpled up the sandwich wrapper, and sighed. Her dad did the same. He put all the garbage in a bag and smiled at her. Now, explanations could ensue.

"Who's that?" Colden asked, jerking her head in the direction of the truck cab, where a furry black face was resting its chin on the sill of a window opened just enough to allow a dog snout through. She was not quite ready to get into her own story.

"New girl," Dix said.

"Haven't named her yet?"

Dix gave each dog that came into his care a new name. It signaled a fresh start but also allowed the dog to drop whatever negative associations of abuse, mistreatment, or simply yelling in anger the former name might be carrying. He rubbed his facial stubble and shook his shaggy head of salt-and-pepper hair.

"Working on a few ideas," he said.

"Have any ideas about who might have taken my gas can?" she asked.

"Same person who took Fred's chainsaw?" He shrugged.

"Maybe it's that Sasquatch Gene is always asking me about," Colden said.

"Nah. Sasquatch doesn't have much use for gas," Dix replied, handing her a cookie.

The fat and sugar exploded on Colden's tongue. It was delicious and slightly nauseating.

"Guess I'll have to get a chain and lock for the next time I go in," she said.

Dix offered a long and deep sigh in reply. Colden knew from their many past conversations that he was not sighing for her but for whomever it was whose life was such that stealing a gas can from an ATV deep in the woods seemed like a good idea. Or an obvious, necessary idea. The sigh expressed her father's deep and unassuaged regret that so many people led such marginal lives of poverty and deprivation in such a stunningly beautiful place. It wasn't exactly the scratch-and-peck existences that bothered him—many of the people they knew had actively and consciously chosen this lifestyle and rejected others. It was the poverty of spirit that sometimes came along with material deprivation and caused some people not just to envy others who had more but also to desire their downfall. Colden knew her father didn't begrudge another person a thing. He didn't think the world was a zero-sum game and had no bone for resentment in his body. His sigh expressed his weariness that in spite of all this, one could not afford the luxury of naivete and still had to take precautions against the sometimes-hostile actions of others.

"Bet Sally was pissed when you told her what had happened," Colden said.

Dix smiled that particularly wry grin he reserved for mentions of his wife. Colden and he were both amused by Sally's rather more dim view of the rural poor. They also respected the fact that she had earned these feelings and opinions through her many years as a very effective social worker and advocate for the underrepresented and poorly resourced.

"She had a few things to say, yes," Dix replied.

Sally did not have the same penchant for philosophical tolerance that her husband did. Colden took another cookie. Then another. She needed sustenance. It was time to trudge back to where she'd left her ATV, fill it with gas, and get it and herself back home.

"Why don't you take the truck," Dix said, watching her. "I'll go fetch the ATV and drive it home for you."

Colden shook her head, as she knew he knew she would. This was her mess. She'd clean it up. Just as he would have done if the roles had been reversed. Dix did not insist. Colden knew he respected her stubborn independence. He just waved her off and said he'd see her at home. They'd have a big dinner later tonight, no doubt. She'd indulge Sally's inevitable and affectionate scolding over the perceived risks she took. Sally worried about her, Colden knew. Sally was not an outdoorswoman herself. She was not much for hiking or camping and occasionally sneaked cigarettes—Colden had found a stray butt or two out behind the garage—even though she had promised Dix many times that she had quit for good. Her father worried about her far less. He knew how well her skills and competence stacked up against the environment they lived in and the people they lived among because he'd given her most of those very skills and competencies. He was aware that she had picked up many others on her own.

A stolen gas can was a nuisance, a price to be paid for living here, like putting up with blackflies. She'd just have to be more careful, take more precautions, next time. She knew he wouldn't begrudge her getting the full impact of her error in not locking down her resources in a place where she had much and so many others had so little. It was no different than making sure your animal feed was secured from bears and rodents. She hopped off the tailgate, grabbed a can, and began retracing her steps through the fields.

By the time Colden got back home, the house was filled with rich smells of onions, garlic, spices, and browned meat.

"Eat or bath, first?" Sally asked when Colden stumbled through the back door and dropped her tired body onto a bench.

"Dinner," Colden said as she shouldered off her pack and unlaced her boots. "No, wait. Bath. For your sake as much as mine."

"How about beer?" Sally asked as she handed her a cold brown bottle.

Colden took a long and grateful slug and soon heard the sound of water pouring into the tub—Sally, who always protested she was not very maternal, was prepping a hot bath for her daughter. Colden levered off her boots, released her feet from her socks, and examined a blister forming on her heel. She peeled off her muddy pants and her reeking shirt and walked to the bathroom in her bra and underpants. A thick layer of bubbles grew atop the steaming water. Sally waved Colden in, backed herself out, and shut the door. As she waited for the tub to fill, Colden looked at herself in the mirror. Her hip bones and collarbones appeared more prominent than usual. The muscles of her arms and legs seemed to push against her skin, unprotected by even a thin layer of feminine fat. A few light bruises from her pack straps were starting to bloom where her shoulders and arms met. There was a scratch she didn't recall receiving, like a mark from a red sharpie. Dried mucus encrusted her nostrils. Twigs and a few dead leaves decorated her hair.

No wonder I don't have a boyfriend, she thought.

She turned away from the mirror, peeled off her underwear, and eased into the slippery, sweetly scented water. She closed her eyes and listened to the sounds coming from the kitchen. Muffled and intermittent conversation, the clatter of plates and silverware, the scrape of chairs—familiar, companionable things. She soaked; she scrubbed; she drained the cooled water from the tub and showered. Then she dried off with a thick, blanket-size towel, slathered herself with lotion, wrapped herself in a robe, padded to the kitchen, and served herself a heaping plate of sausage, tomatoes, onions, and peppers from the pan on the stove. Sally and Dix had already eaten and were in the living room, reading. Colden joined them there. She put a forkful of the still-hot food into her mouth and tasted last summer's tomatoes and basil. She was suffused with feelings of well-being but also irritated by lingering sensations of disquiet. Her parents let her eat in peace. When she put her empty plate on the coffee table and tucked her feet up underneath a blanket, Dix set down his newspaper, and Sally put aside her case reports.

"Well, what the hell was that all about?" Sally asked.

Colden knew they'd all been puzzling over the same things separate and apart. So much so, it was almost as if they'd been conversing together.

"I don't know what to say." Colden shrugged. "I don't want to get paranoid. Maybe it was just someone whose own vehicle ran out of gas and they couldn't, you know, leave a note."

"Nice of you to take that position," Dix said. "But there have been a lot of incidents recently."

"Have there been?" Sally wondered. "Or have a couple of things led us to look for, to see, more than there really is? How much do we even really know? Are they all actual thefts, or in some cases, was it just someone too stoned or drunk to remember that they lost or loaned something to someone who never returned it?"

"You're referring to Gene?" Dix asked.

"Gene. Joe. Dave. Rick. Whoever. Nothing new there."

"I think, in general, you're right to be cautious about us finding patterns and causality where there's just coincidence," Colden said. "But things are adding up in strange ways. There's the camping gear, food, and magazines Dad's clients told him about. The equipment vandalism that my, my"—Colden wasn't sure how to refer to him—"friend. That my friend Drew asked me about. Most of it isn't enough to report to the police, so it's hard to know what's really going on."

Dix rubbed his chin. "Any recent prison escapes? Runaways?"

Sally shook her head. "Inmates all accounted for. And there are always runaways. There are always teenagers out causing trouble. There are always addicts and idiots doing stupid stuff. Like what happened lately out at my grandmother's place."

Colden and Sally looked at Dix. He'd have an answer. He usually did. If not, he at least would have a better question.

"The motivations seem to be different. Between the robberies and the vandalism, I mean," he said quietly. "The robberies may be totally unconnected. Teenagers in one place, forgetfulness in another, a needy friend or neighbor in another. Or a resentful friend or neighbor. People do plenty of silly things out of spite. Could even be copycat stuff. Someone trying to make one theft look the same as another in the hopes they can get away with it. That they'll catch one guy and assume he did them all. The vandalism? That's different. That's someone trying to make a point. A statement. Whoever did that doesn't get anything other than the satisfaction, such as it is, of knowing they messed somebody over. It'd be one thing if someone took credit. But so far, no one has."

"So, where does my missing gas can fit in?" Colden asked.

"Hard to say," Dix replied. "I'd go with opportunistic theft. Hunter or trapper would likely be the only ones out that way and also the only ones with the need and temperament to do something like that. Unless, of course, there's someone out to get you that you haven't told us about."

Colden flinched. Of course, he was joking, because who'd be out to get Colden? What had she ever done to anyone? But she knew about the Sasquatch e-mails, and Larry's hostility, and the night with Liam. They did not. And she wasn't going to tell them. These were her mistakes, her issues to deal with. She didn't need them worrying about her. She didn't even know what, if anything, there was to worry about.

Colden spent the next couple of weeks mostly in her cottage, focused on her PhD research. She tracked moose movements, studied maps, overlaid data, plotted beaver dams and pond sizes. She was acutely aware that she was studying the outdoors from the indoors. It irritated her, but it was necessary, even though she had more aches from being in front of her computer for hours every day than she ever did from the most strenuous backpacking.

At least I'm not getting any blisters, she thought.

The days grew warmer. She was serenaded to sleep by spring peepers and woken before dawn by chirping birds. She opened the windows during the day, and the pungent scent of damp earth tickled her nose. The outdoors beckoned. She needed to survey a couple of beaver marshes and collect her own data cards. She also needed to get out of the house.

She told her father she was planning to be gone again for a few days; he crossed his arms over his chest.

"What?" she asked.

"I've been thinking."

"Always a dangerous idea."

"I'd like you to bring a handgun with you."

"Oh, please. No way."

She was in the closet of her childhood bedroom, looking for some extra tent stakes, and turned to stare at him, shaking her head in disbelief. Dix filled the frame of the doorway to the hallway. The creases on the sides of his mouth looked raked in.

"I'm serious, Colden."

"I'll bring my fishing pole. I can hook someone if they mess with me."

"You said yourself that there's weird stuff going on out there."

"Nothing that requires a damn gun."

"Not yet."

"C'mon. I have a black belt, remember? All the tournaments you schlepped me to?"

"That was a long time ago. And no use against someone who might be armed. Which every hunter and trapper out there will be."

"A gun in a pack is dangerous," Colden pointed out.

"True," Dix confirmed.

Sally showed up alongside Dix. He moved to let her through.

"So, here. Carry this instead," Sally said, handing Colden a can of pepper spray.

"I have bear spray, Sally."

"Great. This is douchebag spray."

If only I could use it on a certain professor down in Albany, Colden thought.

She took the canister from Sally. It was a small item with little weight that would be easy to carry and would make her parents happy.

"OK, OK, I'll carry the douchebag spray."

Dix and Sally dispersed and left her to her preparations.

Colden found the snows almost fully retreated and the woods filled with multitudes of greens so fresh, they seemed to glow. The ground squished under her boots. The air was scented with moist earth and damp decay. Birds twittered in the air, and chipmunks rustled in the undergrowth. She had left the ATV at home and was happy to be carrying all her needs for the next few days on her back. By late afternoon on her first day out, she made it to the reed-filled shores of a small lake she wanted to survey. She set up her tent in the soft duff under a cluster of trees, then sat and listened as the loons sent their laments over the dark, flat water.

Colden was alone. She was sure of it. Like any animal comfortable in the wilderness, she had an acute sense of when her kind was near. There had been many times she'd paused on a trail, felt a breeze of caution cross her skin, and then let her eyes drift until they found a camouflaged hunter sitting in a deer stand, completely unaware of her. Other times, she'd paused on a rock outcropping for a rest or a snack and inexplicably felt compelled to move away to a more private spot, just before a group of hikers appeared and settled themselves, chattering like crows, right where she'd been. She had been out assessing lakes like these and found herself stepping into deeper cover just as a canoe with two fishermen silently paddled into view. At this moment, at this lake, she was confident and serene in the conviction that, for a very comfortable distance, it was just her and whatever other wild creatures were making this area their home.

Colden spent two days surveying beaver ponds and documenting new construction and chewed saplings, along with moose prints, scat, and browse. She found a fresh shed of butterfly-shaped antlers, noting the tiny marks where mice and chipmunks had been gnawing at the nutrient-rich rack. One evening, as she stood outside her tent sipping tea, a large beaver appeared in the lake, swam closer to her, then slapped her spatula tail on the water, the sound loud enough to report and echo off a rock outcropping nearby.

"No worries, my friend," Colden whispered into the quiet after the beaver had retreated. "I'm here to protect you."

Colden found a small flat rock at her feet, cocked her arm backward, and skipped the stone across the lake. Twelve bounces. Her Dad had reached eighteen or more. Her record was fourteen. Too bad no one was there to see, she thought. Only, not really. Colden didn't require or even desire a witness to her life. She was alone, yet not lonely. When she'd had a regular boyfriend, or even just a guy interested in her, even if she really liked him, she had also felt constrained, like she was wearing shoes half a size too small. Invariably, the guys became vaguely dissatisfied with her. They complained that she was always busy. Too self-contained.

One had said she didn't need him enough. She'd responded that she didn't need him at all. It was clearly not the response he'd been hoping for.

Colden knew she was fortunate to "do the work you love," as has been so often advised. Yet, standing on the edge of the lake, skipping rocks and watching the distant beaver, she felt content and also remote from the passion she'd once felt for this sort of work. The ebb and flow of enthusiasm for a project was normal and expected. Helicopter rides were exciting; crunching numbers, not so much. This was a different sensation. She was starting to feel like she was just doing an assignment. She chafed at the restrictions, the reporting requirements, the consensus building.

She was aware this was a fault in her, not the project. People called her ambitious, and in their mouths, the word always sounded like an insult. But the accusation was true. She wanted to make a difference somehow, and she wanted her life to have meaning. She wanted to accomplish all this in her own way, and that was ambition, pure and simple.

For two days, she'd forced herself to focus on beaver and moose. She'd done the work she needed to do. Now, she could go hunt down the camera traps on her personal project. The thought and effort were thrilling. She broke her first camp and hiked deeper into the mountains to the places where she'd set the camera traps. One camera had become dislodged somehow and was dangling from its perch. The others were where she'd left them. If hunters or trappers were in here, they hadn't found or had chosen to ignore her equipment. It took her two more days to find each spot, pull the data cards, clean the lenses, re-secure the equipment. Another full day to hike all the way back out to her truck. She grabbed a premade sandwich on her way home, got back after dark, bypassed the house, went straight to the cottage, and without even removing her boots, opened her laptop and began clicking through grainy black-and-white images.

The cameras were triggered to take pictures by motion. She saw crows. A fox. Deer. Nothing. Nothing. Nothing. A waving branch over and over and over. Nothing. Nothing. Nothing. There was one data card left. She sighed, rubbed her face, closed her eyes, and said, "please, please, please" out loud to whatever science gods might be listening, then began clicking. The first few images were strange, still pictures of the small clearing and stump where she'd directed the camera. She'd hoped the stump would be a likely scent-marking spot. She stared at the screen. Odd. She saw no creatures or movement. A bird or a branch just out of view must have set off the motion detector. Then she saw the tail of another fox. Then something else. Tail and hindquarters, mottled gray fur, bushy tail. Her heart raced with hope and excitement far ahead of her thoughts. She reined them in. The animal was lean. Maybe sixteen inches tall. Nope. Not big enough, tail not brushy enough, hindquarters not beefy enough. Maybe a young animal? No, too early in the season. She clicked to the next photo. A shoulder. It was just a coyote. A normal coyote.

Damn. Oh well. What did she expect? People had studied wolves in the wild for years before getting a glimpse of one, relying on scat and kills to gather information. Besides, the animal she was after might not exist at all. There was nothing to do but to keep trying until she got something or gave up. She wasn't much of one for giving up, though, and this thought made her both determined and exhausted.

There were a few more pictures to go through. A couple of blanks set off by who knows what. Then, an image with a dark, indistinct shape filling half of the frame. A bear? Maybe. They'd be coming out of their winter torpor and be very hungry. Her bait would certainly be attractive. Odd, though. It would have to be a bear standing on its back legs. Whatever this was was tall. Maybe a bear reaching up to scratch or something. There was another shot of the coyote. This time, she could see its muzzle. Yep, a coyote for sure. She was disappointed but not discouraged. She'd get some more cameras. She'd try another area. There was no hurry. She had no deadlines and no one to report to.

She stretched her arms over her head. Scanned the news. Some celebrity scandal. Some political scandal. It all seemed so far away and irrelevant. She checked her e-mail and deleted a few dozen solicitations, announcements, LinkedIn notifications, and science-nerd LISTSERVs. The only personal correspondence was a note from Drew. The subject line said, "Sugar." She couldn't figure out why. Then she remembered he'd said at dinner that someone had poured sugar into the tank of a skidder. He'd commented that it didn't do the damage that people generally and erroneously thought it would, but this person had also cut the machine's gas lines and punctured the tires, as if for good measure. His note was brief.

Hey girl, any news?

The e-mail made her feel annoyed at him for some reason, for no reason. Maybe just annoyed in general. She didn't want to be pressed.

My dad and I are asking around, she typed, knowing that she was doing no such thing and unsure if her dad was or not.

Gotta be circumspect, you know? she added.

She hit "Send." She should have been nicer, she immediately thought. This was a familiar self-reprimand. She was more prone to irritability than she liked to admit.

There was one more e-mail in her in-box, this one from an unfamiliar address. The message also began with the words, *Hey Girl.* At first, she thought it was another note from Drew. There were only a few sentences. The writer asked how she was. If she was around, in the area, on certain dates. Liam. She reflexively checked her calendar. The dates he suggested were next week. She had a flash of insult. *Way to give me warning,* she thought. Then she reminded herself that she hadn't checked her e-mail in more than a week. And that the note contained a specific apology for the late notice. Said an unexpected trip her way had come up. She felt her face flush and her heart speed up like a revved engine as she stared at the name at the end of the note.

Not sure, she tapped into a reply. *Nice to hear from you.* She deleted this sentence. Then wrote instead, *Is your wife coming along on this trip???* She quickly hit "Send" before she could change her mind and was immediately bowled over with a crashing wave of regret.

It's not like they were dating. It was just a one-night stand. She didn't know if he was married. The source of her information was unreliable. But still. She should have been more subtle. Or more polite. Just told him she heard from someone that he had a wife, and she wasn't interested in participating in infidelity. Why had Larry even told her? What a jerk. She wondered if he treated everyone the way he treated her. She'd have to ask around. But whom would she ask? She'd be seen as a complainer, someone looking for trouble. Or labeled "too sensitive." The standard way to keep ambitious women just a rung or two below where their skills would otherwise take them. Just brush it off; just ignore it—that's what they'd say. Or not say, but imply. She needed a beer or a cup of tea. She needed a bath and some sleep. The sandwich she'd picked up sat next to her computer, still wrapped. Her head ached, and her stomach rumbled. She wrote another quick reply to Liam that just said, *Sorry. Heard a rumor. None of my business, really.*

Her e-mail pinged. She hoped and feared it was Liam with either an explanation or insulted outrage at her rudeness. She wanted something, anything, that could close this chapter with a definitive door slam. Or opening. The e-mail was from Drew, asking if she would be in Albany anytime soon. Could they have coffee or dinner?

She hadn't planned on going to Albany anytime soon. But it might be good to check in at her office. She was caught up, for the moment, on fieldwork. She had to get the data cards back into her camera, but there was no deadline on that. Albany was just a couple of hours' drive.

She tapped a reply saying that, yes, she was going to be there next week. There. Now she had a real reason to say no to Liam, no matter what he replied. If he replied.

THIRTEEN

The next morning, when Colden wandered up to the main house from the cottage, Sally was sitting on the back deck, her feet propped on the rail, her fingers wrapped around a cup in her lap. Dix and his truck were gone.

"Not going into the office today?" Colden asked.

"Nope. Decided to take a mental health day. Too beautiful to be inside."

Colden looked around her. The lawn was a rich, iridescent haze, and the trees glowed with an amber light made by rosy buds just starting to unfurl into green leaves. Robins were busy hopping around, cocking their heads, and then tunneling their beaks into the grass. A dog barked protectively in the far distance. The sunlight was warm against her face. A slight chill in the fitful breeze and a large patch of dirty snow plowed up at the end of the drive were the only reminders that summer could be a slow-to-arrive and reluctant guest in these tangled mountains.

Sally lifted her mug. Colden took it, went indoors, and came back with two full cups. She pulled up a chair and paralleled Sally's slouched-down, feet-up posture. They interrupted the morning silence with intermittent conversation about quotidian things.

"Guess your cameras didn't pick up anything interesting yet?" Sally eventually asked.

"How'd you know?"

"Figured you would have told me by now if they had."

"Science is an uneven process."

"Like the rest of life."

Something in Sally's remark sparked something within Colden, creating a fast and electric connection between the cameras, their funding source, and her internal yearn to strive, to search, and that apparently similar drive within her mother. Her real mother. Well, her biological mother. A question she didn't realize had been latent within her was suddenly set free; it fluttered tentatively within her, a butterfly released from a cocoon. She sipped her coffee. She waited. The back of her throat tickled, the question itself trying to take flight.

"Sally?"

"Yeeeesssss?" She drew out the word, playing off Colden's obvious reluctance.

"Can I ask you a question?"

"Of course."

"Am I much like her?"

Colden didn't feel any need to further define the "her" she was referring to. Sally stared fixedly into the distance.

"Wow. That's a tough question," she replied, her voice noticeably quiet, a bit weary.

"I realize that," Colden said. "I mean, I think I do. What do I really know about her, anyway?"

"Not much, I guess," Sally conceded. "Maybe that's our fault. Maybe that's a mistake."

Colden considered.

"I don't think so. You've shared stuff in a natural way. I've just never been that curious. Not that interested."

"And you are now?"

"Not much. Just a little. From time to time, she seems to pop into my awareness in a way she never has before."

"I want you to know that you can ask me anything about her, anytime," Sally said.

Colden realized that perhaps she had been incurious, but perhaps she had also been afraid to bring up her own mother, not wanting to burden Sally or Dix with painful memories. Not wanting to put the specter of Miranda between herself and Sally. Or Dix.

Sally rolled her neck.

"Well, to your question. You are so very much like your father in so many ways," she said. "I usually only see the mirror of him when I look at you. Your jawline. The expression you have when you're concentrating. Something in your gait. Your quiet stubbornness. But you have some qualities he does not. He wants to improve the world around him, for sure, as do you. It's your energies about the effort that are different. You are more restless. More ambitious, I guess."

There was that word again: *ambitious*. But Colden felt, instinctively, the hardwired truth of Sally's observations.

"Did you know her well?" she asked.

"Yes and no," Sally said. "Not as well as your dad did, obviously. But maybe there were some ways I knew her better."

"How do you mean?"

"Because I am a woman. I understood her from that pretty primal perspective. Also, I wasn't in a romantic relationship with her, so I had more clarity about who she was. I loved her but wasn't in love with her. And, well, she didn't hurt me the way she hurt your father."

Colden flinched. It was hard to imagine her father loving anyone other than Sally. They had such tenderness between them. She had seen its manifestations countless times. A hand on the lower back. A kiss to the top of the head. A shared and knowing grin. A cup of tea delivered without being asked for. Colden wondered, for the first time, if Dix's big, messy, earlier love for Miranda was a sore spot for Sally. If she ever felt like she was some sort of consolation prize plucked from the ashes of Dix and Miranda's burned-out relationship. They seemed two such different women: Miranda, beautiful, airy, idealistic, spoiled, and self-absorbed; Sally, handsome, pragmatic, fierce, and loyal.

"It's hard for me to picture them together," Colden said. "They seem, well, not that I really know anything about it, but just not well suited."

"Sure, but since when has being ill-suited kept a couple from falling in love?" Sally replied, without rancor.

Colden took in the scene around her: the aged stone wall and walks bordered with beds she knew harbored bulbs and perennials just starting to stir within the dark soil; the line of deciduous and evergreen trees that fringed the lawns, creating a soft wall of security against the encroachments of the outside world. She allowed herself to feel how grounding and comforting this place was. She realized it wasn't so much that she hated, for instance, going to Albany; she just hated to leave here.

"What do you think she was looking for?" Colden asked. "By going to that commune?"

"You mean, why would she cut out on such an awesome place and wonderful man?" Sally asked.

"Well, yeah, I guess," Colden said. "I mean, sure, how could she leave this? But also, why there?"

"Do you want the groovy answer or the clinical answer?"

"Can I have both?"

"I'll need more coffee for that."

The women laughed, briefly, but neither moved. Sally sighed and shifted in her seat.

"Maybe the groovy and clinical answers aren't that different," she said. "Everything had been given to her, and little or nothing was asked of her in her life. Then, way too much was asked of her all at once when so much tragedy hit, one right after another. She lost her older brother to a car accident, her father to a tree branch in a thunderstorm, her mother to grief and strokes and dementia. She also lost the big coddling arms of lots of money when she realized that her father had wasted so much and owed so much. I think she yearned to make her own life, she wanted to find a way to do some good in the world and not just take on another life that was handed to her by her parents or by Dix on yet another silver platter. Sadly, ironically, but typically—because this is what we dumb-ass humans do—the Source turned out to be a repeat of the same pattern. She set out to find a new path and, psychologically speaking, ended up bumper hitching on someone else's journey again."

Another sigh escaped Sally's lips.

"And she was depressed, Colden. Clinically. She'd suffered so many losses, one on top of another, and she never got the help she needed. Because poor little rich girls are too privileged to, you know, actually feel those pesky things called emotions. Even if she did feel them, she wouldn't have been allowed to discuss them, share them, talk about them."

Now, Colden sighed.

"It's rule number 4b in the WASP handbook. Comes right before, 'Wearing strangely mismatched clothes does not matter as long as they are from L.L. Bean or Brooks Brothers' and right after, 'As long as you don't start drinking until after four, it doesn't matter how much you drink.'"

"Does this mean I'm a WASP, too?" Colden asked.

"Seems to me that being a WASP is like being a Jew," Sally said, somewhat comically. "There's genetics, and then there's culture.

You have to have both to fully blossom into either. And truth be told," she added, her voice growing more serious, "I guess your mom wasn't even as much of a WASP as her parents pretended to be. Her father's parents were strictly working-class. Part of why he was so incredibly snobby. Classic overcompensation."

"I've been given everything, too," Colden said.

"True, but things were expected of you. And you're naturally a hard worker who needs little and wants mostly to make her own way in the world. Plus, some people, like you, seem to enter the world with more resiliency than others."

"How old was she when she died?" Colden asked.

"Let me think," Sally replied. "I guess, well, I'm not exactly sure, but around your age."

"*My* age?"

Sally nodded.

"Thereabouts. Mid- to late twenties."

Colden swore under her breath, and unwelcome tears sprang to her eyes. She swatted at them with the back of her hand.

"Your mother was a very tender and timid soul," Sally said.

Your mother. The phrase sounded so strange to Colden, referring as it did in this instance to someone other than Sally, coming from Sally. She felt sadness swell inside her, a dry sponge suddenly soaked with rain.

"Did you ever want to have kids?" Colden asked.

It was a question that, as it came from her mouth, Colden realized she had long been wanting to ask. Sally shot her a look. Colden didn't lift her eyes; she didn't want to see Sally's face.

"I do have kids," Sally replied mildly.

"I mean, more than me. Other than me," Colden said.

She couldn't, wouldn't, use the term *your own* kids.

"I wasn't referring to you," Sally said.

A small grin broke on Colden's face. Sally was teasing her, making a veiled reference to what she called "OPCs," her shorthand for *other people's children.* Sally had helped, monitored, and mentored hundreds of OPCs. Colden felt a warm pride in Sally's work suffuse her body. But she didn't want to give in to Sally's familiar and slightly snarky redirects of topics that veered toward the personal or sentimental. Colden understood these were the protective reflex of a woman who'd not had an easy upbringing, who understood the many varieties and shapes of financial, cultural, and social poverty, and whose best professional efforts on behalf of her clients were more often than not received with anger and frustration that she couldn't or wouldn't do more. Sally called this phenomenon the "unique sense of entitlement of those with nothing and therefore nothing to lose."

"I'm a scientist, Sally," Colden countered, pushing Sally to answer honestly and sincerely. "I know biology matters. Lots of animals kill their stepchildren."

"Well, of course, there were times when I considered it," Sally parried. "Killing my stepchild, that is."

Colden snorted. Then Sally cleared her throat and changed her tone.

"Certainly, we thought about it, your dad and I. Talked about it. But in case you hadn't noticed, I'm not very maternal."

Colden shot her a glance.

"What? C'mon. You are an awesome mom."

"Easy to say when I'm the only one you've known," Sally said.

Sally was teasing, but the remark stung Colden. Not because it was directed at her—Sally was being self-deprecating—but because it reminded Colden there was an important fact in her life that she had largely ignored. She did have two mothers. One here, present, available; the other opaque, mysterious, absent.

"Sorry, Colden," Sally said. "I don't mean to be dismissive. These are important questions, and I'm glad you're asking. The truth is, your dad and I never actively tried to have kids, but we also didn't try *not* to have kids. It just didn't happen. Which is honestly fine with both of us. If we'd gotten pregnant, that would have been fine, too. We settled very quickly into being a tight and happy trio."

"How did you two actually meet?"

Colden heard this question as if it had come from someone's mouth other than her own. She squirmed in discomfort at the intrusion it seemed to represent. But when she looked over, Sally was smiling indulgently at her. She seemed almost relieved to be sharing this information, as if this was a conversation she'd been waiting for, wanting to have, but wasn't sure how or when to initiate.

"Well, it certainly wasn't a typical first date!" Sally said. "More like, 'Hey, you don't know me, but I'm here to tell you that the commune your ex-girlfriend left you for is housed in my dead grandmother's house, and I've been living there, too, only because I am in a rough spot in my own life, not as part of the commune—just, you know, keeping an eye on things, even though it's like watching a slow-mo train wreck—and oh, by the way, enough about me, what I really came here to say was that I just discovered that the woman who broke your heart died a few days after giving birth to a baby you didn't even know was yours, and the commune leader is trying to hide the infant so that he can raise it in some freaky, back-to-nature way, and I want to help you with the legal fight that's required to get you your daughter.' Not exactly high romance."

Colden exhaled, a harsh sound of spent air, and squirmed in her chair.

"Sorry, honey," Sally said.

"It's OK. I mean, I guess I knew that in a general sort of way. Just strange to have it all laid out like that. To think, 'Wait, that's actually me we're talking about.' It's not just some story. It's the way I came into the world."

"Colden, I want you to know one thing above all others, and that is that you were always loved. Deeply. By Miranda and your dad and me and even that whack job, Darius, who ran the Source and by the women who cared for you out there after your mom died—and even by the foster family that kept you while we were proving Dix's parental rights. You ended up with only two parents, but for the first months of your life, you had many, and they all adored you and cared for you."

Colden considered this. She noticed changes in her physical sensations. It was as if Sally's words had turned on some latent source of heat that was now gently warming her body fluids. Then the switch turned off, and she grew cold again. Maybe she had begun her life in love. But it was a love born of betrayal to her father. A love from people whose actions she found abhorrent. It was a love she didn't want. She wouldn't tell Sally this. Or her father. It would only make them sad for her, make them feel the heaviness of Miranda's legacy. Which she was quite sure, and equally relieved, that she could neither remember nor feel within herself, no matter her biological connection to Miranda.

Colden realized that she'd never closely considered the impact another person could have on her. She'd certainly never considered how much impact Sally, in particular, had had on her. She always felt thankful for her life, but she'd never thought through how tenuous her good fortune actually was, how differently things might have turned out.

"Thank you, Sally," Colden said. "Thank you for saving me from them. Thank you for helping my dad. Thank you for being my mother."

Sally met Colden's eyes. Her cheeks flushed, and her eyes dampened. Colden's did the same. Neither of them was accustomed to tears, so they each looked away, but the moment between them held.

Colden left for Albany the next day. She crashed at her condo and then went to the office early the following morning. It was dark and empty when she arrived, just as she liked it. Larry's office, she noted with relief, was unoccupied. She flicked on a light switch, and the fluorescent fixture over her area flickered and then illuminated. She went to her desk and got to work. Eventually, more lights came on, voices entered the space, and people began rustling papers, coffee cups, and chairs.

Colden sensed someone coming up behind her. She froze. Then a familiar voice said, "Hey, stranger."

She relaxed and turned her chair to see Jack, a cup of coffee in hand.

"Same back 'atcha," she said, smiling.

Another passing colleague, Sam, stopped at her desk. Colden introduced him to Jack. They gave each other quick rundowns on their research. Sam, who studied songbirds and their population decline, asked for some details on the work they'd been doing. There wasn't anything revelatory to report, but Colden pulled up the maps that showed the patterns of moose activity. She overlaid these with maps of known beaver ponds. They saw how the moose were spending increasing amounts of time near these marshy areas as the season warmed and the waters thawed. Interesting, but not unexpected.

The dull grind of science, Colden thought silently.

As she clicked through images, some of the initial collaring work popped up. Sam leaned in toward the pictures of downed moose with their stark eye coverings. He straightened up to a photo of the entire team posing in front of the helicopter: Colden, Jack, Darryl, Larry, and Liam, who stood almost a full head taller than the rest of them.

"So, that must be Sasquatch," Sam said.

Colden's skin tingled as if a spider had just run over her arms.

"What are you talking about?" she asked, her voice scratching against her suddenly dry throat.

"The big dude. What's he, an Aussie? Larry talked about him when he got back. Kept referring to him as Sasquatch. Said he was a real asshole who tried to keep him off the project."

Colden felt Jack go very still. She was afraid to speak. She hoped he would.

"Nope, not an asshole," Jack finally said, quietly. "Real pro. Nice guy. Fun, too."

"Yeah, I figured," Sam said. "Larry's always complaining about someone. Well, thanks for the show-and-tell."

He started to walk away.

"Sam?" Jack said.

"Yeah?"

"His name is Liam. A very high-quality person. I've worked with him for years. Can't recommend him highly enough."

"Cool. Good to know," Sam said, then disappeared around a corner.

Colden wanted to ask Jack what he meant by a "high-quality person." She also wanted to ask him if Liam was married. She didn't do either.

"Fucking Larry," Jack muttered under his breath. "Keep up the good work," he told Colden and then walked away.

Colden kept working. It was the only way to keep her emotions at bay until she was ready to deal with them. But thoughts and questions swirled in her mind like garbage against a curb during a rainstorm. Larry. The Sasquatch e-mails. Could all this be a strange vortex of coincidence? She collected and connected the data she had. Larry called Liam Sasquatch, accused him a being a philanderer, and gave her a hard time for being with him. Did this mean that Larry was sending the e-mails as part of some harassment strategy toward her? But why?

Animals do things for reasons, she told herself—to eat, to help their family members succeed, to breed. They repeat behaviors that are rewarding in some way. Everything else is a waste of precious and hard-won energy.

Humans thought they were above the petty survival squabbles of other animals. Colden knew better. She tried to imagine what reward Larry was getting for his behavior toward her. In many species, low-ranking males often used sneaky strategies to get mating rights or to obtain status. Larry seemed a low-ranking male—unattractive, awkward, marginally successful, and even that seemed to come with significant baggage. He certainly wasn't trying to breed with her, and she was not in the way of his status. Or was he? Or was she? There were only so many seats at any research and funding table. Academia was wildly, if often passive-aggressively, competitive. She didn't like to admit it so blatantly, but she knew her colleagues liked her, respected her, and enjoyed working with her. She was always a first pick for a team. Larry must see her as a threat, she realized. It was incomprehensible to her how or why she would represent a threat, and yet, that was the conclusion the evidence was leading her to.

The office was quieting. People heading out for lunch and afternoon classes. She felt rattled. She should go get some lunch. Maybe she could get a nap in before her dinner with Drew. She was embarrassed that she hadn't done much on Drew's behalf; the only "asking around" she'd done was of her father. She would take some time this afternoon to think of a more directed plan, and she'd share that with him tonight.

One last quick check of e-mail before she left. And there it was. A response from Liam. How strange and coincidental the timing. Her hands trembled slightly as she clicked it open.

> *Colden,*
>
> *I'm sorry. You should have heard it from me. I am married. Technically. However, we have lived apart for a couple of years. My traveling so much was hard on her. She asked for a divorce so she could have a full-time partner. We agreed on an amicable settlement. Then she got sick. Very sick. We stayed married so I could keep her insured. I assume you heard something from Jack? You can ask him for confirmation of my story, if you want. He knows*

my wife. She's in hospice now. So yes, I'm married. But it looks like I won't be for much longer. Be well. I have nothing but fond memories of you and know you will do great things.

Liam

P.S. I remembered, finally, how I knew Larry. I hate to speak ill of a colleague, but please be cautious around him, my friend.

Colden read the e-mail several times, her insides growing more still and quiet with each perusal. She was embarrassed that she'd attacked Liam without understanding the full story. She was mad at Larry for telling her things that led her to take actions she regretted. She felt manipulated and outmaneuvered. The sensation was familiar. This was how she had felt when a sparring match went against her. It was time to calm down, stop reacting, think, plan, and decide on a fresh or different approach to the person she saw as clearly an opponent. Even though she still wasn't clear what they were fighting for or over. She reminded herself that the best approach was not to attempt to beat the other person, but better protect and better maneuver yourself.

Still. She felt in vague yet real danger.

She didn't respond to Liam's note. This time, she'd think before she typed and hit "Send." She turned off the computer and left her office. On her way out, she noticed that her mailbox, the real one, the physical one, was stuffed with papers and envelopes. She always forgot to check and clean it out. She flipped quickly through the memos and magazines, the junk mail and university correspondence. Most got jammed into her pack to be read more carefully later.

As she turned to go, she noticed her name on a plain brown box on the counter. It was a regular box from Amazon, about the size and heft of a large book. She thought carefully. She hadn't ordered anything from Amazon, and if she had, it would have been delivered to her home. But there it was, addressed to her. The date on the label showed the box had been sitting there for three weeks. Of course, it had. She hadn't been expecting anything.

A door opened and closed in the hallway. Someone laughed. A car alarm went off in the parking lot and was quickly silenced. The brown package seemed a living, dangerous thing, poised, waiting to strike.

Colden's keys were in her hand. She used them to stab at the tape and release the cardboard flaps. Inside, she found three small paperbacks: *Bigfoot, My Love*; *Sasquatch and Me*; *Take Me to the Woods*. Subtitles told her that each was an installment in the seven-book Sasquatch Erotica series. She quickly covered the books with the packing paper and closed the flaps.

Larry had just made things a lot easier for her, Colden thought. Larry had just given her evidence.

FOURTEEN

Brayden had dreams not of what his father had done to him, but of his own rage and escape from unseen tormentors. They were not nightmares but live-action sequences from a movie where he was the star scaling walls, leaping across an abyss, scrambling up and down ladders and fire escapes and in and out of windows. There were also dreams where he screamed at someone whose face he could never see, dreams from which he woke sore and hoarse, as if, indeed, in his sleep, his voice had ricocheted from his throat to the walls of his cave.

Lying there in the damp darkness, trying to rouse himself from the fog of an unrestful night, thoughts of his sister always came to him. Memories of her played in his mind like a ribbon in the wind, twisting, turning in on themselves, pausing just within reach and then dashing away.

There was the time Belinda had crawled into bed with him in the middle of the night and held on to him until dawn, their breaths silently syncing as they lay, wakeful, together. He had thought at the time that she was there to comfort him, that she knew what their father was doing and thought by being there herself, she could keep him away. There was the time he saw the tracery of fine scars across her forearms, and he didn't ask her what was wrong, just rubbed his forefinger over the crosshatches and watched as tears dripped from her eyes. The time he found her shoving her belongings into a suitcase, and the way she watched him with such deep resignation as he took everything back out and returned it to her closet and drawers. And then the time that he was walking down the long, silent hallway, thick with pale carpeting, and saw his father—his adoptive father, he always reminded himself; he shared no blood with this monster—come from the bathroom, pull the door closed behind him with a hard finality, and then rub his hands together as if he was drying them. Brayden was seventeen years old. His father had given him a hard look and said, "Don't go in there. Your sister's using it."

That time, outside the bathroom, in the hallway, Brayden had quickly turned, frightened of his father, and gone back to his own room. Where he'd recently installed a lock. Which he slid shut before crumpling all of his six-foot-four frame into a puddle on the floor and sobbing with the sudden, guilt-racked realization that she was getting it, too. She hadn't been trying to help him; she'd been trying to get help from him. He'd been so stupid, so caught up in his own pain. He'd never told her what their father was doing to him because he didn't want to burden her. He'd also assumed that if the same things had been happening to her, she wouldn't be like him. That she would tell someone. Because he always thought that she had more courage than he did.

Then, the morning after that horrible night when his father closed the bathroom door on her, his sister was gone.

He asked his father where she was. He shrugged and said he didn't know. He asked his mother, and she looked at him with a pained expression, then shook her head in a way that closed off further inquiry. He quietly waited another day. Then he kept asking. His father told him to mind his own business. Another day passed. He started asking why they weren't looking for her. His mother's face got tight. His father, sitting on the sofa, reading the news, told him to forget about her. That she was a little whore, and wherever she was, it was good riddance to bad rubbish. His mother, across the room in a straight-backed, upholstered chair, gulped a bit, pressed her knuckles against her teeth, and said nothing, did nothing. His father shook out his newspaper and went back to reading.

That's when the rage lit up within Brayden, roaring through his body like a brushfire on a hot, dry, desiccated day.

Mind his own business. That's what he had done. And look what that had done to his sister.

A whore. Not his sweet sister.

Brayden grabbed what was nearby. A chair. A birch-twig chair that sat next to the front door. Where he had often paused to remove his shoes. His father hated people bringing mud into the house on their shoes. It was a classic, Adirondack style. They'd made it together, a father–son project. Even collected the birch branches from the woods nearby. He was behind the sofa, unseen by his father. The man had no idea what was happening. Brayden, his anger rendering him silent, lifted the chair high overhead and brought it down onto his father's head. The chair seemed to explode with a sudden release of all of Brayden's unexpressed fury. Twigs flew off in every direction. Brayden remembered that his father had misdirected him in its construction, had cut corners. What a flimsy thing it turned out to be. It broke apart so easily. He watched his father crumple sideways on the couch, his body littered with birch branches. Brayden's mother didn't move from her seat. Her hand dropped to her side, leaving her mouth open in a perfect O.

Shock, Brayden thought. That's what shock looks like.

Brayden turned and left the room. He ran to the basement, where he had a pack stuffed with emergency supplies. It was something his father had made him do, so they'd be prepared in case of an emergency. He'd never said exactly what kind, but his paranoia came in so many forms, it hardly mattered.

This was certainly not the sort of emergency his father had had in mind.

Brayden grabbed the pack and fled the house.

Go quickly, *he told himself.* Before your mother comes out of her spell. Before she calls the ambulance. Before your father shakes off the debris and comes after you.

Brayden was bigger, but his father was meaner. Brayden knew that made the older man more dangerous.

Now, months later—how many months exactly, he wasn't sure, but judging by the seasons, it had to be six or more—here he was, idle in the woods. It was wonderful, in its way, to be so free. He had his chores. These kept him grounded in reality. These many small tasks of staying alive and keeping his camp clean. He had the paperbacks and magazines he'd swiped from the camps. In the beginning, he'd read them over and over to fill the time. But now he was content to sit. He stared into space. He watched leaves move in a small breeze. He noted the retreat of a small patch of snow in the spring warmth.

He needed this quiet.

And yet, the memories of his sister kept up their noisy onslaught in his mind. He was her big brother. He was supposed to protect her. That was what he'd done all the years they were in foster care, standing over her when other kids picked on her, giving her his portion of food when there wasn't enough to go around, warming her with his own body when they didn't bother heating the room where they slept.

Then when they got to the fancy Victorian house on the hill, he'd let down his guard. It was supposed to be their forever home. These parents were supposed to be solid citizens. His sister turned into a straight-A student. A star soccer player who tutored other kids. How could she do all that, be all that, and also be suffering under the same burden that he was? He had found that the weight of it made it almost impossible to concentrate in class, to make close friendships, to smile, to be happy.

His own agonies were nothing compared to the anguish of realizing that he had not been there for her. That she had not felt she could share her torture with him, that she could not ask for help. And that he had been too blinded by his own shame to see hers.

Guilt.

Guilt was so much harder to bear than shame.

FIFTEEN

Colden went back to the mountains. She set aside her experiences in Albany—the note from Liam, the books, her dinner with Drew. She wasn't sure what to do about any of it and decided to be cautious. It was surprisingly easy to put everything, literally and metaphorically, into the unused drawer of a small desk in her mind and in her cottage. She was accustomed to taking action. She thought it would be hard to leave these things to stew. Instead, it was a relief.

Summer came on early and suddenly, a jolt of light, heat, and biting bugs after the gentle lull of a mild winter melding into a brief spring. Her father had been extremely busy as the new season took hold. So much so that she'd been joining him on his rounds, helping him with getting homes opened and aired out, beds cleaned up and prepped for planting, tasks and repairs checked off various to-do lists.

Then, a couple of weeks after she returned, Dix said, "I have something for you."

They were in the shop. Dix was cleaning one of his mowers and removing the blades for sharpening.

"News of our phantom vandal?" Colden asked.

Dix shook his head in a way that was not exactly a "No" but more of a comment on the sorry state of the world.

Colden was sitting on a stool at his workbench. The seat wobbled. She stood, turned the stool upside down, got a screwdriver from the pegboard on the wall in front of her, made a few turns, and righted the stool.

"I kinda liked that stool the way it was," Dix said. "Now you've gone and wrecked it for me."

Father and daughter grinned at each other. Dix flicked the switch on his grinder and pressed the edge of a mower blade to the wheel. Colden watched the steel spark against the stone, smelled the tang of old grease and fresh grass.

"You said you had something for me?" she said.

Dix used his chin to direct her to a stack of papers on the far, and clean, edge of his workbench. Printouts from a website and an online article. Of course, he wouldn't just send her a link. He was perfectly computer savvy, but she realized that he wanted to watch her reading whatever it was, in his presence, so he could gauge and manage her response.

The articles were about something called "Conservation Dogs." A program took crazy, obsessive-compulsive dogs from shelters and redirected their drive to sniffing out invasive species, finding orca poop in the ocean, and tracking wildlife scat in the woods. Colden read and tried not to let anything show on her face. Her father kept grinding his mower blades—turning, wiping, testing—shooting an occasional low glance her way. Once he was done, he turned off the spinning stone, and quiet settled back into the shop.

Colden set down the papers. Her father waited for her. His preternatural patience was somewhat exasperating. She felt peevish. She didn't want help with her project. From him or from a dog.

"I don't know anything about dog training," she said.

"I do," Dix replied.

Colden liked dogs just fine, but she wasn't interested in them as a species or a pet. She looked somewhat askance at companion animals, thinking less of them than their wild cousins, as if they were somehow complicit in their own domestication and subjugation. They'd had animals around the house. Somewhat aloof cats who occasionally wrapped themselves around her legs or nestled with her in bed but were kept mostly to keep away rodents. A handful of hens for the fresh eggs, but when a coyote or fox or mink or hawk got one or several, she'd always found herself rooting, silently, for the predators. They'd had a sweet, gimpy dog when she was a kid. Lucky. A dog Dix had found in a trap in the woods. But Lucky was always old and infirm in Colden's memories, limping around, looking for a patch of sunshine to warm her aching joints.

She remembered how her father had cried when the vet finally came to the house to put Lucky down. The fat tears had rolled silently down his face, an endless stream that continued as he placed the dog in the grave he'd dug, covered her body with dirt, and planted a lilac to mark the spot. It was the only time in Colden's life that she'd seen him cry. She'd been embarrassed for him then. A lanky, laconic, competent, practical man crying over a bag of old bones in a shabby fur sack. It shook Colden to see her father so exposed with raw emotion. He'd looked old to her then. The first time she'd ever seen him that way. She didn't want a dog. She didn't want to make herself vulnerable to that sort of feeling.

"So, you think a dog would be better at finding a coywolf than my game cameras are?" she asked, her voice larded with skepticism. "A nose better than the latest technology?"

Dix looked at her and raised his eyebrows. He knew that Colden hadn't gotten much from her game cameras.

"I assume you read the part about the exquisite sensitivity of a dog's smelling abilities," he said mildly. "Far exceeds your technology. Many others as well."

She had. She knew. She changed her approach and her complaint.

"I don't know, Dad. I really don't want to deal with a dog."

"Always the solo operator."

"You're one to talk."

"Apple doesn't fall far from the tree."

Colden felt her stubborn resistance harden. Then a fresh idea occurred to her. She'd give it a try just so she could prove him wrong.

"Bet you have a candidate in mind," she said.

"That I do."

"Bet he's nuts."

"That *she* is. But she won't be once she has a job to do."

Colden sighed. This was going to happen. Her dad didn't pick battles often, and when he did, he always won, even though he never actually fought. He simply let circumstances play themselves out, waiting patiently until his solution became the most obvious.

"Plus," Dix added, "she'll be good company for you when you're out there in the woods by yourself."

"I have no need of company."

"Maybe company has no need of you."

"What you mean is that she'll be good protection."

"Wouldn't hurt you to have a companion with sharp teeth and keen senses."

"Thought that's why you taught me how to use a gun."

"Which you won't bring with you."

"I could bring my archery set."

"Little heavy and cumbersome for your backpack."

She was out of arguments and sarcasm. Dix began wiping his hands on one of those red rags always hanging out the back pocket of his Carhartts. His fingers were grease stained, large knuckled, and multi-scarred.

His life, Colden thought, *is etched in his hands.*

For the first time, she wondered if those enlarged joints ever ached or caused him pain. If so, he never showed it. Dix crossed his arms over his chest and faced her.

"I read something once, Colden," he said. "It was some research. Something Sally had. They'd asked guys who were incarcerated for burglary if they'd rather face a dog or a guy with a gun when they went in to rob a house. They all said they'd rather face a guy with a gun. When asked why, they said, 'Because dogs don't hesitate.'"

"You've never worried about me in the woods before."

"That's true. But this feels different."

"I still think it's probably just bored high school kids trying to get booze from summer homes and stuff like that," Colden said.

"Maybe. Maybe not."

"It could be someone needy who figures the rich people won't really mind 'sharing.'" She made air quotes with her fingers. "Figure they have so much already, what's it to them to replace a bunch of gear they probably never use, anyway."

"Could be," allowed Dix.

Colden looked at her father. Deep furrows made his brow look like a plowed field. There was more salt than pepper on his unshaven cheeks. He was slightly stooped at the shoulders, as if from a lifetime of ducking his head so that it didn't strike anything. His arm, injured decades ago, seemed stiffer than usual, more often than usual.

"Can she pack in her own food?" Colden asked.

"Of course."

"You bought her a pack already, didn't you?"

Dix dipped his chin in affirmation.

SIXTEEN

Colden drove up the quarter-mile-long, steep, and winding driveway to the property Dix had converted to an animal shelter. It was slow going. He, who usually maintained things impeccably, had allowed the drive to acquire and keep its seasonal array of frost heaves and holes because the rough road discouraged lost or curious people from approaching his sanctuary. If someone persisted, they'd find themselves dead-ended at a locked gate with a call box in the middle of a six-foot wall of fencing adorned with several "No Trespassing" signs. Dix had thoughtfully put in a small turnaround to make it easier for those misguided few to return from wherever they came.

In general, Dix was against fencing and posting property, preferring to leave things open to both wild animals and people who wanted to wander, roam, hike, hunt, ski, snowmobile, or fish, legally. However, the animals at his shelter needed to be kept safe from coyotes, raccoons, bears, tourists, and people angered that their animals had been removed from their care for reasons of abuse or neglect.

Colden knew Dix was trusting of people, to a point, a friendly yet guarded man. She'd never heard her father say a mean word to a person. He neither gossiped nor boasted. Yet, he also rarely engaged people. She saw that people had a tendency to give way around him. When he came into a store or ran into a person at the post office, the response to his presence was usually a soft, "'Lo, Dix," and then a careful stepping aside, as if he were a fragile thing they wanted to avoid damaging. Or maybe a dangerous thing they wanted to avoid irritating. He was respected for his equanimity, evenhandedness, and modesty but also known as someone you didn't want to cross—not because he would come after you if you messed with him, but because he wouldn't. He would quietly and completely cut you off and out. Which meant others, who respected him and his judgment, would do the same.

These thoughts about her father blew in fitful gusts through her mind as Colden punched in the security code, made her way through the gate, and approached what had once been her mother's family's summer and vacation home. It was the sort of place that people from downstate or away called a "cabin" but that was two to three times the size of a typical year-rounder's home, outfitted with more luxuries and amenities than many locals would ever see, much less use.

While among themselves, the locals scoffed at the absurd extravagances, they kept their mouths shut around visitors because maintaining and caring for these seasonal homes provided one of the few forms of steady employment in the area. The locals liked tourist dollars, even if they didn't think much of the tourists themselves. Money made in urban places like Wall Street allowed many of their neighbors just enough income to live in the wild, rural environment they preferred.

She slowed her truck as the imposing log building with a wide front porch came into view. Colden had collected bits and pieces of the story about her grandfather flouting a bunch of laws and regulations as he built this place. Logs acquired illegally in Canada. Septic not fully permitted. Add-ons not part of the original permit built anyway with a possible kickback to the inspector. This was the place Miranda had to abandon because she didn't have means or the heart to bring it up to code. This was the place Dix had bought, anonymously, before he and Miranda were a couple, just because he could. Because he liked to fix things. Because it would help Miranda. He didn't want any attention for the deed because gratitude would somehow wreck the experience for him.

At that time, Miranda probably still thought of him as just the family's handyman, content as her family had been in her erroneous assumptions about him, with no idea that he was both college educated and land rich. His parents had been architects. He was an only child. He had slowly acquired property over the years, mostly just to preserve it. No one knew, no one even suspected, how much he owned.

People always underestimated her father. She had always considered that a failure of imagination on their part. Maybe, it occurred to her, he liked it that way.

Dix was sitting on the front porch talking to the caretaker. One full-time person and a changing cast of down-on-their-luck humans, dogs, and various other critters lived here. There was a barn and a handful of other outbuildings, along with several large corrals and two pasture areas. The lawn was well tended. There were baskets full of colorful flowers hanging from the porch rafters. Comfortable, birch-twig rocking chairs on the deck. It looked like a rustic B&B or inn, not an animal shelter.

It hadn't always been like this. Colden remembered the first time her father had brought her here. She must have been eleven or twelve. Small trees grew in the gutters, shutters hung askew, windows were boarded up. Paint peeled from the sides of the outbuildings. Dix had, uncharacteristically, let the place return to a feral state. They hadn't gone inside on that visit. They didn't even get out of the truck. They'd bounced up the muddy drive, he'd given her a huge oatmeal cookie and a cup of hot chocolate from her own kid-size thermos and unscrewed the black cup from his man-size thermos of coffee, and they'd just sat there a while, sipping and chewing.

She remembered she had waited for him, wondering why they were there, knowing a story would come. Colden had had a sense, even as young as she was, about what she was going to hear, and she didn't want to rush it. Dix told her a lot that day. About the history of the house, her mother's family, how Miranda had sought out a sort of life that he wasn't able to give her. He never said that he had failed Miranda. But Colden could feel the regret and self-recrimination in his voice. He never said that she'd gone wrong, just that he had. He'd not done enough to save her from herself and from the man who led the commune.

After that day, he had begun to put the house back together. At first, he did the straightforward things to arrest the decay and destruction wrought by simple inattention. Then, repairs began to overlap with collecting more wayward animals. A tenant had left a couple of dogs behind. A feral cat had kittens in the barn. Someone left a dog tied out at the post office. He found a starving horse in a small pen outside a falling-down trailer when he was driving down a back road.

Dix built a few dog runs in the shop. The garage was given over to the cats. He built an enclosed "catio" off the back, enclosing a couple of trees so the felines had natural climbing posts. An ornery donkey, a potbellied pig, and a crippled sheep joined the horse in the barn.

Back then, all this work on the outbuildings alone made Colden think that Dix was afraid to take over the house itself, as if he was worried about disturbing ghosts that might still haunt the long hallways and dark corners. But eventually, he did open the doors and fix the broken windows. He removed the mouse nests and replaced the oakum between the logs. He furnished the place with secondhand finds that were no strangers to dog hair and hired a caretaker, someone Sally had followed in a series of foster-care homes, a young woman who needed a safe haven as much as the dogs and other creatures did. This woman eventually went away to college and was replaced by a middle-aged woman with a teenage daughter fleeing an abusive husband. Dix sealed the place's fate the day he put up a small sign on the door naming it "Ragtag Farm." The property's transformation from rich person's getaway to animal sanctuary was complete.

Colden hadn't spent much time at the farm. She had been busy with her own pursuits, and her father did not ask for her assistance or interest. She did have vivid memories of her first visit to the house once its rehabilitation was completed. Wandering the space, she'd tried to imagine what it was like when the dining room was set with silver, china, and crystal instead of a veterinary exam table and supply cabinets; when the back deck was used for cocktail parties instead of as a puppy playpen; when the shop had a lounge chair, humidor, and bourbon decanter instead of half a dozen dogs and innumerable shredded blankets and chew toys. She found she could only conjure images from some period drama set in Victorian England. Her mother and her mother's family were not just unknown to her, they seemed mostly unknowable.

The animals didn't care what the house had been. They made it their own. This was a lesson the humans eventually learned, as well.

On this warm May day, Colden slid from the seat of her truck, slammed the door, and listened to the resulting cacophony. A chorus of barks began within the house and garage. Chain link fencing jangled as dogs jumped against their runs. A donkey brayed. Guinea fowl and geese made a screeching racket. A swayback horse trotted lamely up to the gate and whinnied. Her father watched her approach, grinning.

Colden could not help but smile at this untidy assemblage and especially at the grin on Dix's face. Something came over him when he was here. Or perhaps it was more accurate to say that something fell away from him. Dix was not exactly serious, but he took things seriously. Yet, when he was here, his movements were looser, his expression less guarded, and something approaching joy animated his features.

Dix waved at her, rose from his seat, met her in the yard, and directed her to one of the corrals. There, a sleek, well-muscled, medium-size black dog with a square head and a strong jaw was leaping vertically up and down, putting a couple of feet between her back legs and the ground every time. Colden was equal parts impressed and intimidated by her manic athleticism.

"Isn't she great?" Dix asked.

Colden looked at him to see if he was serious. He was.

"*Hyperactive lunatic* are the words that come to my mind," she answered.

Dix led Colden through the double gates, into the dog's yard.

"This is Daisy," he said, crouching in the dirt.

Daisy wriggled toward them, and Colden reached out to pet her. The dog jumped aside, avoiding her touch.

"I thought you said she'd make a good companion," Colden complained.

"She will. She just doesn't know you yet," Dix explained.

"She certainly doesn't seem interested in getting to know me," Colden said.

"She has no reason to," Dix said. "We need to give her one."

Daisy was staring intently at Dix's hand, which held a yellow orb. He cocked his arm and threw the tennis ball as far as the quarter-acre fenced yard would allow. Daisy raced after the ball, caught it on a bounce off the chain link, then ran back and dropped it at his feet. They repeated this routine several times.

"She's not exactly friendly or affectionate, is she?" Colden observed.

"You're not exactly warm and fuzzy or soft and cuddly, either," Dix replied, handing Colden the ball. "You're both focused on work. You'll make a great pair."

Colden stiffened. Independent, self-contained, not needy: she'd always thought those qualities were good things. But these same adjectives had often enough been used as accusations. Especially by the men she had known. It was no wonder she liked being a field biologist. It was a way to be alone. There was a reason she preferred wild to domestic animals. They didn't want to curl up on your lap.

Colden threw the ball. Hard. It clattered against the chain link and made a wild bounce. Daisy caught it, anyway. Then brought it back to Dix. He looked at Colden, questioningly.

"I'm not criticizing you, honey," he said, picking up the ball and handing it to her. "It's just an observation."

Colden threw the ball again. Less hard. Daisy brought it back, and this time, she dropped it at her feet. But when Colden bent to pick it up, Daisy snatched it away, chomped on it a few times, took a couple of steps backward, and dropped the ball again. Colden closed the distance and reached for the ball. Again, Daisy snatched it away. This time, she kept it in her mouth.

"Drop it!" Colden demanded.

Daisy and Dix both looked at Colden in mild rebuke.

"She won't listen to me," Colden pouted.

"Why would she, when you talk to her like that?" Dix asked.

Colden threw up her hands, crossed her arms, and rolled her eyes.

"Yep, a perfect match," Dix said. "Stubborn and demanding. Training you both is going to be a blast."

He held out his hand. Daisy placed the ball in his palm. He threw it for her, and she raced away, her body shining and rippling in the early summer sun.

Two weeks later, Colden was at one of her regular trailheads, sticky with sweat and itchy with mosquito bites. Her arms were crosshatched with scratches from briars and scrub and pockmarked with welts from blackflies. There were several ticks crawling up her legs, their tiny bodies black spots against the beige of her pants.

She brushed the ticks off her pants. They seemed worse when she was with Daisy. She got a bowl from the truck and squirted some water into it from her bottle. Daisy's messy lapping sprayed the water onto the dry, gravel ground of the turnout. The dog emptied the bowl and looked up at Colden expectantly, her red tongue lolling out the side of her mouth. This had been their first time camping and working together in the field. It hadn't gone well. Daisy chased deer and chipmunks instead of scent. Colden knew she was to blame for most of the problems—she'd let the dog off lead when she shouldn't have; she pushed her too hard, too fast; she didn't do as her father had instructed her.

It was so easy to resent the dog; she knew she really resented her own incompetence around the dog.

She didn't want to face her father, his excruciatingly patient instructions, his natural facility with Daisy. She wasn't ready. She was stalling. A solution presented itself. She'd go see Gene.

The air was still and the light flat when she pulled up to his cabin and got out of the truck. Colden felt chills wriggling up and down her arms as she stood in the yard. It wasn't just the cooling air on her skin that caused the sensation. There were no dogs running out to greet her. Colden listened for the slight whine of Gene's wheelchair. She cocked her ear, hoping to hear the dull thumps of his crutches. Quiet. Nothing but quiet.

Colden called out, "Hello? Gene?"

A small movement at the front window of the cabin caught her attention. A curtain was moved and then dropped back into place. She heard the familiar sound of crutches against a wood floor. A lock scraped.

A lock? Since when did Gene lock his house?

The door opened. Two dogs pushed each other through the opening, and then Gene rocked his way out after them, followed by Buck. Killer and Jake swarmed Colden's legs. Buck laid down on the porch with a grunt. Gene lowered himself to his well-used rocking chair. He looked worn out. Wrung out. Colden waited. She tried to look through the gap of the front door.

"Where's Lucy?" she asked.

Gene shook his head and compressed his lips.

"Gene?"

He wouldn't look at her. He closed his eyes, and Colden watched reluctant tears squeeze their way free and roll down his cheeks. She pushed past the dogs and sat on the raw edge of the porch. She reached up to touch Gene's leg but thought better of it and pulled her hand away.

"Gene, what happened? What's going on?"

Buck got up and rested his chin on Gene's lap. Gene stroked the dog's head and sniffed away the tears. He stutter-started his story several times. Colden held on to each disconnected piece of information he offered, waiting for enough details to emerge so that she could put together a complete picture.

He'd heard a strange sound. He'd been asleep. He'd had trouble sleeping lately. He'd taken something, smoked something. It was hard to wake up. He was a little foggy. Something had come onto his property. It was the middle of the night. Maybe it was early in the morning. Still dark. So late, it was actually early. He heard some rustling around out by the barn. Whatever. This was nothing new. Probably just a raccoon. Nothing to worry about. Anything a raccoon might want was locked down. Must have been a young one. One that didn't know any better. The dogs barely lifted their heads. At first, anyway. Something fell. There was some kind of metal-on-metal clattering. Then the dogs whined and barked for a bit. Everything got quiet again. Lucy wouldn't settle. He wasn't going to let them out. What if it was a bear, not a raccoon? A bear would rip the dogs open with a single swipe. He got out his gun. He went to the window. He looked out and saw that the door to the barn was half-open. Had he left it like that? He couldn't recall. Honestly, he'd had one too many that night. Maybe a few too many. There was only a tiny bit of light. There was something out there that was just a shade darker than what was left of the night itself. He went to his back door, opened it a bit, listened, heard more rustling, and popped off a warning shot. The dogs started barking again. He looked around the door. He saw some large, indistinct shape slide out the barn door and begin shuffling away. He shot again. This time at the shape. If it was a bear, it was a nuisance. He wanted to scare it. He heard a yelp, and the animal shuffled off. The dogs stopped barking. He set the gun down. Killer, Jake, and Buck looked at him from where they were on the sofa, paws on the windowsill that faced the barn. No Lucy. He called. Whistled. The dogs in the house came to his side. He called Lucy's name over and over. Nothing. The other dogs looked stressed. They wouldn't move, wouldn't go out the door.

Gene got a flashlight, stumbled out into the night, and found Lucy by the barn. She was lying on her side, bleeding out. She looked at him, took one deep breath, and was gone. It wasn't the bear, or whatever the visitor was, that had killed her, though. Gene had done it. He'd shot her. He hadn't meant to, but there it was. He'd shot his own dog. She must have slipped out the back door, he hadn't noticed, and then he'd shot her in the dim, predawn light. After all she'd been through, all she'd recovered from, all he'd nursed her through, this was how she had to die—at his hands.

His bad sleep, his damn eyes. He needed glasses, but where was he going to get the three hundred bucks it took for an exam and specs? He'd been saving up for new teeth. He'd lost so many, he was cooking everything down to mush these days. He had thought his teeth were more important than his eyes. He saw perfectly well close-up. It was just the distance thing. Those damn painkillers, too. A friend had given him a few he'd had left over from some dental surgery. His back had been hurting like a son of a bitch. Lucy had gone out the door because she was trying to protect him, and he, the fool, had shot her.

What a dog. The best dog. Now she was dead. He'd buried her out back. With a bunch of tennis balls and toys she loved. With her bed. He hoped she'd forgive him. He'd saved her, and then he'd killed her.

"Some shit just isn't right," Gene murmured. "Some shit just doesn't make any sense."

Tears dripped down Colden's face. Killer licked them off her cheeks.

"Oh, Gene. Oh, Lucy. I'm so sorry, Gene," Colden said.

There were no words to comfort him, so she sat and simply tried to share the sadness. The sun lowered, taking the light with it. The mosquitos came out. The dogs snapped at them. Colden slapped at her arms and legs. Gene sat totally still.

"Brutal year for the skeeters," Colden said.

"Time to go in," Gene answered.

Colden wanted to say something like, "It's not your fault. Accidents happen." But remarks like that would be unwelcome. Lucy's death was Gene's fault. She knew it. He knew it. It was an accident, yes. It could have been prevented. And it wasn't. This was Gene's fault and now his burden. Colden knew that any effort she might make to mitigate his justifiable regret was nothing more than a cheap papering over of ugly emotions. They were emotions he needed to have and work his way through. She respected his anguish and self-condemnation.

She stood and left him with no more words between them. Sally and Dix were eating dinner when she got back. Colden washed her hands, put some kibble in a bowl for Daisy, served herself salad and shepherd's pie, and joined her parents on the screened-in porch.

"Don't take this the wrong way, Colden, but you look like crap," Sally said by way of greeting.

"Well, it's been a crappy few days," Colden replied miserably.

They ate in silence, the only sounds cutlery scraping against plates and mosquitos tapping against the screens. When the plates were empty and set aside, Colden sighed and told them Gene's story, which conveniently saved her from having to tell her own. When she was through, Dix sucked his teeth and asked if anything was taken.

"Taken?" Colden asked. "What do you mean?"

"Stolen."

"What would a bear want to steal? Other than food?"

Dix sipped his beer. Sally watched him. Colden glanced from one to the other.

"Maybe it wasn't a bear," Dix said, his voice subdued.

"More of those silly robberies? Is that what you're suggesting, Dad?" Colden asked, incredulous and annoyed. "It's not like Gene has much of anything worth stealing."

"True, but someone might not know that until they checked."

"Well, I didn't think to ask him," Colden said. "Given how upset he was, it wasn't, you know, a great time to start playing private eye."

Daisy wandered into the room and shoved her nose under Dix's hand.

"Well, how did things go with this girl?" he asked hopefully.

"Horrible, if you must know. You'll see the scrapes on her belly from crashing through the brush when she ran off after a deer or something. Yes, it was my fault. Yes, I took her off the line, like you told me not to. It's a total pain to hike in the backcountry with a leashed dog. Of course, nowhere near as much of a pain as spending forty-five minutes bushwhacking and hollering for her. I'm sure we scared off any and every wild animal in three counties. Not very helpful for my research. Oh, and she barked at night in the tent. Every tiny sound caused her to bust out yapping. I hardly got any sleep. She didn't mark on any coyote scat. She dug after chipmunks, destroying old stumps. She ate deer poop and then licked my face. It was all frustrating, disgusting, totally unhelpful. A complete waste of time and effort."

Daisy was panting and wagging her tail as Colden spoke, glaring at her. Dix methodically stroked the dog's sleek sides.

"I told you it wouldn't work," Colden pronounced.

She stood and left the room. No one followed her, not even the dog. She went to the bathroom, slammed the door, stripped down, and took the shower she'd been longing for. She let her warm tears mix with the cool water cascading over her face.

Wow, she'd been so bratty, she chastised herself.

Unreasonable. Unfair. She was just so frustrated. She was getting nowhere with the coywolf project—a dozen cameras checked several times and no signs of anything that could viably become a research project. The moose and beaver work had become totally rote and boring. She was supposed to go back to Albany for some departmental meetings and reports. She didn't want to see Larry. She had never written back to Liam. She had nothing to tell Drew. She was lonely. Yet, all she wanted was solitude.

Stop. Stop, stop, stop, she told herself. *You're tired. It's been a rough day. Focus on finding something unexpected out there. Find the thing that no one else is looking for. That's what you need to do. Find the thing no one even knows is out there.*

The following morning, Colden hunkered down at the cottage. She felt bruised by her own behavior the previous evening. She wasn't ready for human company. But as she sat on her little porch sipping tea and watching the day brighten, she saw Sally walking down the path toward her.

Sally never came down to the cottage. Well, almost never. Colden expected, almost hoped, Sally would give her a stern dressing down. She certainly deserved it. She was also not ready to give up her foul mood, and a reprimand from Sally would help preserve her misery.

There were two rockers on the porch. As Sally got close, Colden shook the dry leaves from the cushion of the extra chair. Sally sat down with a mug of coffee. She sipped and stared out in front of her. She didn't even say good morning.

"Why aren't you at work?" Colden eventually asked.

"Thought I'd take the day off."

Colden waited a few moments before replying.

"That worried about me?" she half joked.

Sally turned and looked at her full in the face. Her frank regard caused hot tears of frustration to spring to Colden's eyes.

"Um, yeah. Little bit," Sally said sincerely.

"Sorry if I was a jerk last night." Colden had difficulty getting the words out of her thickened throat. "No—I mean, sorry I *was* a jerk last night."

"You weren't a jerk," Sally said. "Well, maybe a little bit of a jerk. That's not what concerns me. I just want to know why. What's going on?"

"It's just the research."

Sally didn't respond. Her silence told Colden she wasn't buying the excuse.

"OK, it's not just the research," Colden finally conceded. "It's a lot of things."

"Spill," Sally said.

Colden didn't want to tell Sally everything. People were always coming to Sally with their problems. She was a professional listener and fixer. Colden didn't want to be yet another person burdening her with their petty foibles. But Colden knew she'd worried several strands of her life into a knotted ball. Sally was the best person to help her untangle things. So, she gave in and started talking.

"It's just . . . I don't know. Things don't seem to be progressing. I feel so frustrated. The PhD stuff is fine, but it's honestly not as interesting as I'd hoped. So much drudgery, collecting tiny bits of information and trying to find patterns, which at the end of the day seem so obvious and anticlimactic. I'm not getting anything on the coywolf stuff. I'd had high hopes. Silly, I know. Unrealistic. But still. I wanted, I don't know, I wanted to discover something. I wanted to make some sort of a difference somehow. To have an impact."

"Impact?" Sally asked, skeptically.

"Yeah. OK, to make a splash. To get noticed. To get my career going. To do something. Something meaningful."

"Wow."

"Wow, what?"

"You sound so much like your mother."

Colden flinched.

"Sometimes I worry I'll somehow make the same mistakes she did."

"Nope. You'll make your own mistakes," Sally said.

Colden drank some tea. She shifted in her seat.

"I feel like I've made a few recently."

"Go ahead," Sally urged her. "Tell me. There's nothing I have not heard before."

Colden slouched in her seat and told her about Liam. Everything up to and including his last e-mail, which was sitting, cowardly unanswered, in her in-box.

"Sounds like a pretty great guy to me," Sally said when Colden was done.

Colden looked at her in genuine surprise.

"What? Seriously? Don't you think that's incredibly weird about his marriage?"

"Not in the least. On the contrary, seems incredibly mature and realistic."

"You and Dad would never do anything like that," Colden insisted.

"You don't know the slightest thing about what your father and I might or might not do," Sally countered.

Colden was shocked—not just by what Sally said, but by the definitive, corrective way she said it. She looked at Sally, blinking in the harsh light of her reply.

"When you're young, you think relationships are all about being *in love*," Sally said. "As if 'in love' can protect you from every obstacle, every other feeling, from anything going wrong. News flash, sorry, honey, love is not going to carry you over all the hurdles of a long relationship. Being in love helps, obviously. It's important. But sometimes, maybe most of the time, making a marriage work is about sucking shit up, making tough choices, plowing ahead. Like your friend Liam did. Even if plowing ahead means ending the marriage to preserve the relationship."

Colden felt confused and miserable. As if she were still an eight-year-old who had just been told that Santa Claus doesn't exist.

"But you and Dad seem so happy. Have always seemed so happy," she said, pouting.

"Colden, how the heck would you know if we were happy or not?"

The rebuke pushed Colden deeper into her chair.

"Look, all you've seen of us is through the lens of a kid. Kids are all self-absorbed. And frankly, you're still a kid. Sort of, anyway. You've had a very sheltered life. A wonderful, rich, engaging, beautiful, but sheltered life. You think we're happy and have always been happy because we kept *you* happy. Believe me, we've had plenty of struggles. We didn't get together in any conventional way. We came into our relationship with all kinds of baggage. We wondered if we were in it for the right reasons. I had fears and insecurities about not being your mother. Miranda seemed like the big love of his life, and we're so very different. Not just in personality, but, petty as this sounds, she was beautiful, delicate, feminine, sweet—not things anyone would ever accuse me of."

"But Sally, you're . . ." Colden protested.

Sally stopped her with a severe look.

"Please. I am many things, but beautiful, girly, all that . . . not so much. Do not insult me with cheap compliments."

"But you two always get along so well. I've never seen you argue," Colden said, unwilling to give up.

Sally shook her head.

"Do you really think we'd argue in front of you?"

Colden opened her mouth to say something, but no words came out.

"Maybe we should have argued in front of you," Sally continued. "Maybe that would have been more honest. Given you a better sense of what really happens in a relationship. Sometimes I worry that you don't really get it. I mean, sometimes I worry that you don't realize that struggles aren't signs of a *bad* relationship, they *are* the relationship. They are the things that bind you. Assuming, of course, that you struggle together, fairly, and with love. Even when you really dislike each other. Even if you've hurt each other."

"Well, Dad never seems to struggle with anything."

"You sound like your mother, again."

Colden stared at Sally, surprised.

"That was a core problem for her with your dad," Sally said. "She was always comparing herself to him. He always seemed to have it all together, to be good at everything, to not have any issues at all, to just cruise through life in his own bubble of competence. Not true, of course. He does have fewer doubts and worries than most. He simply doesn't fret much about what he can't change, being kind of naturally Buddhist, I guess. But to say he has no doubts, regrets, or concerns is terribly unfair to him. It limits and constrains him. He's not an island."

Colden groaned and put her face in her hands.

"Ugh. Sounds like what most of the guys I've dated have said about me. Too independent. Too self-contained."

"You are nowhere near as Zen as your father, but I'm sure you seem pretty insulated to most people. There is no reason to change—likely, you can't change—but be aware that these qualities can be hard for other people to bear. Your dad doesn't really get that. It's a blind spot. It keeps people at a distance in a way he doesn't see. Sometimes it even pisses people off. Makes them poisonously jealous."

Colden thought about Larry. He seemed irrationally angry at and competitive with her. She wasn't dating him, yet it occurred to her that he was treating her like a spurned lover. She decided to tell Sally about him, too, about the way he treated her, the way he tried to elbow in on her work and seemed to want to take her down, as well.

"Well, there you have it," Sally said when Colden was through. "Perfect case study of unreasonable and yet dangerous personal and professional envy."

"But why?" Colden moaned. "We're not even in the same field. Not really. Why doesn't he just focus on his own work?"

"Ah, why focus on making yourself better when it's so much more fun to try to bring someone else down?" Sally asked. "You're just there, Colden, that's why. Doing well. Respected. Get along with your colleagues. Doing interesting work. Making it look easy. Most people are not as well equipped as you are. The fact that you don't seem to realize how competent and smart and playing-way-above-the-hoop you are makes it even worse for other people. And then you're pretty, and you don't even notice or care that you're pretty. It can be a maddening combo for other people to have to witness."

Colden was intensely uncomfortable with everything Sally was saying but had to admit that it was all wise and true. Colden had a cushy life and had taken it all for granted—not because she was spoiled or entitled, but because she'd never had any setbacks. Not yet, anyway.

She was not without empathy. After all, she was surrounded by people who never even got far enough ahead to have a setback. She had compassion for them. However, it had never occurred to her that she could ever be one of them. That her life could turn and take her in unimaginable downward directions.

Colden thought of Miranda, sitting on this same porch, wondering about her own life but from a very different vantage point. She must have been scared to death of the future. She'd been cut adrift from so many hopes and dreams that had seemed so inevitable. So much of Miranda's life never got the chance to take place because her parents had failed her in a multitude of ways. Colden felt swamped by an overwhelming rush of gratitude for her own life and for Sally and Dix.

"So, what do I do, now, Sally?" she asked, her voice low and strained.

"Write back to Liam and apologize because he deserves that. Ask your lawyer friend for advice on Larry because he needs to be carefully managed. Keep doing the work you love and are really good at. And don't be any less wonderful for anyone."

"OK," Colden said.

"And let your dad help you with the damn dog. Stop being so obstinate—admit you don't know what you're doing, and he does."

SEVENTEEN

Colden didn't tell Sally this, but she'd already asked Drew for help with Larry. She hadn't meant to or wanted to, but over their last dinner, right after she'd gotten the Sasquatch erotica books, the story had come out. She had considered canceling dinner with him since the topic of conversation was supposed to be what she'd found out about his vandalism project and she didn't have anything to tell him. She had never done what he'd asked, and she wasn't sure why not. Some kind of embarrassment. Both toward him on behalf of her neighbors and on behalf of her neighbors for allying herself with an outsider. Complicated and conflicting loyalties. However, when he texted to confirm, instead of making an excuse, she asked if they could meet at the same Italian place they'd been to before. She wanted the familiarity and comfort, as limited as it was, of him and of that restaurant.

When she arrived a few minutes early, Drew was already seated. Again, she'd wanted to get there before him. Again, he'd beat her. Colden waved and weaved her way to his table, tucked into the far corner of the room. Drew surprised her by standing up, pulling out her chair—well, that wasn't the surprising part—and then kissing her cheek.

She was unsure if she liked or resented his gallantry. Was there something vaguely misogynistic about it, or was she being ridiculously political about simple politeness? Maybe she was just unused to being treated this way. Maybe she didn't want to admit that she kind of liked it.

The waiter came over and, with a dramatic flourish, shook out her white napkin and placed it in her lap. The action flustered her. She stammered when he asked what she would like to drink. Drew intervened and suggested a small pitcher of Chianti to share. Once again, there were many animated and distracting conversations going on at tables nearby. She realized she was avoiding meeting Drew's eyes, which made her more uncomfortable. He seemed to be waiting for her to say something.

She took a deep breath, then a sip of water, forced a smile onto her face, and asked him about his house. He started telling her a convoluted and comical story about a plumbing mishap, leaning across the table to show her a large blood blister on the outside of his hand. She had a hard time following but nodded and smiled, even laughed at the appropriate moments. After the story wound down, they each drank some wine, and then he pulled back against his own seat and regarded her warily.

"What?" she asked.

"I was about to ask you the same thing."

"What do you mean?"

"Something is wrong. I can see it on your face."

"Just some stuff at work," she said, waving her hand in the air dismissively.

Drew leaned forward and touched her hand. His face was filled with concern.

"What's going on?"

Colden noticed one of his front teeth overlapped the other slightly, like crossed ankles. Why hadn't he had braces? Too expensive for working-class parents. She felt inexplicably sad. Her concerns were so petty. She twisted her wine glass in her fingertips. Drew crossed his arms over his chest.

"I'm not saying another word until you tell me what's upsetting you," he said.

Colden snorted, as if she was laughing at a joke. Drew was serious. His lips were closed. She wanted to see his teeth again.

"OK," she said, sighing. "It's just . . . Well, there's this guy . . ."

Drew did not move. So, she told him all about Larry. Which meant she had to tell him about Liam, too, at least a little bit. Drew took it all in, nodding, staring at the tablecloth, pursing his lips from time to time, thinking, shaking his head here and there. In between her sentences, he somehow quietly placed their order. Food came. He showed her how to twirl her spaghetti onto a large spoon she hadn't understood how to use. She found herself talking not only about Larry but also about her work. Her frustrations. The boredom. The mind-numbing acquisition of minute details about animals, on which publication and careers depended but on which she was not clear the animals' lives depended. Also, the raw beauty of the landscape where she worked. What it was like to see a moose lift its head, antlers dripping wet and strung with aquatic plants, from a marsh created by a beaver. She even told him about the coywolf project. She seemed unable to stop talking. Finally, the words sputtered out. Drew watched her for a bit, as if waiting to see if she'd start up again. He wiped his plate with a piece of bread, crossed his knife and fork over the edge, and settled back into his chair. She looked down at the few ivory-colored strands of spaghetti left on her plate, the remnants of red sauce. She'd monopolized the entire meal with her story. It was discomfiting.

"I'm going to help you," Drew said.

"I thought I was the one who was supposed to be helping you. And I haven't been doing a very good job at it. I haven't been doing any job at it, honestly."

Drew waved her concerns away.

"You'll get to it. The vandalism has stopped recently, anyway. And you've obviously been a little preoccupied. In the meantime, get me whatever info you can on this Larry guy. I'll see what I can find out."

"Seriously?" Colden shifted in her seat. "I don't know. Is that OK? I mean, I don't want to get anyone in trouble."

"Colden, if someone is harassing you, they should get into trouble," Drew said.

"I guess I'm not sure if this is harassment. That's such a strong word. Maybe it's just, you know, being a jerk."

"Tell you what," Drew said. "We won't get him in trouble. We'll just see if he is in any trouble already."

"Maybe I'm just being paranoid and making a big deal out of—"

Drew put up his hands.

"Stop it, Colden," he said, not unkindly. "If it's him sending you these weird things, then it's unlikely this is the first time he's done it. Or the last time. If people like you don't come forward, someone else will suffer. It may get worse. A lot worse. Believe me."

Colden looked at him questioningly.

"I've represented people in situations like this," he said, explaining the strength and clarity of his opinions. "You know. Pro bono. On the side."

Colden nodded slowly. Volunteer work. Giving back. This was a good man. Better than she had given him credit for. She should do that. Volunteer work. She'd been meaning to do that. She was so fortunate. She should share some of what she had been given. Take some disadvantaged city kids on an adventure in the wilderness. Anything to get out of her own head for a bit.

The waiter arrived with two Italian flags and dessert in a glass.

"What's this?"

"Tiramisu," Drew said.

Colden didn't know what tiramisu was. She'd never heard of it.

"But we didn't order it," she protested.

"It's a gift, Colden," Drew said. "A gift of deliciousness. All you need to do is say thank you and enjoy it."

Such good advice, Colden thought. So difficult to take.

EIGHTEEN

Sometimes Brayden thought about leaving his lair in the woods. It was not so much of an idea or a plan that he would implement, but more of a "what if?" The way people think, "What if I won the lottery?" A fantasy. No, more of a necessity. Because a fantasy was something you wanted to have happen. Brayden didn't want to leave; he just wasn't sure he could stay.

He always felt something or someone would somehow compel him to walk free of the line of trees, with nothing more than whatever his backpack could carry, and then he'd have to go start a life. A real life. It was just that this life, his life beneath the trees, felt more real than anything he'd ever experienced.

He liked listening to the birds singing and the chipmunks rustling in the leaf litter. He liked watching the leaves moving in the breeze and the water trickling in the nearby rivulet. He enjoyed all his small tasks, from checking his fishing poles and gathering berries and mushrooms to cooking up a trout and boiling water on his campfire. He spent hours and hours listening, watching, observing—well, in fact, he didn't know how much time he spent doing this or that because his watch had stopped working.

And what difference did it make, anyway? It's not like there was anywhere else he had to be. It's not like there was anyplace else he wanted to be.

The only thing he wanted from that other world, that world beyond the trees, was to see his sister. He didn't even need to see her. He just wanted to know if she was OK. If he saw her, well, that would bring it all back. For both of them. So maybe not seeing her was OK, too. As long as she was all right. As long as she wasn't with their father and was somewhere better than where she had been. That's all that really mattered.

NINETEEN

Colden finally wrote to Liam. She apologized for being a jerk, made some crack about hitting "Send" before thinking, told him she was sorry to hear about his wife, and said she hoped they'd work together sometime in the future. Originally, she wrote that she hoped to see him in the future, but she changed it. It seemed keeping him at a professional arm's length was the most prudent approach.

She clarified that it wasn't Jack who'd mentioned his wife, but Larry. She didn't want Liam to be erroneously mad at Jack. She also wanted Liam to share what he knew about Larry, but she didn't want to ask. She hoped that by calling him out as the gossip, she'd get some info.

For encouragement, she added, "Larry's kind of a jerk—I shouldn't have listened to him."

She was surprised to get a reply the next day.

Colden,

Thanks and no worries. Totally understandable. And yeah, hope to be up in a 'copter with you this upcoming winter. As to

Larry, he is a bit of an ass. I don't normally gossip about people, but I'll give tit for tat to that guy. Here's a tip: his name isn't really Larry Stevens. It's Lawrence Steven Rivers.

All the best,

Liam

Colden read the "'copter" remark several times, wondering if there was any flirtation there. Maybe everything Liam said was a flirtation. Even though she had created the distance between them, that didn't stop her from wishing he'd try to close it. Regardless, there was more important information in his reply. Larry's full name. She popped Drew a quick note telling him that a friend had given her Larry's supposedly "real" name—maybe he could find something out from that. She thought about doing a deep Google dive herself but didn't want to go on the hunt for more dirt. She'd had enough of Larry for the moment. She'd see what Drew came up with.

Which reminded her that she had promised to help him. And that she had been avoiding Gene since she found out about the accidental shooting of his dog. It was time. She needed to check up on him and check in with him.

Summer was in a high, June mood, full of sun and birdsong, when Colden again drove over to Gene's. She'd wanted to bring him something. A sort of peace offering. He waved off gifts as readily as he did assistance, but her father had just baked a blueberry pie. Gene loved pie.

He was sitting on the porch when she arrived, his eyes closed and his face turned toward the sun. He did not change his position until she was all the way to the front step.

"Your dad make this?" he asked as she handed him the pie and a plastic fork she'd brought.

"Of course," Colden answered. "You know he's the only one in our house who cooks."

"He's good at it."

"He's good at everything he does."

"Pretty annoying, ain't it?"

Colden nodded, smiled, and sat down. Gene ate in silence while she pet the dogs. When he was finished, he crumpled the foil in his hand and looked at her.

"Why you here, Colden?"

"Why are you asking?"

Colden was getting used to being called out by people on the feelings she thought she was skilled at obscuring.

"Something's up."

"I can't just be making a social call?"

"You can. I enjoy your social calls. But something else is going on. I can tell."

"Maybe. OK. Yeah. You busted me."

"So, tell me."

"You first, Gene. How are you?"

"Pickled, seasoned, hardened, and grumpy."

"You know what I mean."

"I miss my dog, if that's what you're driving at."

"It is."

"Well, there's nothing to be done for it. She's gone, and I'm an idiot. It's not the first stupid mistake I've made in my life, wrecking one thing while trying to fix some other thing. I'm certain it won't be the last."

"You're hard on yourself, Gene."

"Life is hard on me, too, Colden."

She nodded. There was too little fairness in the world. It was something she'd had the luxury of not considering too closely for the bulk of her life.

"I'm so sorry, Gene."

He cleared his throat.

"Tell me what else brought you out to this little patch of hell today, Colden."

"OK," Colden conceded. "So, I have this friend—"

"Boyfriend or *friend* friend?" Gene asked, interrupting her.

"Just a friend."

"So far, just a friend, you mean."

"Gene."

"OK, tell your story."

She did. About Drew and his employer, the vandalism, and his search for an under-the-radar solution.

"Your pa mentioned something about this a while ago. He wasn't quite so direct about it, though."

"Yeah, well, I asked for his help. Because I was too cowardly to ask around myself," Colden confessed. It felt good to be honest about her failings.

"Is this friend of yours a good guy?" Gene asked.

Colden thought about that for a moment. Gene would do anything for her but was, with reason, suspicious of outsiders.

"Yes, Gene. Yes, he is a good guy. I really think he is."

Colden meant it.

"Is he a fair guy?"

Colden nodded. She believed that to be true of Drew, as well.

"Hmmmm," Gene said.

"You got any ideas for me?"

"Maybe," he replied. "Might take more than a piece of pie to get it from me, though."

"Like what kind of more?" she asked cautiously.

"Guarantees."

"What sort of guarantees?"

"No prosecution."

"Told you, we have that. What else?"

"You sure?"

"Yes, what else?"

Gene didn't speak. Colden waited in the silence, petting Killer, who was lying peacefully at her feet. This was the kind of dog she wanted. A serene dog who would rest his chin on your thigh, not that hyperactive Daisy who wouldn't even look at you unless you had a ball in your hand. Then again, Killer would never work for you the way Daisy would. He'd follow you through the woods right up until he became bored, and then he'd turn around and go home on his own. He didn't have the drive that Daisy had. That Colden had.

"Here's the thing, Colden," Gene finally said. "The dude what's done this feels sorely wronged. These guys come onto property that's been in his family for generations and just took it and used it for themselves. They didn't ask. They were not polite."

Colden didn't speak for a few minutes. She didn't want to argue with Gene because she needed him to be on her side.

"I'm a little confused," she said cautiously. "I was told that they sent letters and tried to get in touch, but they never got a response. They only had a blind post office box to send to, of course. Also, I thought that property boundary had been settled a long time ago."

"Depends what you mean by settled," Gene said.

"Well, moving a fence line doesn't automatically reestablish a property line."

"Well, it should. If the line wasn't correct to begin with. The fence is just making a point that the deed should have. Some folks don't have high-priced, fancy lawyers to make their points for them. Some folks have to find other ways to make themselves heard."

"How much land are we talking about?" Colden asked.

"Eight feet."

Colden looked at him incredulously.

"Eight feet?"

"Eight feet for about a mile."

"That's all?"

"May not be much to you, but it's still his land. They're using it to get to their lands."

"And there's no other way to get there," Colden said.

"Not without either building a road through a swamp or blasting through a mountain of granite."

"So, what's your friend want?"

"Payment. Payment for the land or for an easement to use the land. And an apology."

"I'll look into it," Colden said. "Tell your friend I'll look into it."

"K. And Colden?"

"Yes, Gene?"

"He ain't my friend."

"Sure, Gene."

Colden stood to leave. Whoever this guy was, he seemed to be trying to make things difficult just for the sport of it. Lengthen your own line, her martial arts instructor had always said. Easy advice for a woman like Colden to follow, she reminded herself. Not so easy for those who didn't have a line to start with, much less one to lengthen.

"Thanks for stopping by," Gene said, brightening up. "Always nice chatting with you. And thanks for the bribery. I mean, the blueberry pie."

"Anytime."

"Hey, Colden."

"What, Gene?"

"You oughta learn to bake. Bet you'd be even better than your dad."

TWENTY

Colden was determined to make her and Daisy's next trip into the woods productive. She would be patient. She would work with Daisy at her level. She would not take her off lead. She would try to enjoy the process. She would remember to play, not just train.

The morning dawned cool and dry, the air free of the normal, oppressive summer humidity and swarms of biting bugs. Colden picked up two egg sandwiches, one for each of them, and a cup of coffee for herself. She had a waist belt and a ten-foot lead, which they had practiced with on shorter hikes. Daisy was finally sticking close by and had given up tugging Colden in different directions, following the scent of every critter she could find. They'd also been working on basic manners training, and Daisy was much more focused on Colden than she used to be. Working with the dog had allowed Colden to apply some of her knowledge of animal cognition. She was even starting to like Daisy, to look forward to seeing her wiggling body, damp nose, and ample tongue. These surges of primal affection made Colden feel vulnerable and raw, but she was starting to welcome the feelings.

They hiked for hours in the soft air beneath the trees. Colden asked little of Daisy, just rewarded her attention and enjoyed her company. They got to the farthest camera trap at midmorning and a second site a little after midday. Colden collected the data cards and decided to take a break for lunch. She found a spot to sit and offload her pack. Her waist belt and the bright yellow lead that tethered her to Daisy became entangled. She squatted and fumbled with the webbing and the nylon. Then, in the slow-motion way that disasters unfold, Colden watched the leash handle pull away from where it was woven into the leash itself. With nothing to resist, the lead slipped through Colden's hand, and as if Daisy been waiting for this very moment, as if she'd made it happen herself, she was off, after a scent. Colden looked dumbly into the space the dog had just occupied a moment before. She was gone, completely disappeared among the ombré shadows made by the latticework of tree branches overhead.

Colden stared, stunned into silence and immobility. It was not possible that one moment the dog was at her side, sniffing around, and a second later, she was a flash of black amidst the undergrowth.

"Daisy?" Colden called tentatively.

She was greeted with mocking silence.

"Daisy! Daisy!"

A few crows flapped away.

"Daisy? Here, Daisy. Daisy, come! Come on, girl. Daisy?"

Colden trotted to and fro, a few steps here, a few there, like a frightened rabbit. Everything around her settled into stillness.

Think, she told herself. *Stop and think. Make a plan. Execute the plan. Just follow the dog. She can't have gone far. It's only been a few moments.*

Colden reshouldered her pack and set out in the direction Daisy had bolted. After a few minutes of angry strides, she realized her plan was useless. Completely ineffective. The dog could be anywhere. She could have turned and doubled back dozens of times. She was fast and agile in an environment where Colden was slow and plodding. In the little time since the leash had unraveled in her hands, the day had heated up, bringing on waves of humidity and bugs. Colden found herself standing in the middle of nowhere with several black and red smears on her arms and face from slapping at blood-filled mosquitoes and blackflies. All her formerly soft and liquid fondness for Daisy had been replaced with a hard knot of anger at herself and the dog.

"Dammit."

Colden sat down, pulled out her map and compass, and got her bearings. She took some rope from the pack and hoisted it into a tree, where it would be safe from bears. This way, she could leave it behind and move more quickly. Unburdened by weight and gear, energized by frustration, she walked briskly in one direction for a set amount of time, calling to the dog, forcing her voice into a falsely upbeat and welcoming tone, then came back to the center and set out in a different direction, creating an invisible pattern of spokes radiating from where her pack sat in the crotch of a tree. By the fourth return, an hour and a half had passed.

This wasn't the first time that Daisy had gotten free of Colden and her confining leashes. But in the past, she always found her way back to Colden within forty-five minutes. Colden's hot anger was steadily being supplanted by cold fear. Her head hurt. She'd never had lunch. She'd been hiking for more than six hours without a break. She retrieved her pack, drank some water, and ate some granola mix. She wondered if she should go back to the truck—maybe Daisy had gone there. Dogs did that. It would take her hours to hike out. Daisy would have covered that distance in much less time. If that's where she went at all. And if she wasn't there, then what?

Colden wanted her father. Not just for his calm counsel and assistance but in the visceral, vulnerable way of a child. She sent a text, even though there was no signal. Maybe it would find its way out of the woods on some passing bit of electronic ether. Her face fell into her hands, and tears dripped through her fingers. She let them flow because she could not stop them. She'd cried more in the past month than in years.

After a few minutes, she told herself to get a grip—there was work to be done. She lifted her head, wiped her nose with her sleeve, checked her phone, stashed it away, and tried to think. Daisy would be better at finding her than she was at finding Daisy. Maybe she should just sit here a bit. Maybe Daisy would return to her. Colden wished she had a nose just a fraction as sensitive as her dog's. The things she could find. The work she could accomplish. She took several slow, deep breaths, steadying herself. She listened to the chickadees peeping around her. She watched a nuthatch on its head-down, hopping descent of a large pine tree. In the distance, she heard a woodpecker's methodical hammering against a dead tree on its assault after bugs.

Then there was another sound. Colden held her breath and heard only her own blood pumping through her veins. There it was again. Erratic and insistent. Angry and frustrated. Just like she felt. A dog barking. Colden jumped to her feet, grabbed her pack, and started scurrying in the direction of the yips. She ran a bit, twigs and branches slapping her in the face, scratching at her bare arms; then she paused to listen and adjust course. The barks were becoming less frequent, but more frantic. They were also not moving.

"Shit."

Colden ran, as best she could, through the thick understory of ferns, viburnums, and birch and maple saplings. Her breath came ragged into her lungs, filled with pollen-laced, moisture-rich air. A bramble tore a gash in her pants. She stumbled over a rock. She fell to her hands, gouging her palm and scraping an elbow.

"Get your act together. You're no use to her if you are injured," she said out loud.

Colden slowed down, became more careful in her progress, and followed the barks. She was close now. She looked at her watch. She'd only been running for about twenty minutes. It seemed like hours. There. There in a dip in the land, a gap in the understory, there was a dark patch, the filtered sun reflecting white on something shiny and black. Daisy. Sitting. Panting. The leaf litter around her was roughed up, as if there had been a scuffle of some sort.

"Daisy. C'mon, Daisy," Colden urged, squatting, holding out her hand.

Daisy whined and stayed where she was. Colden felt Daisy's fear and was mortified that the dog was afraid to approach her.

"C'mon, Daisy girl," she whispered. "It's OK. C'mon, girl."

Daisy lunged toward Colden, then yelped and fell back.

"Fuck."

Colden scrambled toward Daisy, sweat and tears blinding her. She wiped her arm across her face, but her high-tech wicking shirt would not absorb the salt water and smeared debris across her eyes instead.

"Stop crying, you idiot," she demanded of herself.

She stroked Daisy's heaving side. She ran her hands over her body. Scratches. A little blood. Then her front leg. Swollen. Serious edema. There. There it was. A thin wire just above her elbow. A snare. No, not a wire. A thin cord. Whatever. Her dog had been caught in a rabbit snare.

Colden sat back on her heels and spoke softly to Daisy, urging her to be still. The dog's struggling to get free had tightened the string, so it was almost hidden in her flesh. Already. If Colden simply released the snare, blood would immediately rush into the leg. She didn't know if that was good or bad, but it had to be painful. The snare was a simple, homemade thing, the kind described in everything from Boy Scout manuals to survivalist treatises. She tried to loosen the slipknot. Daisy squirmed and nipped at Colden's fingers, which were already wet with the dog's blood; Daisy had bitten her own flesh as she tried to free herself. Even though Colden tried to go slowly, suddenly the string was loose, and Daisy was licking and biting frantically at her leg. Colden stroked the leg, trying to soothe the pain, her fingers mingling with Daisy's tongue and teeth. Daisy flopped over onto her side in exhaustion. Colden took everything out of her pack, stuffed it in the exterior pockets, unzipped the front, and maneuvered Daisy in. The dog squirmed and wriggled a few times, then settled. Colden zipped her up, snugged the top gently around Daisy's neck, slid her arms through the straps, stood up with forty pounds of dog on her back, and started her trudge through the forest.

She paused only once, and that was to send her dad another text. She just said that Daisy was injured, she was on her way out, and she would go directly to the vet. When she got there almost three hours later, he was there, waiting for her.

"Snare. Front leg," was all Colden had to say when he came to the door of the truck.

Dix lifted the dog from the passenger side. Her broad, pink tongue flashed repeatedly over his face. They went into the office together, handed the dog over to a tech, and sat in the waiting room, silent and grave.

"It's my fault," Colden eventually said. "I wasn't careful enough. The leash handle broke. I should have bought the more expensive one. I shouldn't have let it slip through my hands. I should have held on."

Dix wrapped one long arm around her shoulder.

"This is too hard, Dad," Colden said. "I was really starting to love her. And then I didn't keep her safe."

"The world is full of tempting dangers," Dix said. "She went and got herself caught up in one. It happens to the best of us."

TWENTY-ONE

Brayden sat on a rock in front of his shelter. It was hot and still. So was he. The bugs were ferocious, but he never slapped at them anymore. He waited. Most times, he found, they didn't even bite. If one did, he slowly, methodically, brushed it off his body. He had become someone who moved as little as possible. Not because of laziness. It was an internal change. It was about economy of energy expenditure. He moved only as required. Plenty was required—collecting firewood, keeping his camp tidy and concealed, fishing, foraging, setting snares. In between what was necessary, he sat or lay or even stood completely still. He could easily watch deer stepping gingerly among the birches and maples, silent on their slender legs and sharp hooves, their fur the color of last year's dead leaves, not afraid of him because they didn't see him, their eyes and brains cued to react to movement. He watched the leaves of the large beech tree just in front of his cave twitch and sashay in the small gusts of warm, humid air that found their way to his retreat. He listened to the sparrows signing their chirping melodies. There was a chipmunk who would now eat directly from his fingertips, even come up his leg and sit on his thigh, nibbling on one of the sunflower seeds he held out for it.

Not too long ago, he'd found a couple of packs a bear had liberated from a campsite and dragged away. The packs were ripped apart, but Brayden was able to open the pockets the bear couldn't get into. There wasn't much, but the few packets of nuts, seeds, trail mix, and ramen he found were a distinct treat for him. One he was willing to share to get the companionship of a chipmunk.

He listened to the rhythmic pounding of a woodpecker not far away, the call of loons from the pond where he fished, a plane far overhead. Then, a dog barking. That was rare. Brayden loved dogs. He'd always wanted to have one, but his dad would never let him. Never said why. Brayden thought his father's only reason was just that Brayden wanted one so badly. Another way his dad could control the situation. Could be an asshole, just because, apparently, it felt good to him to be an asshole. The barking kept up. Brayden smiled at the sound.

He'd seen a woman in the woods earlier in the day with a dog. He was out setting some snares. He'd seen her before. Once. He recognized her long, dark-blonde hair, the blue pack, the determined way she walked. That first time, she had been setting up a tent not too far from here. That seemed a long time ago. She didn't have a dog then.

This time, this day, he'd seen her and the dog on a trail. He was only thirty feet or so away, but he knew they wouldn't see him. People didn't see what they didn't expect to see. So busy, they were always looking for what they thought they knew or wanted to be there. He stood very still, mostly hidden behind a tree, moving nothing but his eyes. He watched the dog pause and lift its head in Brayden's direction, scenting on him. The woman pulled gently on the long, bright yellow leash that connected the dog to some sort of a belt around her waist. She never glanced his way. She was focused on whatever was ahead of her.

He had a friend with a dog, he remembered. They'd go into the woods, and the dog helped him hunt coyotes. Raccoons, too. As he sat at his camp, listening to the dog bark reminded him of the way his friend's dog sounded when it treed a coon. That had been fun, being out with a friend and his dog. That was a nice memory. Brayden didn't have many of them. He knew good things had happened to him in the past. His entire life wasn't all bad. He even did some good stuff with his dad. Scouts. Fixing things. Working together from time to time. The sum total of actual time that his dad spent abusing him, it wasn't that much, really. There were so many more hours in the day, so many other days in the year. There was more to his life than just that horrible stuff.

So, why didn't his agony match the actual quantity of abuse? Why did it seem that one bad thing, the really bad thing, that happened only a few times, well, maybe several times a year for a lot of years, why did that thing take over every other thing? He didn't understand. He wished it wasn't so.

The dog barking stopped. He wondered if it was that woman's dog. Already, he could barely remember what the dog looked like. It was just a fleeting memory. She must have gone home. Home. He imagined her in some nice log cabin, dog asleep at her feet, fire roaring. Well, not a fire now. It was too hot these days. But still. Brayden's home was behind him, behind a tarp and a layer of evergreen boughs. Not that different from the home his chipmunk kept in his hollow in a punky log. Brayden's home was simply a bigger hollow under a very large rock. Still. It was the best one he'd had.

TWENTY-TWO

The e-mail said that Drew was coming north. He had a meeting with his clients, information to share, and he asked Colden if he could meet Gene. He said there was no need for her to keep being an intermediary. Colden didn't want to, in any case. She didn't like the cloak-and-dagger vibe of the situation. She also wanted and needed to be with Daisy. The vet had removed her leg. There was just too much damage from the couple of hours without blood flow, and they were concerned about infection, paralysis, and nerve damage. The vet told Colden not to worry, that dogs don't have an emotional attachment to their limbs and that she'd be getting around perfectly well as a "tripod" in no time. Still, Colden was miserable about the situation, and Daisy needed her help while she healed and adjusted to her three legs.

Dix said he'd take Drew over to Gene's. Something in his tone made it seem that this was not just a courtesy, but preferable to all parties. This made Colden uncomfortable. She didn't like the idea of these distinct and disparate parts of her life colliding, especially when she wouldn't be there to supervise or even observe. But there was no way she'd send Drew over to Gene's alone. An intermediary was essential.

Drew arrived at her house in a little Subaru. Colden was surprised. She'd expected a BMW or an Audi. Didn't lawyers always drive nice cars? She was somehow pleased and disappointed by his choice of vehicle. Mostly, she was glad to see him. His broad smile and crooked teeth had somehow insinuated themselves into her psyche and become a familiar and welcome sight. She introduced Drew to her father in the driveway.

"Well, shall we go?" her father said, surprising her.

"Sure!" Drew replied.

They got into Dix's truck and left. Colden had hoped for some time to see them together, to sheepdog some conversation. Men. Like dogs, it didn't take them any time at all to simply connect and get to the work at hand.

They were gone for a few hours. It seemed longer than necessary to Colden. She wondered whether the extra time meant things were going well. Or perhaps, not well. She heard the truck coming up the drive before she saw it. She looked over at Daisy. The dog was zonked out in her crate. Colden went outdoors. Dix and Drew got out of the truck, smiling and chatting. Colden felt a flash of jealousy. She was peevish that she'd been left out of something, something important.

They lowered their voices when they saw her, like teenagers seeing a teacher coming down the hallway. The three of them stood in the driveway, a bit awkward with one another. Colden asked them how it went. Her voice felt falsely cheerful.

"Great," Dix said.

"Really well," Drew quickly added.

Colden looked from one to the other, hoping for more. She didn't get it.

"Beer?" Dix asked, turning to Drew.

"Sure! Why not?" Drew replied.

Colden felt vaguely alarmed that Drew was about to come into her house and it was not at her invitation.

"How's Daisy?" Drew asked.

"She's sleeping."

Colden crossed her arms and planted her feet. No one moved toward the house.

"What's going on? Why are you two being so weird?" she demanded.

"Nothing's going on," Dix said, stepping away from the truck and waving Drew forward. "We're not being weird."

Colden watched them walk away, wishing they'd return, wondering what had happened out at Gene's, and then followed. Dix and Drew were already pulling on beers when she stepped into the kitchen. Dix handed her one.

"Such a beautiful area," Drew said to Colden. "Your dad showed me around a little."

Colden took this in, her father and Drew joyriding.

"You're staying for dinner, right?" Dix confirmed, speaking to Drew.

"Love to," Drew said as he tipped back his bottle. "Long drive ahead. Nice of you to offer."

"Oh, don't drive back to Albany tonight," Dix said. "Not if you don't have to. We've got plenty of room here."

Colden looked from one man to the other.

"Wow. Quite the male bonding went on out there at Gene's, apparently," she said.

Dix and Drew stared at her, neither responding.

"So, what did you guys find out?" she continued. "Who's the culprit?"

Dix dropped his eyes. Drew did the same. When he looked up, he took a long swig of beer before answering.

"Uh. Well, Gene wants to keep that confidential. However, we got it all squared away. Came to a great agreement. Nothing a few Benjamin Franklins and a good chat couldn't resolve."

"Confidential? Well, surely that doesn't apply to me," Colden said.

Drew bobbed his head up and down. So did Dix.

Drew shrugged and said, "'Fraid so."

Dix mouthed the word *sorry*.

Colden was about to protest further but was interrupted by the sound of Daisy whimpering and the back door opening at Sally's arrival. Colden left the kitchen—Dix could handle introducing Sally—and hustled to Daisy's side. She used a sling to lift her up and help her limp outdoors.

In the lowering light of the summer evening, Colden pouted. She didn't like being excluded. She didn't understand why or accept that it was necessary, especially in this instance and with these people. She could not imagine why Gene would not trust her with whatever information he had.

Daisy squatted awkwardly to pee, lost her balance, was caught by the sling, and then looked up at Colden, her tail slowly wagging and her tongue hanging out. She looked slightly confused but not in pain. She was a little drunk on medications. She tried to lick her stitches and almost fell over again. Her ears pricked, and her eyes focused on something in the yard. A bright yellow tennis ball in the faded grass. Tears sprang to Colden's eyes.

"After all these weeks of wishing you'd stop chasing the damn ball, now that's the only thing I hope for, my friend," she said.

Colden turned to lead Daisy back to the house. As she did, she saw, through the kitchen window, Sally, Dix, and Drew laughing at something. They made a bright circle of smiles. She found it terribly unsettling that Drew had broken free of the secure mooring she had created in Albany and was now floating around the rest of her life.

Daisy and Colden took a few small, slow steps. Daisy stumbled. Colden leaned over and lifted the dog into her arms. She pressed her nose against Daisy's neck. She used to smell like cut grass and pond water. Now, she smelled like iodine and alcohol. Together, they stutter-shuffled their way back into the house.

The next hour was busy with dinner preparation and small talk. Colden let her irritation go. It wasn't until they had almost finished eating their meal that Sally asked Drew if he'd found out anything about Larry. Colden glared at her.

"What?" Sally said. "I'm not allowed to ask?"

Colden didn't really want her personal embarrassment shared over the dining table. Apparently, it was too late for her to be delicate in this way. Her parents were treating Drew like an old family friend.

"It's OK, Colden," Drew said, smiling at her and laying his hand on her arm. "In fact," he said, addressing everyone at the table, "I did find out a little bit."

Drew told them that at first, the Larry trail held only a few breadcrumbs. Then, things changed when Colden got his former and full name. Drew had found that Larry, Lawrence, had a few glitches in his professional career many years earlier when he worked at a small college in the Southwest. He was accused of some irregularities in his research, then of sexually harassing a colleague. Nothing stuck in either charge. Everything was dropped, and his record was basically clean.

"Do you think there's a connection between those things?" Dix asked.

"Likely," Drew said. "Not provable, but the person he allegedly harassed was listed as a coauthor on a few papers. There's some connection."

"So, someone he worked with found out he did something wrong in his research, charged him, and then he started to harass her?" Colden suggested. "Tried to silence her for daring to cross him?"

"Maybe," Drew said.

"What else could it be?" Colden insisted.

"Innocent until proven guilty," Drew said.

"Where there is smoke, there is fire," Colden shot back.

"I think," Sally interjected with a pointed calm in her voice, "The issue we should be considering is what we can or should do from here. We can't do anything about what happened in the past. We just want to stop him from bothering Colden. And from harassing people in the future."

"I'm not *bothered* by him," Colden said defensively.

"Well, I am," Drew said cheerfully.

"Unfortunately, we have no proof," Dix said. "There are no literal or figurative fingerprints that connect him to the e-mails or books."

"Unless he was stupid enough to use his own credit card to order the books," Sally said.

"Unlikely," Drew replied. "And even if he did, we have no way of getting that info. It appears that we have no case to pursue at this stage."

"No case unless he does something worse," Colden noted.

No one spoke for a few minutes.

"I read something interesting recently," Dix said after taking a few swallows of water. "There was this woman, a columnist or comedian or something. She was harassed by someone online. Social media stuff. There wasn't much she could do, legally speaking. So, she did something completely unexpected. She talked to the guy. Well, one of the guys. The worst one, I guess. She confronted him, kindly, and basically asked him why he was doing what he did. Told him how she felt. He stopped."

"Yeah, right," Colden said.

She was not happy with her own tone, but she was having a hard time overcoming her petulance.

"No, it's true," Drew said, pointing his beer bottle toward Dix. "I read that, too. Guy even got his act together. Said it really turned him around. He'd just been bitter and miserable and jealous of her success. Felt marginalized by it. Silly, but common enough."

Colden didn't say anything for fear of saying the wrong thing.

"Might be worth a shot," Dix said, looking at her. "You could just talk to him. Not like you're accusing him. Like you're requesting his help."

"The damsel in distress," Colden said. "Classic."

"No," Dix said. "The woman in charge of her own life. You have nothing to lose by trying," he added.

"That's not entirely true," Sally said. "He might escalate. If he feels threatened."

"I can handle myself," Colden said. "It's not like there's been or likely to be any physical contact."

"If he did escalate, then maybe we'd actually be able to bring a case," Drew surmised. "But I think that's an awfully big risk. To you, Colden."

"Yes, but if we don't do something, as you've pointed out in the past, he may find another victim. Someone without the same resources I have."

"You mean someone without skills in martial arts and firearms?" Drew said.

Colden glared at her father. She had never told Drew these things about herself. He must have. He shrugged and smiled at her.

"I hear you are also good with a bow and arrow," Drew continued. "But I wouldn't recommend that approach. Let us torture him legally, if need be."

Colden couldn't tell if Drew was trying to get her to soften her mood, or if he was just perennially cheery. She busied herself with folding and refolding her napkin.

"In any case, I recommend we sit tight for a bit. Maybe I can get more info," Drew said. "Colden, you should try to avoid him, and if you can't, be as neutral as possible, and document whatever misbehaviors you can."

Colden opened her mouth to say something but didn't know what to say. She didn't like all this planning and activity and directives going on around her, about her. Daisy started whining. Colden stood up, thankful for a reason to stop the conversation.

"I'll go," Dix said, stopping her with a hand on her arm.

"No," she said. "I'll go. She's my responsibility."

Colden almost said, "She's my fault."

Drew took the guest room and Colden the sofa, where she'd been sleeping for the past week so that she could be close to Daisy and the door. She slept fitfully, waking repeatedly to bad dreams she could not remember. As the sky outside the windows moved from pitch black, sprinkled with the shiny salt of stars, to the soft gray of a predawn summer day, she gave up on sleep, tossed back the blankets, and put her feet on the floor. Daisy thumped her tail and opened her big mouth, panting her good-morning greeting.

What a happy girl, Colden thought. *Nothing bothers her. She holds no grudges.*

She opened the dog's crate and felt her tongue on her fingers.

I should take a lesson from her, Colden told herself.

They went outdoors, where the heavy dew soaked through Colden's sneakers and caused Daisy's legs to slip out from underneath her. She sprawled and panted, then gave up and rolled onto her back, pumping her three legs in the cool air. Colden gave in as well and laughed as she rubbed the dog's velvety stomach. They wandered slowly in the low, morning light, Daisy sniffing happily at invisible things. Colden wondered what images those scents conjured in the dog's mind, what she was finding and experiencing with her nose. She wished she had a fraction of this dog's sensual sensitivities.

The house was still, everyone asleep, when she came back in. She quietly fed Daisy, returned her to her crate, and made coffee.

Now, Colden thought, would be a good time to look at the data cards she'd pulled that day that Daisy got injured.

She hadn't had the heart or time to review them so far. She expected disappointment, and she'd had enough of that recently. She'd use this quiet hour before anyone else was up to skim through them and get that small chore off her to-do list.

Shafts of yellow light were streaming in the windows by the time she heard footfalls in the hallway. She was sitting at the dining room table, her laptop open, her cup long empty, when Dix came and stood behind her. She smiled up at him and pointed to her screen. He was silent as she toggled back and forth through half a dozen images.

"Sally needs to see these," he said.

He left Colden and got coffee to bring to his wife, and then they both came back and sat at the table. Colden angled the laptop so that they could see and move between the images. Moments later, Drew joined them. Colden smiled at the sight of his hair standing up in different directions and the pillow crease on his cheek. It was a welcome contrast to his usual good grooming.

"Wow," he said as he sat at the table and ran his hand over his head. "Haven't slept that well or long in forever. Helps when there aren't car alarms going off outside your door."

"Coffee?" Dix asked.

"I'll get it, thanks," Drew replied without moving. "What are you all looking at?" he asked instead.

Dix sucked his teeth.

"What? What is it?" Drew asked.

"That's what we're trying to figure out," Sally said.

"Something from Larry? More Sasquatch images?"

"No, not from, Larry," Colden explained. "Although Sasquatch seems to be a theme in my life these days." She directed his attention to her computer. "These are pictures from some game cameras I set up out in the mountains. I was hoping to find a hybrid species, a cross between a wolf and a coyote. There's been some reports of an unusual animal out there. But the cameras picked up something else instead."

"A different sort of unusual animal," Dix remarked.

Drew stood so that he could see the laptop.

Colden toggled back and forth between several images. A large, hulking figure filled a corner of one picture. An image from a greater distance showed it was not a Bigfoot but the back of a man. He was wearing a long-sleeve shirt and pants, a backpack hanging from a shoulder. His hair was black, straight, and unkempt, and it appeared long uncut. In one image, he was hunched over, with only the curve of his shoulder showing. In another, he was standing, something in his hand, hanging from a rangy arm.

"Rabbit," Dix said, pointing. "Bet he got it in a snare."

"Like the one that caught Daisy," Colden said.

"Is that legal?" Drew asked.

"No, not legal," Dix said. "But sometimes necessary."

"Sometimes people are just plain hungry," Sally added.

"Bet he's our vandal, too," Colden said.

"Wait," Sally said as Colden flipped through the images. "Go back. Can you zoom in?"

Colden stopped on a picture that showed a part of the man's face. He was in profile, his head turned over his shoulder as if he'd heard something. He had a patchy beard. His hair hung lankly over his broad forehead.

"Jeez," Sally said, staring fixedly at the screen, her eyes darkening with concern.

"What?" Colden asked.

"Sally?" Dix urged.

Sally raised her finger to the screen and stroked the man's face.

"I think I know who that is," Sally said. "His parents have been looking for him."

Sally swore them all to secrecy and explained what she knew of the situation. The young man and his sister had been in foster care. Biological mother was an addict. Meth. Alcohol. Liver blown all to hell. Noncompliant with any and all services offered. Biological father was who knows. The brother and sister got adopted as teens. The adoptive mother was a bit of a type. Mousy, weak, emotional. Had been trying to have kids for ages. Decided to adopt so that she could "do some good." The father was a blowhard and a jerk. Everyone knew that. No secret there. But they were financially comfortable, had a big home, and it's not like anyone else was stepping up to adopt these kids, what with their age and background. All the home checks went fine. The kids were sort of shut down, but that was normal in these situations. The girl started doing well in school. The boy was more withdrawn, quiet—nothing strange about that. He was a Boy Scout, and she was a cheerleader. The family went to church.

Then, last fall, the father ended up in the hospital with a head injury, cuts on his face, bruising. Like he'd been in a fight. He wouldn't say what had occurred, wouldn't press charges against anyone. No one would have thought much of it because this guy had made enemies in business and among his employees. He was also not above throwing a few punches himself. But at the same time, both kids disappeared, stopped going to school. Again, the parents would not offer any details, just said there had been a family argument, it was a private matter, all families had their problems, and the kids simply overreacted, ran away. All they wanted was to find them and bring them home. Friends of the kids were interviewed. There was some rumor that the girl might have gone to Canada with a secret boyfriend or something. The son had seemingly vanished. Maybe he followed her. No one seemed to know. The case was open, but the leads had all dried up. The parents may have hired a private investigator. She wasn't sure.

"Think he's been out there this whole time?" Drew asked.

Sally shrugged. "Maybe. Wasn't with any of his friends. They wouldn't have been able to hide him for this long if he was. My suspicion is that he and his father got in a fight, and he left. Must be afraid to come back. Afraid of his father or of the cops."

Dix whistled softly.

"It's entirely possible to make it out there. Especially if you have basic backcountry skills," he observed.

"And aren't above stealing some canned goods and warm sleeping bags," Colden added.

"Good thing it was a mild winter," Sally said.

They all stared at the picture on the screen.

"I think I've met him before," Dix said. "That workshop I gave to the high school kids on carpentry and furniture building. He was there. Nice kid. Hard worker. Very quiet. Very reserved."

"Do you know his father?" Colden asked.

"Mostly just by reputation," Dix said. "He's the sort of guy I try to avoid."

"There's got to be a good reason, good to him, anyway, why he's hiding out there, beyond just one fight, physical or not, with his father," Drew said. "The home life must not have been all chocolate chip cookies and warm milk, or he would not have bolted. He wouldn't stay out as long as he has if he had a warm bed to return to."

"How do we help him?" Dix asked. "Can't imagine calling the cops is the right approach."

"Well, here's the thing," Sally said. "He was a minor when he took off. But he's not anymore. That's affected the state's interest in the case. It seems he's had a birthday in the midst of all this.

He's now an adult, so he can technically do whatever he wants. He's a missing person, but he doesn't need to be brought back to his parents. And he probably doesn't know that his father, for better or worse, seems to have softened his stance toward his son."

"Yeah, but if he's been stealing things," Drew said, "there's that."

"We don't know if the thefts were made by him," Dix said. "Nothing stolen was very expensive, in any case. Not like he's up for a felony."

"Technically, he's overstaying his time camping. That's pretty serious," Colden said sarcastically.

"I wish I could just talk to him," Sally said. "If we could just talk to him, we could figure out what's going on and get him the help he needs. Hopefully track down his sister, too."

"Need to do it in a way that won't spook him," Drew said.

"We can find him," Dix said. "Colden and I can. If she can get us back to where the snare was, I bet we can find where he's hanging out. He's met me before. I think he'd trust me."

"It's weird, though, Dad. I've been in that area so much over these last months. Traipsing all over the place. And I've never seen a trace of him."

"You weren't looking for him," Dix pointed out. "You know how easy it is to disappear in there."

"I want to come with you," Sally announced.

Dix and Colden shifted in their seats and looked away from her.

"What?" Sally asked, taking offense.

"It's going to involve a lot of backcountry hiking," Dix said softly.

"Maybe even, you know, camping," Colden added in mock horror.

Drew looked from face to face, trying to get in on the joke.

"Bugs," Colden said, smirking. "Dirt. Ick. Squatting to go pee."

Sally crossed her arms over her chest.

"The wild outdoors is not exactly Sally's favorite place to be," Dix explained to Drew after he kissed the top of his wife's head.

"Well," Drew said, "perhaps even more important is that—no offense, Sally—you're part of the system. A system that failed him. If he trusted social workers and foster care, he would likely have reached out to someone he's worked with before instead of running away."

Everyone was quiet. Colden wondered at Drew's wisdom on these issues. All that pro bono work he'd done.

"You're right, Drew," Sally said, sighing. "Poor kid. Can't come out or won't come out. Thinks no one wants him, he has no one to trust, and he has nowhere else to go."

Colden had to head to Albany for a departmental meeting. She would make it a quick trip. Sally was doing some research on the case while she was away, and then Colden and Dix would go out looking for the young man in the woods.

Brayden, Sally had told them. His name was Brayden.

Colden was not looking forward to Albany. She was never looking forward to Albany but especially not now that there was a good chance she'd see Larry. Drew's advice was in her head, to lay low and remain neutral, but all she wanted to do was confront Larry. She wished she had a smoking gun, some piece of incontrovertible evidence she could pull out of her backpack and wave in his face. She'd been considering reaching out to Liam to see if she could tease any more information out of him, but she didn't know what tone to take. She wanted to keep it casual and light, to keep doors open between them, and she also wanted help but didn't want to admit that she wanted help, and she didn't want him to know exactly why she needed help. She started and deleted an e-mail several times. Finally, she forced herself to tap him a quick note and hit "Send" before she had time to overthink what she'd written.

Hey,

How are things in the 'coptering world? Do you know yet if you'll be our pilot for moose surveys this upcoming winter? You guys are such pros. Anyway, on a slightly different topic . . . was wondering what you meant about Larry. Just checking cuz the world of research and academia is often enough scarier than the wild animals we study, right?

Hope you are well. Thanks.

Colden

She'd sent the note more than a week ago, but Liam had yet to respond. She got down to the city, went to her meeting. It was all pretty standard planning stuff. Schedules, classes, granting opportunities, interns, graduate assistantships. Budget cuts. Colden offered to help with a couple of big grants and agreed to cover another professor's intro-level biology class when she was on maternity leave the following spring. Larry was there, but he said almost nothing. Colden avoided eye contact with him. When the meeting was over, she grabbed a pile of paperwork from her mailbox, went back to her office, and sat down to read through it all. She was deep into a long treatise from the IT department on updates to the online class portal when a voice came from behind her.

"Nice of you to offer to work up those grants," Larry whispered. "That should ingratiate you to the department head even more than usual."

Colden turned her chair, crossed her arms, and set her expression.

"Can I help you with something, Larry?" she asked.

"No, as a matter of fact, you can't," Larry said. "There's absolutely nothing you can do for me."

Larry stared at her. Colden stared back. He didn't look well. His eyes seemed watery, his face bloated.

"Nice computer," Larry said, his eyes flicking over to her MacBook. "Daddy buy that for you?"

Colden stared at him.

"Christmas presents? Along with your Patagonia parkas, boots, and backpacks?" Larry sneered. "You and all your designer gear."

Colden opened her mouth to correct him, but no words came out. Her parka was Patagonia, but her boots were not. Brand-name gear wasn't exactly "designer." Not really. It was about ensuring quality. It was about getting the best tools for the job. In the backcountry, good clothes were essential to staying warm, dry, and on the job. Patagonia didn't even make boots, did they? She'd looked at Patagonia packs but didn't like the feel of them. The one she'd bought, well, truth be told, it was even more expensive. But it was important. She needed it. She used it all the time. It had to be comfortable, durable, well made. An image of the stiff, woven birch packs that natives and early explorers had used flashed in her mind. Good enough for them. But that was then. This was now. Of course, she'd take advantage of the best-quality equipment. Why was she even thinking all this nonsense about brands and logos? Why was she so defensive, even to herself? She remembered Larry's outdated and inappropriate clothing when he'd tried to come with them. Jealous. Out of his element. Bitter. That's all this was. She remembered what her father had said. Just talk to him.

"What's wrong, Larry?" she asked him. "Why do you care what kind of coat or computer I have?"

He glared at her.

"I don't care about you or your damn computer, or your silly little projects and grant proposals. You're just playing at science as an excuse to take nice long walks in the woods and fly around in helicopters. The rest of us actually have to work hard and make sacrifices to do, you know, real science, Colden. And then we get no credit because we're not spoiled little rich girls that the university hopes will donate big bucks back to the program someday," Larry hissed in an angry whisper.

Colden was struck dumb by the vitriol that larded Larry's speech. She was indignant at his insults, at the way they dismissed her genuine interest in conservation and her years of hard work in the classroom and field. But she also finally recognized that his anger was bigger and beyond her. All the discussion with her parents and Drew had helped her realize that she was not a person to him but a representation of some injustice he'd suffered and never recovered from.

"Larry," a masculine voice said, interrupting her thoughts.

Jack appeared over the wall of her cubicle, his voice bursting the bubble of hate Larry had blown up around her.

"Hey, man," Larry said, moving his eyes from her to Jack, who had his hand extended.

"Just wanted to say good-bye and good luck," Jack said, pumping Larry's arm.

Larry nodded and smiled, clapped Jack on the back, then turned and walked away. Colden felt her heart squirreling in her chest.

"What was that all about?" she asked Jack once Larry was out of earshot.

"Didn't you hear?" Jack whispered. "He's leaving. Some kind of family issues. Among other things."

"Larry is leaving?" Colden repeated.

"Yeah. Did you know he's got a special needs kid? Think his wife isn't that healthy, either. They're heading back to, I don't know, Iowa or something. No, Indiana. Be closer to family. Poor guy. Keeps getting hosed on tenure. They kind of screwed him over here. Made big promises but didn't keep them. He felt pretty marginalized. And without tenure, well, you know. He's going to teach at a community college."

"Well, how can he expect to get tenure without publishing?" Colden demanded, miffed at Larry but also at all she apparently didn't know about this guy.

"Oh, he's published plenty," Jack corrected her. "I mean, in the past. He's a passerine specialist. A good one. But he got blindsided by his coauthor who was tweaking the results, fabricating research. He had no idea. She wasn't even doing the fieldwork she said she was. She was independently wealthy, paying her students to do work she was supposed to be doing, giving them no oversight. Turned out she was also having an affair with the department head. Who had helped her get papers published. She blamed it all on Larry. Tried to make it all his fault. Even accused him of sexual harassment, which also wasn't true. Just a distraction. She had plenty of money for lawyers. He didn't. First in his family to go to college, actually. It was a big mess—all the papers got pulled; the university tried to cover it up. The guy's such a jerk personally, even though he's a good scientist, he hadn't made any friends. So, no one came to his defense. They were too worried about their own careers to go out on a limb for him. The whole thing was a disaster. Really tainted, well, kind of wrecked, his career. He never regained his groove. Or found a new one."

"Doesn't seem to have made him any nicer," Colden said.

"Nope. Not nicer. Just more angry at the world. Too bad, really. He's actually a decent scientist. That's not enough to make it in academia, though. You know that."

"So, the harassment thing wasn't true?" Colden asked.

"Apparently not. She admitted it, eventually. Pulled her charges. Sadly, it was too late for Larry. The damage was done. She didn't need her career. But Larry needed his."

"How do you know all this?" Colden asked. "How do you know what's even true or not?"

"Friend of mine worked with him. Helped him get the job here."

"He was always such a jerk to me," Colden complained.

"Yeah, no bedside manner in that one, that's for sure," Jack allowed. "Maybe you just brought back bad memories. You look a little like his former research partner."

He grinned at her, waved, and walked away.

Colden sat, stunned, at her desk. So many strange and unfamiliar sensations rattled around inside of her, filling her head with noise. This brief pulling back of the curtain on the private trials and tribulations of Larry's life left her feeling confused about what and how to feel. She was resentful of his remarks but also sad that he'd had such a difficult life. And there was still the mystery of the e-mails and books. Did this new information mean Larry didn't, couldn't, wouldn't harass her in that way? But, if not him, then who? And why? Colden was reluctant to give up on him as the prime suspect. Maybe this was his way of getting some revenge, if not on his original persecutor, then on someone who reminded him of her.

It was time to pack up and get going. She had to get back upstate. She and her dad had another mystery to solve. The offensive e-mails had stopped, in any case. There'd been no more books. She might never see Larry again. She might never find out exactly what had happened. Then her e-mail pinged. It was a note from Liam. He had answers for her, but the information he gave left her feeling worse than ever.

TWENTY-THREE

It didn't take Colden and Dix long to find the spot where Daisy had been caught. The snare itself was gone, but there were still signs of the dog's scuffling, a smear of her blood on a rock, and even a few black hairs caught on a broken twig. Dix pulled a topo map from his pack. They'd work in spokes and circles about a mile from the snare site, looking for clues. The terrain was rough, unmarked by hiking trails, with plenty of steep hillsides and enormous rock outcroppings that would make getting around slow work. They had two-way radios but agreed not to use them except in an emergency or if either of them found something significant. They had set up their own campsite and planned to meet back there in a few hours, share info, set out again. They'd widen their circle as necessary.

Being back at this spot made Colden feel sullen. It reminded her of her failure with the dog but also with Liam. With Drew. Even with Larry. It seemed she didn't have any natural talent with domesticated creatures, human or otherwise. She noticed that Dix did not ask her about her mood. Which did not mean he didn't notice it. He just tended to let these things ride themselves out. If Sally had been there, she might eventually push Colden for explanations. Dix rarely did. Maybe this was because he was taciturn himself. Maybe this was because he understood Colden at an intuitive level that words could not reach.

She and Dix set out in their respective and opposite quadrants. They were looking for something out of the ordinary, something not quite nature-made. They were both deeply and instinctively connected to what the landscape looked like when left alone for nature to take her course of growth and decay, life and death. They believed they'd notice anything, or at least most things, that seemed like it had been disrupted by a human hand or foot.

They doubted he, Brayden—he was Brayden to them now—would have any kind of regular camp. He would have been found by now if he did. Then again, maybe not. It was easy to miss things out here that seemed incredibly obvious once they were right in your face. Especially if it was one small tent in a multi-million-acre wilderness. They also didn't know how much effort anyone had put into looking for Brayden. If he'd been a convict, they'd have brought in Staties and dogs, helicopters and ATVs. But Brayden was a runaway, a former foster kid with combative parents who had not made any friends in the system. Cops and social workers had seen tons of runaways disappear. There was little they could do, especially with the Canadian border so close by. Kids headed up there and never came back. Or they stayed away until life on the street finally got worse than whatever life at home was like. Sally had brought home story after story of kids like Brayden and his sister. Besides, Brayden was now an adult. He was free to do as he wished. There was a primal beauty in these mountains. Colden knew how compelling it could be. As well as how compelling getting away from other humans could be.

Colden welcomed the distraction that concentrating on her surroundings required. Looking at every punky log for signs that a hiking boot had scraped off a light layer of moldering wood, checking saplings for branches broken off by the pressure of a passing human body, bending down to small game trails through the leaf litter on the ground, searching for well-disguised snares . . . it all took her mind off her own concerns. She knew her worries were minimal. She'd also come to think they were mostly self-inflicted. This realization made the feelings worse.

She tracked back and forth in a slow, methodically widening zig zag across her assigned quadrant. She tried to imagine what she might do if she were Brayden. She wondered if he had planned to stay out here, to essentially move to the wilderness, or if a temporary escape had unintentionally become permanent due to simply having run out of other options. He'd need to stay warm and out of the weather. A small cave or large crevice in a rock outcropping could provide that necessary protection and shelter. Sleeping bags had been stolen, perhaps by him. Food as well. Even reading material. Something to stave off the boredom, perhaps. Nothing had been stolen in many months. He'd likely gotten good at foraging, fishing, and hunting. There was bounty out there if you knew how to find it. Maybe he'd planned ahead, packed well, and the robberies were just a weird coincidence. The scientist in Colden had never put much stock in coincidence—recent experiences had started to change this attitude.

It had been a mild winter, fortunately. Holed up in a tight, dry space with plenty of down all around him, Brayden would be OK. He was young and tough. His snare was well made. He obviously knew something about camping and surviving in the wilderness. Maybe he'd been to one of those outdoor programs. His father seemed like the boot-camp type. Even a dedicated Boy Scout would know enough to make it in the woods. For a time, at least. As long as he didn't get injured or ill.

They'd found pictures of him from high school. A long-unused Facebook page. He'd been a heavyset kid back then. That would help. Buy him time. The photos from the game camera showed he'd lost plenty of weight. He was still large and imposing, but after nine months or so in the wilderness, he appeared to be more deer than bear.

The hours passed. Sparrows and chickadees serenaded her while she worked. The oppressive heat of a few weeks prior had left the air. Some of the trees, those already stressed by attempts to grow in less-than-ideal locations, already had hints of fall color in their leaves. Soon enough, it would be back-to-school season. Which meant back to work, for her. To Albany, to the classroom, to regular meetings, and to time at a desk. There would be no more Larry. She was glad he was gone but also annoyed that the situation with him remained unresolved.

The thought of Albany meant thoughts of Drew. Even he seemed to have slipped out of her grasp. He had somehow created an independent relationship with her father and with Gene. He'd solved his own problems almost entirely without her help. Even though she had facilitated things early on, she was being excluded from the details of the final resolution. For some reason, it had all become secret. It seemed the men around her had closed ranks to the clubhouse, and she was no longer allowed in. Everything was irksome.

She called her father on the radio. She wasn't supposed to. Emergencies only. Screw it. She'd had enough of the boys making the rules. She told him, in a hushed voice, that she was staying out for two more hours, moving over to the next quadrant, instead of trekking back to the camp. She'd meet him there later. She'd found nothing yet. There was no need to waste time and energy connecting up at camp when there was no information to share. Dix answered with just an OK and out. There was no way to tell from the single utterance if he was annoyed at her. Actually, she did know. He wasn't irritated at her not because she didn't deserve it, but because he didn't get annoyed. Which in itself was annoying. Time to move on. Time to focus on the small, shoulder-height branches of the trees and shrubs, the damp spots on the ground that might hold boot prints, to look for rock faces that might offer crevices, overhangs, or caves large enough for a man to hide in. No, to live in.

Nothing, nothing, nothing. She found nothing.

Seems to be a life theme these days, she thought.

She was late getting back to their campsite. Only by about forty minutes, which was not enough to be alarming but enough to show her disregard for their original plan, as well as her own revision of that plan. Dix already had their two small tents set up, as she suspected he would. He was not one to wait for someone else, even when there was no rush and waiting would make the task at hand easier. He even had the bear line strung up and the camp stove set out. Colden sat on a log he had placed near the stove for just that purpose. She sighed and unlaced her boots. She peeled off her socks, found a pair of sandals, and took a long draw of water from her bottle. Dix put a pot of water on the stove. She knew he was leaving her be.

"What's that stuff?" she asked, pointing with her chin to a few twigs of varying lengths leaning near the flap of his tent.

"Found another snare, as well as an ad hoc fishing pole that was set into the ground so that it didn't need tending."

"You think it's a good idea to dismantle them? Won't it make him suspicious?"

"Better to have him suspicious than to have another dog injured," Dix said mildly.

Colden watched Dix as he lit the stove. She wanted to see if she was exasperating him yet. She didn't understand why she wished such a thing was possible, even when she knew from long experience that it was not. He would not be drawn into the tangle of other people's emotions when they had nothing to do with him and he knew he was not the cause of whatever feelings had gotten twisted up. He busied himself with setting out a small tarp and arranging the cooking implements and packets of freeze-dried food.

"Stroganoff or chili?" he asked her.

Colden shrugged in reply.

"Something you want to talk about?" he finally said, sitting back on his heels, eyes flicking back and forth from watching the stove to watching her.

Colden shrugged again. Then hot tears sprang, shockingly, embarrassingly, to her eyes. She pulled her baseball cap down over her forehead and busied herself with extricating a light jacket from her pack. Dix did not press her. Instead, he settled himself onto the other log he had set up for a seat and told her of his efforts in the woods. He spoke slowly and carefully, almost to himself, as if he was thinking it all through, out loud. He hadn't found much to report. He tried tracking back from the snare and the pole, but whatever trail there may have been was too faint or old or nonexistent for him to follow. The snare may have been set out weeks or months prior and forgotten. Dix wondered if Brayden was still in the area. If he might be moving from one place to another. Maybe he had a permanent camp. Maybe not. Maybe both. A well-concealed home base and then other spots where he went to forage or hunt. Or steal.

"I wish you wouldn't use that word," Colden interjected.

"Steal? Why not?"

"It's so hard. So condemnatory."

"It's just descriptive. It's just what happened."

"Well, maybe he did it. Maybe someone else did. Maybe whoever did it needed to. For survival."

"True. But stealing is still stealing. Regardless the reason."

"Those people won't miss the stuff he took," Colden said. "Probably don't even use it. Rich folk. They can easily afford to replace it."

"Someone stole your favorite down bag, you'd be pretty upset, I bet, even though you can afford to replace it."

There it was again. The accusation. She was rich and comfortable and could have nice things, and this made her spoiled and separate and different from other people. People like Larry. Jack. Even Drew. She knew she was being irrational and unfair to her father, but she couldn't stop herself.

"Whatever," she said dismissively.

Dix handed her a bowl with some dry ingredients and a spoon; he poured hot water over the food. She stirred the concoction methodically.

"Did you find anything interesting in your travels?" Dix asked, ignoring, as usual, her foul state of mind.

"Not a one," Colden replied.

"Where you want to start tomorrow?"

"Guess the next quadrant. Like we planned."

They fell into silence as they ate. Then Colden collected the bowls and cutlery, took them down to the nearby pond, and scrubbed them with sand from the shoreline. She took longer at her chore than was necessary. She scanned the distance for beaver activity. She knew there was none. She'd been at this pond earlier in the year. Sparrows skimmed the still surface of the water. The day was coming to a close, darkness dropping its opaque curtain slowly, unwillingly. She put everything in a pile and was about to return to her tent when, instead, her father appeared at her side. He sat next to her and reached into his pocket. He handed her a candy bar. Extra-dark chocolate. With salted almonds. Her favorite. A peace offering, even though she was the only one arguing, and the disagreement was totally within herself. She took the treat, peeled back the wrapper, broke off a large hunk, handed it to him, then took a piece for herself. The sweetness and bitterness melted together on her tongue, dissolving the hard spot that had been at the back of her mouth all day.

"Sorry, Dad," she said quietly. "I don't know what's gotten into me."

"Oh, I bet you actually do," Dix said. "Why don't you try telling me? Might make you feel better."

Colden took in a long breath and blew it out through her lips. He was right. She just wished he wasn't.

"It's just . . . I feel like . . ."

She didn't know where to begin. Then she admitted to herself that she did know. She didn't want to start there. She was embarrassed. She wasn't used to being embarrassed. She was used to getting things right. She began again and spoke quickly, a tumble of words rushing out in an effort to get the pain of admission over with.

"So. I guess I was totally wrong about Larry."

"Really? Do tell," Dix said.

Colden relayed the story that Jack had told her.

"That's all very interesting," Dix said. "I feel bad for the guy. Quite a lot of trouble for one person to manage."

"Yeah. Makes me relieved at least that the truth came out before I added to his woes."

"What do you mean? What does any of his professional and personal struggles have to do with all the e-mails he sent to you?"

Colden dropped her face into her hands.

"This is so embarrassing."

"Honey, what is it?" Dix asked. "It can't be that bad."

"He didn't send the e-mails. I had it all wrong," Colden wailed.

"What?" Dix asked, leaning forward, trying to comprehend.

"He didn't send the e-mails or books," she repeated loudly, forcefully. "It wasn't him. I totally screwed up."

Dix raised his eyebrows and sat back, taking in this fresh and strange information. Colden knew he was going to wait her out. He'd let her talk when she was ready. His patience was maddening and also just what she needed. She sat in the thickening silence for a few moments, then plunged forward again, diving straight into the deep end. The first thing she had to tell him was about

Liam. She'd never discussed this part of the story with him, only Sally. She kept the details to a minimum, but she had to tell him they'd been intimate. Not information she wanted to share with her father.

As she talked, stumbling over her words, she got the feeling that this was not news to him. Of course—Sally would have told him. It's not like Colden asked her to keep it a secret. Still, she was both relieved and irritated that they'd discussed her private life. Couples. The things that passed between them. She didn't understand the bond, all the things that were shared offstage, in private, at night, as they lay in a darkened bedroom. They were her parents and a long-married couple. Telling one something was as good as telling the other.

The specter of being an outsider rose up again, this time shadowed with a sense of betrayal. They'd been a trio. She always believed this. Now, she realized she was really just an appendage to a duo. They were the grown-ups. She was a child. Still and forever. Colden wondered if Dix and Sally had laughed, or rolled their eyes, or tsk-tsked about the romantic mishaps of their naïve daughter.

Dix was trying to not let on that he already knew. Colden knew he wasn't going to betray his wife, and he also didn't want to make her more uncomfortable by telling her that what she was sharing was not news. He was going to let her work through this the messy way. She could barely see her father's face in the twilight. She was glad this meant he couldn't see hers, either. She kept talking. She said that Larry seemed so bitter, so suddenly, toward her after her night with Liam that there seemed to be a connection between his attitude toward her and her hooking up with the helicopter pilot.

"OK, and now you're thinking this isn't the case?" Dix asked.

"I know it's not."

"How?"

"Liam and I had a few e-mails afterward," Colden continued. "He told me that Larry was a jerk and to watch out for him. This made me even more suspicious, of course. One day at my desk, as I was looking through some pictures of the trip, a colleague made a reference to 'Sasquatch,' saying that's what Larry called Liam. That seemed like evidence. I jumped to a conclusion. Not good science."

"And then?"

"I didn't want to bug Liam. I didn't want to seem like I was, I don't know, after him or something. It all was feeling so weird. So, middle school. I should have asked him about the nickname, but instead, I wrote and asked him what he knew about Larry. What was he talking about when he said to "watch out" for him? He told me basically the same story Jack had, but he had a lot less sympathy for Larry. Made it seem he'd been such an arrogant ass that he almost deserved what he got. Sort of."

Dix chewed a piece of chocolate. Colden took a deep breath and plowed forward.

"Then, at the end of this note, where he's telling me what a loser Larry is and making me think that maybe Jack had it wrong, maybe Larry is at fault, Liam asks me, like a total afterthought, if I got his e-mails. If I got the books he sent. Didn't I think it was so funny, he asked, all the connections? Said he'd sent them from another e-mail address to keep me guessing. I had no idea what he was referring to. Like what connections. Then it hit me—the e-mails had come from him; the books had come from him. He was Sasquatch. He was teasing me about himself and about us. He told me that he'd come back into town a few weeks later, after our moose-collaring job was done, for some reason or another, and was sitting at a bar, talking to some woman, just making friendly conversation, and she tells him that she and her husband were in town doing research on 'Sasquatch erotica.' She wrote books in this genre. Apparently, it's a thing. I had no idea. Neither did he. He thought it was a riot. You know, with him being nicknamed Sasquatch and all. He thought I knew that was his nickname—didn't everyone? Sure. Everyone but me! He thought I was in on the joke and that everything would be obvious. Then, when I didn't respond, he decided to up the ante by sending me a few of the woman's erotica books. Didn't I get the card in the box, explaining it all? Of course not, because I was too busy being delicate and paranoid and blaming the wrong person and didn't look for a card. Which I eventually did find because, in my whole Perry Mason mode, I had actually saved the packaging to use as some kind of gotcha evidence against a totally innocent if completely annoying colleague. It was all just a joke. Ha, ha. Didn't I think it was hilarious? Sasquatch erotica. His nickname. Our night of passion. The author's husband was apparently short and bald. Which made it all that much more comical."

Dix chuckled.

"It's not funny, Dad."

"Well, it kinda is, honey. I mean, I'm sorry it got so convoluted and that you got caught up in it in the way you did. But you gotta admit. It is funny. Now. I mean, if it happened to someone else, you'd think it was very entertaining."

"It could have been very ugly."

"Well, let's just be thankful it didn't turn out that way."

Colden squirmed and sighed.

"It's just a misunderstanding, Colden," Dix insisted. "You made some mistakes and some assumptions. Lesson learned, I'm sure."

"Yeah, but it's a misunderstanding that was blown up, out of proportion, in the wrong way, because of me. I got you guys involved, and I almost accused someone of sexual harassment just because I got weird. I feel so stupid. Like a complete idiot. Worse than an idiot."

"You'll have to tell Drew. Get him off the case, as it were."

"That's the most embarrassing."

"Oh, I bet he'll get a chuckle out of it. No harm done."

"Yeah, all you dudes think it's so entertaining. Totally awesome. Like a frat-club prank."

"Colden, what are you really mad about?" Dix asked, his voice softening. "You could simply be relieved that no one was actually harassing you and that you got the real story before it was too late. Why not look at it that way? There's something more going on here. Maybe it's not funny to you, but why are you so miffed about everything?"

Colden picked at a thorn that had gotten lodged in her pants.

"I just feel like I'm getting things wrong these days," she said, pouting. "A lot of things."

Dix waited for her to continue. She paused and then rushed on.

"I'm annoyed with the moose and beaver project. It doesn't seem to be going anywhere. I'm just collecting data anyone could get. There's no news there. No discovery. Beavers are coming back, they're creating habitat that moose like, so moose seem to be starting to do a bit better, too. Whatever. This is not a project that's going to do anything for my career. I'm not getting anywhere on the coywolf thing. That's some fantasy project that's starting to seem like a complete waste of time. I almost accused someone of sexual harassment who was not only totally innocent but was basically a victim of it himself. I screwed up with Daisy big time. I suck as a trainer and handler, I have no patience, and she got badly injured because of me. I feel like, well, Dad, I feel like what Larry accused me of being. A dilettante. Some spoiled brat trying to turn what's a luxury for most people into a real career and failing at it. I wanted to do something more, something that's meaningful. That actually changes things."

Dix sighed.

"You sound a lot like someone I used to know," he eventually said, his voice quiet with memory.

Miranda. Colden was stung with the comparison. But of course. This uncomfortable striving she felt was not in Dix or in Sally. It was in her mother. That's where it came from. Miranda, the searcher for meaning who hurt people in her self-indulgent quest. Who hurt herself most of all.

"Yep. My mother. The ultimate poor little rich girl," Colden said.

"It's not that simple," Dix warned.

"Isn't it?"

"No. It isn't."

"Please tell me why not."

Colden and Dix had rarely talked about Miranda. He'd never hidden anything from her, nor had he offered much to her. Other than that one visit to the log house, he answered questions as they arose in the context of their life together. Not many had. Colden hadn't wanted to ask, hadn't wanted to open his old wounds. As she sat by the still pond, getting stiff in the cooling air, waiting for her father to answer her question, she realized that this conversation had been hanging between them, unspoken, for years. Some children wait for the awkward parental chat about the birds and the bees; Colden had been waiting for this.

"Your mother was a beautiful, earnest, sweet woman, Colden," Dix said. "She started out rich, yes, financially so, and you know what happened there. More important, more damaging, anyway, was that the family was poor in spirit. In soul. She was unlike the rest of them, there. She had an abundance of spirit and soul and no idea what to do with those qualities. She tried tutoring disadvantaged children, working at an organic farm, even learning to knit so she could make mittens to give away. She was attracted to the Source because she honestly, earnestly, thought they were going to help teenage runaways. She went out into the world, looking for something she had never experienced. She had no map to find what she was searching for, and she got lost. I'm sorry you didn't know her."

Colden hadn't known her mother had tried these things, that she'd had such a large charitable impulse within her. But she still felt a deep disregard and dismissiveness toward this woman she'd never met. The feeling was strange, overpowering, and while she knew it to be unfair, it was totally irresistible.

"I don't think I would have liked her," she said, full of spite.

"That's an unkind remark," Dix stated. "I loved her. Sally loved her. You would have loved her, too."

"She hurt you. She hurt Sally. She likely would have hurt me, too."

Dix regarded her closely.

"She hurt people only because she was so hurt herself, Colden. She lost everything in a short time period. She suffered huge losses. She tried to rebuild herself. She tried to do something that had meaning for her and that would help others. She truly, and naively, believed that there was a larger goal and purpose at the Source. She was led astray by a charismatic person who preyed on her vulnerability and generosity."

"Yeah, and in the process, she threw away the one good thing she had, which was you."

Colden didn't know why she was being so hard on Miranda. She didn't know why she wanted her father to fight with her, even though she knew he wouldn't.

"We were not a good match," Dix said simply. "We loved each other, cared for each other, but were not right as partners. She saw that, and I didn't. You know how I am. I think I can—more fatally, *should*—fix things. It's a form of arrogance I didn't always recognize. She didn't want to be fixed. At least not by me."

Even in the dim light, Colden could feel Dix's unflinching gaze on her; she turned her head away in discomfort.

"I'm sorry, Colden," Dix said. "I'm sorry you never got the chance to know her. If I'd done more . . . no, not more, but different, she might still be here today. Don't be mad at her. Be mad at me."

Colden *was* mad at him. For the first time in her life. The feeling was disorienting and vaguely nauseating, like being tumbled beneath a wave at the beach.

"What hurt you the most, Dad? What was the worst thing she did to you?" Colden insisted on knowing.

"She cut off all her hair," he said quietly.

"What?" Colden was incredulous.

"The women who stayed out there at the Source were required to cut off all their hair. It was a way of repudiating the outside world and their own so-called vanity. Your mother hung out there for quite a while, still living with me, without taking that step. Then she did. Hacked it away. When I saw her with her hair all chopped off, her gorgeous mane gone, I knew I'd lost her for good."

"Wow," Colden said. "And I thought the worst thing she did was hide her pregnancy. Not take care of herself. Indulge in strange rituals in the middle of winter that cost her her life. Might have cost mine, as well. Kinda dumb luck I'm here at all. But it was really all about the hair."

"Stop it, Colden."

Dix almost never rebuked her. She knew she deserved it.

"She failed you by not being here as a mother for you," Dix said. "But she's the one who suffered the most."

"Sally is my mother," Colden said, unwilling to relent.

"Sally has been an amazing mother to you, that's true," Dix said. "But Miranda would have been one, as well. Different, but wonderful. She very much wanted children. She very much wanted you."

"Apparently not enough to take care of herself and stick around to be a mother."

Dix sighed. He seemed unsurprised by Colden's attitude, just saddened by it.

"I loved your mother very much. And I failed her," he again insisted. "I should have protected her from herself. I should have stepped in sooner, faster, more. I was confused by her behavior, jealous, hurt. I didn't see what was really going on."

"You're the one who says you can't save people from themselves. You can't fix someone who doesn't want to be fixed."

"Maybe that's just an excuse for failing to help them enough," Dix said, his voice a whisper. "I couldn't fix her. But I could have done more to help her help herself."

Colden felt the pain and regret that suffused Dix's words. She'd never seen him defeated in this way. It made her wonder at the power of love to build up and also to destroy another. It made her realize she'd never actually felt it before. Not love like this. Not love that made someone full of desire and recrimination in equal measure.

"If Miranda had stuck around, you wouldn't have Sally," Colden said. "Clearly, you love Sally more."

"I don't love Sally more. I love her differently. If Miranda had lived, she and I would not be together, of that I'm sure. But she would be here. For you. And you'd see all the parts of her that you carry within you."

"I see them," Colden said. "And I don't like them."

"They are good things, Colden. I can't convince you of that, but I hope you'll see it one day. Your mother had great gifts that she didn't know how to use. You have all of those gifts—a sense of wonder in the world, a drive to make things better, to make a difference—and you'll use them better than she was able to. You already are."

These words broke something open inside of Colden. A feeling that she had clenched inside squeezed out of her grip, only to ooze and slosh in her gut. Tears filled her eyes and spilled over her lids. She was thankful for the darkness. Mosquitos were arriving in drifts. A loon wailed in the distance. Dix slapped at his arm. Colden wiped at her cheek.

"Time to get under cover," he said. "We have our work cut out for us tomorrow."

They stood, brushed off their pants, and walked back to their tents, each silent and self-absorbed. Dix stooped to crawl under his flap, and Colden called out to him.

"Dad?"

"Yes?"

"Thank you. I know that conversation wasn't easy for you."

"Few things worth doing are, Colden," he said.

Then he disappeared into the darkness of his cocoon for the night.

TWENTY-FOUR

Colden had been wandering in purposeful circles for four hours. She saw nothing but messy, tangled, lovely nature. She was tired. She hadn't slept well or much the night before. The conversation with her father had stirred her up, and she could not settle down. Thoughts of her mother kept divebombing her every time she fell asleep, jolting her back awake. Regret, which was getting to be an all-too-familiar feeling lately, filled her head. She wished she could roll back the hours and have been nicer, kinder to her father. That morning, when they'd emerged from their tents, it seemed Dix was more withdrawn than usual, as if he was wary of her. Maybe he was just tired, too. He could simply be weighed down by the painful memories of an unresolved past. It was as if she'd recently peeled back the skin on several people she thought she knew, only to discover their insides were jammed with all kinds of complex, Rube Goldberg–type machinery she had never imagined before.

She sat on a log and took an apple from her pack. She bit into the crisp fruit and took solace from the sweet, moist flesh on her tongue. She thought she heard something strange and harsh. She stopped chewing. Nothing. She took another bite. Then another squawk. She stopped chewing for longer this time. The sound came again. It took a moment for her sleep-deprived mind to realize it was her walkie-talkie. She fumbled it from her pack, turned it on, and heard her father whisper coordinates. They signed off. He was almost a half a mile away. She trudged as quickly and yet quietly as she could toward him and finally found him lying on his stomach in the dirt, tucked behind a small bush, a pair of small binoculars to his face. She lowered herself to the ground at his side.

The ground fell away in front of them. They were lying on the lip of a rocky basin about twenty feet deep and thirty feet wide, a land formation left behind when the glaciers scoured the area. Dix handed her the binoculars and pointed with his chin. She scanned the stone outcroppings, saplings naturally bonsaied as they clung to small pockets of soil in cracks between the rocks, the thick layer of leaves built up on the ground, a few scrappy evergreens, a twisted birch, a couple of small maple trees. Nothing even vaguely unusual. She moved the binoculars off her face and looked at her father questioningly. He pointed again, this time with his finger, directing her eyes across the way and to the left. Colden squinted, let her eyes drift, and softened her focus.

There. Now she saw it. It was like staring at one of those illusion drawings where you can't stop seeing the young woman until suddenly you can only see the old woman, hidden in plain sight in the drawing. There was a spot where the rock face met the ground. It resolved itself in front of her eyes into a small overhang, cleverly hidden behind evergreens and a few logs set to appear as if they had arranged themselves there naturally. There was a line in the leaf litter, a darkness in the rock face, which became a thin trail leading away from a small cave beneath the overhang. She kept staring, and a rope high in a nearby tree came into view, adorned with a branch-covered bag, hoisted there to be out of reach of bears. There was a small ring of fire-blackened stones. A bent grill leaned against the wall, barely distinguishable from the rock behind it. Colden looked at her father with raised eyebrows and tipped her head over her shoulder, signaling her concern that they were a little too exposed; if someone returned to the cave and had the inclination to look in their direction, they'd be seen. Dix scooted backward on elbows and knees. Colden followed.

"What should we do?" Colden whispered.

"Wait," Dix said. "See if anyone shows up."

Colden rolled over onto her back. She removed a stick that was digging into her side. She put her pack under her head and crossed her hands over her stomach. And then, without meaning to, she was suddenly, deeply asleep.

She woke some time later, groggy, confused, stiff, and sore. Her eyes fluttered, and in her liminal state, she tried to remember where she was, why she was lying on the forest floor. A mosquito bit her ear. She was too befuddled to move, so she tried to concentrate. Slowly, the images of the rock basin came back to her. Memories of the evening before came back as well, her difficult conversation with her father, her restless night. She was shocked she'd fallen asleep like this, right here in the duff. Without getting up, she looked to her right and left. She didn't see her father, but she did see his pack. She rolled slowly, carefully, onto her stomach. Dampness had seeped through her pants and shirt. She looked around. Dix was not there. It was odd that he would have left her sleeping like that, but it was even more unusual that he'd leave his pack behind.

Then she knew, in a sudden rush of awareness, what had happened. And that once again, she'd miscalculated and missed out. She swore silently at herself and inched her way back to the lip of dirt and rock.

There he was. Sitting on a stump by the ring of stones, his knees bent at an acute angle, as if he was on a child's bike. She inhaled sharply, then covered her mouth with her hand to keep herself from calling out to him.

What the hell was he doing? How did he even get down there? And why wasn't she there with him?

Colden kept scanning. The rock face behind him was different—branches had been moved aside to reveal a dark, moss-covered tarp. As she watched, the tarp itself moved, pushed aside by a young man, impressively taller and more broad than her father, with a dark waterfall of black hair cascading over his face. Brayden. Colden held her breath. He had something in his hand. He stepped to Dix and gave it to him. A fistful of twine and wire. Snares. Now neutralized. She saw them share a few words that she could not hear. Then Brayden got a long stick and showed that to Dix. A fishing pole.

They're chatting like Boy Scouts comparing notes about hunting and fishing in the backwoods, Colden thought. Shouldn't they be doing something more important? Like packing up?

Colden didn't know what to do and then realized there was only one thing to do—slide back, stay out of sight, and wait for her father. The forced passivity infuriated her, but she held her position and resisted her impulsivity. If she stepped in, she might wreck whatever delicately balanced relationship her father was forging down there among the rocks. Doing the right thing slightly mitigated her frustration at being left out. A flicker swooped through the forest. A chipmunk scurried among the punky logs at her feet. She waited, checking her watch. Fifteen minutes passed. She'd give it another five minutes. OK, five more. She was just about to move back to the rock edge to see what was going on when her father appeared in front of her. It was as if he had materialized from nothing but air.

"Jesus," she whispered. "You scared me."

Dix put his finger to his lips, picked up his pack, and motioned at Colden to follow him. She got to her feet and followed him in silence for almost an hour. Finally, they were back on the main trail. Colden stopped. Dix kept going a few steps before looking back over his shoulder at her. She threw up her hands in a demand for an explanation.

"He's not ready to come out yet," Dix responded to her silent question. "He's not ready to face, you know, all of that." Dix moved his hand vaguely in the air. "But we talked. He's OK. He's not going anywhere. He promised me. He said I could come back. So, I will. We'll talk some more."

Colden looked at him, her eyes wide and stunned.

"That's it?"

"For now, yes."

"Don't we need to get him out of there?"

Dix shook his head. "No, we don't need to do anything. He's fine. He's an adult. He's healthy. Eating pretty good out there. Misses chocolate. I gave him the extra bar I brought for you. Didn't think you'd mind. Maybe chocolate will entice him to come out."

"What about the thefts?"

"He told me that he took a few things. Couple of sleeping bags and some reading material. Some food. Canned goods mostly. He said he was sorry, but that's what got him through the winter. He didn't take your gas can. No need for it. Nothing to power up. Some other jerk must have done that. He did take the moose leg. Made jerky from it. Gave me a piece. Pretty good, actually."

"Why's he out there? What's he running from?"

"Didn't ask directly. I just met him, Colden. He'll tell when he's ready. Can't be a pretty story."

"Didn't he wonder what you were doing out there?"

"Not really. Lots of people wander these woods."

"Lots?"

"Well, enough that seeing me didn't seem too much of a surprise to him."

"What about me?"

"What about you?"

"What should I do?"

"Nothing. We're going home. I'll come back in a few days. Without you."

"Without me?"

"Yes, Colden. Without you. You're far too scary for this guy. You'd run him right off." Dix grinned at her and started off down the trail. She had no choice but to follow.

TWENTY-FIVE

Brayden came around the edge of the rock outcropping that defined the small amphitheater he thought of as home and saw a man sitting on a stump. His stump. The very seat where he spent hours eating, sipping water, playing with the chipmunk that had become his friend. He was strangely not surprised. It was as if the very thing he had been unknowingly waiting for had come to pass. He paused briefly, a mere hitch in his forward motion, then kept moving forward.

"'Lo," the man said.

Brayden nodded. There was something familiar about him.

"Nice place you have here," the man said.

"Thanks."

Brayden's voice was an unfamiliar sound. He had not spoken out loud in so many months. Just whispers to himself as he pulled in a line, hand over hand, on his fishing pole or worked the thin twine and small branches that set his snare. It was too loud, too sudden, like a sneeze in a library. He stood there, unsure what to do next. There was only the one stump. There was no place for him to sit. The man got up. Now they were both standing, two tall men, looking each other over. The man cracked his knuckles.

Now Brayden remembered him. He'd come to school, taught some sort of woodworking. No, furniture building. That's when Brayden learned how poorly made the chair his father and he had built was. That's when he realized how many shortcuts his father had taken.

The man lowered himself to the ground and sat with his long legs stretched out in front of him. Brayden did the same. If there were not two seats, neither would take the one.

"Please," Brayden said, gesturing. "Take the stump."

He was trying to be polite. Trying to remember manners. His voice, so long unused, cracked. He hoped this didn't make him seem weak.

"My name is Dix," the man said, staying where he was. "I think we may have met before. I came to your school."

Brayden nodded.

"I know your father a little bit. Mostly by reputation."

Brayden sat very still.

"Not a very nice man, your father," Dix said, matter-of-factly. "Hope you don't mind me saying so."

"No, I don't mind," Brayden replied quietly. "It's just the truth."

Brayden had lost the habit of speaking. His voice felt like sandpaper in his throat.

"You fixed this place up real nice. Must have been a bit chilly this past winter, though," Dix said, smiling at him. "Fortunately, it was a mild one."

Brayden wondered how he knew he'd been out here this long. He thought of the sleeping bags he'd taken. He wondered if this man was here to retrieve them. If he knew. If he was going to get in trouble for stealing. He wondered if he'd killed his own father. If he was going to be charged with something. It was hard to imagine the old man dead. He was so tough and mean. Brayden thought it wouldn't be beyond him to die just to spite his son, just to get him sent to jail. He didn't say anything. He waited. They looked at each other. The man pulled at a piece of grass and put it in his mouth. Then he looked away, seemed to be thinking of something.

"So, look," he finally said. "You must be wondering what I'm doing here. Long story, but let's just say it came to my attention that you are out

here, been camping away for quite a while. That maybe you like it here, maybe you don't. Maybe you just don't know where else to go. You should know that your parents are OK and were looking for you. Maybe that's not a good thing. Seems they're just worried about you, but I know that things in families are not always what they seem. My wife. She's a social worker. Maybe you've had some bad social workers in your past, but I can guarantee you she's a good one. The best. She'd like to help you out. We'd all like to help you. Guess you're eighteen now. You don't need to go back to your parents if you don't want to."

He looked at Brayden directly. Brayden kept his head down. He was taking in the man's words. There were a lot of them, and he had grown unaccustomed to words.

"I'll let you think about that for a minute," Dix said.

They both sat in the silence, listening to the forest. Brayden felt each thing this Dix person has said settle in him, like a fresh leaf set free, tacking back and forth on the breeze of a new season until it settled gently on the ground. Dix sighed, signaling he was about to begin again.

"You think you might be ready to c'mon out of here?" he asked. "Or are you happy to stay? We've got a big house, and there's room for you if you're hankering for a shower and a solid meal and a soft bed. Just until we get things sorted out. For as long as you need."

Brayden shook his head. He didn't even realize he was doing it at first. His hair brushing back and forth over his face alerted him to the motion. He couldn't look directly at this man in front of him. He seemed trustworthy. He knew he meant him no harm. But he couldn't leave with him. He didn't know why he couldn't, just that he couldn't. Not yet, anyway.

"OK. I understand," the man said.

"Sir?" Brayden said.

"Yes?"

"Do they . . . does he know I'm out here?"

"Don't believe so. And he won't hear it from me. I promise you that."

"Thank you."

"You need anything? Anything I can bring you?"

Brayden appreciated the respect this man was showing him. He shook his head.

"I'm OK," Brayden said.

"I can see that," Dix said. "Seems you're doing pretty darn well out here. I admire that. Admire your resourcefulness. Can you show me what you're using to feed yourself? Snares? Fishing pole?"

Brayden was glad to have something to do. To stop talking about, thinking about, his father. He went into the cave and came out with the things Dix had asked to see. They looked them over. Dix gave him a few tips that would improve their function. He told him to be careful to not leave the snares unattended in the woods. He said dogs could get caught in them. Brayden hadn't considered that before.

"Well, I better be going," Dix said. "You've probably had more than enough of me." He stood up, brushed his pants with the flat of his large, long-fingered hands. "Would it be OK if I came back sometime?"

Brayden shrugged his acceptance. He wanted to say more, to be more enthusiastic. He liked this man. He wanted to see him again. He didn't know how to express it.

Dix reached into a pocket and handed Brayden a chocolate bar.

"Here. Enjoy. I bet it's been a while since you've had something like this. I know I'd miss chocolate myself. Probably one of the only things I'd miss."

Brayden took the gift. Saliva pooled in his mouth.

He whispered a quiet, "Thank you." Then added, "Thank you for coming to see me."

Dix stepped over to where Brayden was sitting with his head bowed and squeezed his shoulder. Brayden flinched. The man didn't remove his hand. Brayden stiffened. It had been so long since he'd been touched. And he'd so rarely been touched with anything other than . . . than things he didn't want to think about. His eyes burned with tears that would not come. He hadn't realized until right then how lonely he was, how lonely he had been.

The man walked away. Brayden was sorry and relieved to see him go. He would come again, Brayden knew that. He expected he wouldn't have to wait for too long.

TWENTY-SIX

Three weeks later, Colden and Drew were sitting out on the deck behind the house. They'd been there for hours. The sun had set, and the bugs subsided. Dix and Sally had cleared the dinner plates and gone indoors. The house behind them had settled into silence. The two candles on the table had burned down and out, leaving them in a darkness softened by the slow rise of an almost-full moon.

Drew was now a family friend. He had an open invitation from Sally and Dix to come and stay anytime he was in the area. He checked in with all of them about Brayden. And Daisy. And Gene. Not Larry, because now Larry was gone. But Colden knew she had to tell Drew about Larry. She knew she had to clear the air and the record.

Over dinner, Dix told Drew about his visits to Brayden. Dix had been out to see him twice more since the first discovery. He put no pressure on him, just visited and brought him a few things to ease his time in the woods: a bear ball, a camp stove, chocolate, coffee.

"It's like you're taming him," Drew said.

Sally nodded. "Yes, he's gone a little feral."

"He's like a dog that's been abused," Dix said. "We can't push him. We have to be available and gentle, and let him come to us."

"Yes," Sally said. "More than likely, abused."

They'd all gotten quiet at that thought, each caught up in their private imaginings of what Brayden might have been through. Whatever it was, it was something bad enough that it made staying where he was preferable and safer than returning to his parents' home. After dinner, they sat out on the deck and spoke of other things. The weather. Politics. As it got darker, the conversation slowed, and silence settled in. Dix and Sally, at some unspoken cue from each other, got up and went into the house. Drew and Colden sat, neither wanting to rend the quiet that had settled its cloak around them.

Eventually, Colden felt agitation build inside herself as she fretted about how to begin the story she had, so unwillingly, to tell.

"How are you, Colden?

The words were so quiet, Colden almost wondered if she'd imagined them.

Drew waited a beat and then repeated himself.

"How are you, Colden? You seem kind of withdrawn."

Colden sighed. She'd been caught. She was also relieved he started the conversation she could not.

"It's just that I have something to tell you that I wish I didn't," she said.

"Spill it," Drew said. "You'll feel better. Whatever it is, I'm sure I can handle it."

Colden told him, in as few sentences as possible but without holding back any information, about Liam and Larry. Drew listened, his feet propped up on the deck railing, taking occasional sips from a beer, staring straight ahead, letting her speak without interruption. Finally, her story sputtered out just like the candles had some minutes before.

"I'm pretty embarrassed," she said into the gloom.

"No need to be," he replied.

"Could have all gone very wrong," she insisted.

"But it didn't," Drew countered. "That's what matters. You caught yourself in time."

"You're being quite generous to me," Colden said, unwilling to go easy on herself.

"Not really. Dudes can be jerks. He was a jerk to you. I don't blame you for feeling jumpy and suspicious."

There seemed to be some undercurrent of private, personal experience informing Drew's response. Colden had the passing thought that maybe Drew was gay. Maybe that's why he knew what jerks men could be. Maybe that's why he hadn't come onto her. Which made her wonder if she wanted him to.

"You're not speaking very well of your own gender," Colden said.

"Well, I'm a guy," Drew said evasively. "I know how we can be."

Colden wished he wouldn't be so flippant. She didn't know what more to say. She hoped he'd say something, share something. It was as if they were waiting for each other. He took his feet from the railing.

"I should go," he said.

"I thought you were staying?"

"Thank you." He sighed. "But I can't."

Colden felt stung. His tone was strangely abrupt.

"Early meeting tomorrow with my clients," he said. "They've put me up in some hotel in Plattsburgh. Few other folks flying in."

Plattsburgh was an easy drive in the morning. He could stay. She kept these thoughts to herself.

"OK," she said.

"Colden?"

"Yes?"

She hoped he was reconsidering. She wished for company. For his company.

"You think your dad would let me come with him to see Brayden?"

His question confused her.

"Um. I don't know. I guess. Don't see why not. Ask him."

"It's just." Drew exhaled a burst of air. "I would like to talk to him. Call it a hunch about something."

Here it was again, that feeling of being excluded from the boys' club. First Gene. He was her pal; she was the one who talked to him, who got things going, who introduced him to Drew. Then, just when things got interesting, she was shut out. Liam and his Sasquatch nonsense. All the guys had known his little nickname, but she had not, and this gap in her knowledge had caused her a cascade of embarrassment. Drew was her friend. Yet it seemed he'd gotten to be best buddies with her father. It felt disloyal and unfair. Now Brayden. She'd found the guy. By mistake, but still. Now her dad had taken over.

"Well, he didn't want *me* coming along," she said, trying to make it sound like a joke. "But he'll probably feel differently about you."

Drew stood and paused. In the dark, she felt his hand drop onto her shoulder. He squeezed. She was not consoled. But she reached up and grabbed his hand, anyway, and as she did, she had an insight, a brief, sunny break in the clouds that had gathered inside her head.

Whatever is going on with him, it has nothing to do with you, she told herself. *Be more generous, more understanding, more kind. It'd be good for him, but even more, it'd be good for you.*

Daylight began to fade by late afternoon, and the nights came on chilly. A few trees, stressed by location or age, flamed with spots of hot color punctuating the fading abundance of green. The world was hinting at, warning about, the season to come. A slight hustle replaced the slow motion of summer. People and other animals began to prep for what was next, when the outdoors became a hostile place again, full of cold winds, white snow, and black ice, things that could kill you.

Colden had to survey several beaver ponds, looking for changes in activity and conditions. Dix had to clean out gardens, lay in firewood, patch spots where the weather could sneak its way inside his clients' homes. Sally faced the new onslaught of issues and crises that going-back-to-school time predicted in her work. Drew was in Albany and hadn't said when he'd be back. At least not to Colden.

No one was talking about Brayden. But Colden knew the same thoughts were floating through their minds: he needed to come indoors. He couldn't be chased or coerced—he needed to be enticed. No one knew what would work to make him feel safe enough, trusting enough. No one knew if whatever they were—or were not—doing was the right or best or even legal thing. And there was no one to ask because they would not betray his trust by telling authorities or his family. Besides, he was a free man. There was no reason to.

Colden assumed her father had a plan brewing, or maybe several alternative plans, but didn't want to ask what they were. She didn't want to bother Dix, and she didn't want to face the possibility that he'd be unwilling to tell her. So, she focused on her own work. Daisy had healed up and was staying mostly at the farm shelter, playing with other dogs, completely unconcerned about her lost leg. Colden visited her regularly but was in the field a lot. She spent her time at home in her cottage, crunching numbers, organizing data, creating maps, revising her reports.

She didn't work on her coywolf project at all. She needed a break from chasing ghosts. She was freshly determined to find something, understand something, uncover something that would elevate her beaver and moose project from basic conservation science to something more career-making. She stopped waiting for nature to hand her an "aha" moment and pushed herself to find one. She also, reluctantly, reminded herself that good science and effective conservation didn't necessarily require "aha" moments.

September arrived. Colden went out for a few days of collecting moose scat and taking photographs of browse marks on plants and trees near a couple of stable beaver ponds. The work made her tired and dirty, which was fine, but she was also annoyed at the Labor Day campers and hikers she'd had to dodge. There were all these people tramping noisily through what she could not help thinking of as "her" woods. She knew part of the point of conservation was to keep wild places wild for people, as well as animals. She just wished that humans would follow basic rules of common sense and politeness. It only took a few yahoos leaving food unprotected at a campsite to train bears that tents were a predictor of yummy snacks and that hikers were mini-marts on foot. It only took a few dogs off leash to dig out the nests of birds and small mammals and disrupt fish hatchlings in ponds and streams. Just one idiot blaring music from his digital device could drown out the sounds of owls and frogs for anyone nearby.

She was protective. She thought that was a good thing. She was also judgmental. She thought that was a necessary thing.

These were the thoughts and irritations that spun through her mind like the yellow leaves swirling alongside her tires as she drove up her driveway on a bright afternoon just after the three-day weekend. She was so preoccupied, it took her a moment to realize there was an unfamiliar car parked near the garage. Right where she usually parked. Wait. It was not unfamiliar after all—it was Drew's little SUV. Happiness at the thought that he was there, in her house, that she'd see him momentarily, spontaneously swelled inside her. Those same feelings were then gently tamped down with irritation and confusion that she hadn't been informed he was coming.

What if she had stayed out another day or two? She would have missed him. Maybe he texted her; she hadn't looked in days. She tried to shake off her annoyances as a dog would water from its coat, left her belongings in the truck, and walked quickly to the back door of the house. She expected to hear the chatter of voices and the clatter of plates that she associated with Drew's visits, but the house was silent and still. They would have seen her, heard her come up the drive. Yet, no one came to greet her. The kitchen was empty, the counters bare.

"Hello?" Colden called. "Anyone home?"

Of course, they were home. Her question held the hint of a rebuke at being ignored.

"We're out here."

That was Sally, calling from the far side of the patio off the dining room.

Colden finished prying off her boots and walked through the house. She opened the sliding door and froze in place. There, sitting somewhat somberly in chairs, were Sally, Dix, Drew. And Brayden.

Colden felt stuck in the doorway. Sally and Dix stared at her. Brayden stared at the ground a few feet in front of his feet. Drew stared at Brayden. Then he got up, grabbed an empty chair, and set it down next to himself.

"Colden, come join us," Drew said, smiling at her. "Brayden, this is Colden, Sally and Dix's daughter."

Brayden flicked his eyes in her direction—she saw some shiver of recognition—and then dropped his head again. Colden looked at him. She wondered if they'd met before, but no, that was impossible. Her gaze flitted from one person to another. Something big had passed between them all, some sort of knowledge or story or experience, and she had no idea how to catch up to wherever they had been and wherever they had ended up. A breeze drifted by, bringing the smell of sweat from her shirt to her nose. Her face itched with dirt and salt. Her stomach growled. She was thirsty.

"I'm going to get a beer," she said. "Anyone else want one? Brayden, can I get you something?"

"I'll take one," Drew said.

No one else said anything. Colden felt slightly giddy. A little lightheaded.

"OK. Well, I'm also starving, so I'm going to order a pizza. Or two. Maybe three?"

At the word *pizza*, Brayden looked up. His dark brown, heavy-lidded eyes opened a bit. The suggestion of a smile played at his lips. Colden felt a sudden surge of joy. She almost laughed. She'd had miraculously found a secret key into the locked castle of this young man.

"Pizza, yeah?" she asked him.

Brayden nodded.

"Nothing quite like a pizza after a long stint in the woods, is there?" she said. "What's your favorite?"

She ticked off ingredients and watched Brayden nod or shake his head at each one. Then she went into the kitchen, opened the fridge, and bent over, pushing things aside so that she could get at the six-pack on the back of a shelf. When she straightened up and closed the door, Drew was standing there. He didn't say anything to her, but his face was full of feeling, and his arms were open. Colden couldn't tell if he was offering or asking for a hug. She'd never hugged him before. She put her drink on the counter and stepped into his embrace. He wrapped his arms around her shoulders, rested his cheek on the top of her head, and held her.

"Can we go somewhere, just the two of us?" he asked her, his voice a soft whisper. "Tomorrow. Pack a lunch, take a hike? Can you take me someplace, I don't know, someplace beautiful?"

"Yes, yes, of course," Colden said. "Tomorrow. We'll go tomorrow."

"There's so much I want to tell you," Drew said, not letting go. "There's so much I have to tell you."

TWENTY-SEVEN

Brayden was lying on the ground, staring up at the leaves swaying in the breeze that rustled the topmost branches. His backside was damp and cool, soaking up sensation from the earth, while his front was dry and warmed, as was the air around him. He heard a slight disturbance. He felt the vibration of footsteps. He didn't move. There was no reason to hide. It was undoubtedly that tall guy, Dix.

He'd come by twice before. Brayden liked him. Dix didn't ask anything of him. They sat and talked about fishing, trapping, and hunting. The woods. Best way to start a fire. The weather. He'd also brought him a stove with some fuel, some freeze-dried food, a couple of apples, a stack of granola bars, and packs of hot chocolate. All welcome things, delicious things. Dix had also brought him a bear ball, a little keg-size plastic container that was smooth all over so that a bear couldn't get into it and you had to open with a coin. It was a neat device. Easier than stringing things up in the tree all the time. It was useful to him, and for that, he was appreciative.

The footfalls got closer. Brayden sat up. He listened. There was something different about the approaching steps. He waited, staring at the gap in the rock wall where Dix had appeared last time. Ah, there he was, filling the narrow space. Brayden used to have to squeeze through it sideways when he first found this hideaway. Now, he was so thin that, like Dix, he could step right through. He did. And there was another man right behind him. At first, Brayden thought it was a mistake, some trick of the light. No, definitely another man. Shorter, darker, but clearly there with Dix. Brayden scrambled to his feet, startled. They were both smiling at him.

"I brought a friend with me," Dix said. "I hope that's OK."

Brayden had no idea what to do. He struggled between fear, discomfort, a desire to flee, and a competing desire to be polite to his new guest. There was nowhere to go, in any case. He was in an oversize rock bowl with high walls, and the two visitors were standing in front of his only escape route.

Dix and the other man stepped forward and lowered themselves to the ground. Brayden followed suit. He picked up a stick and poked at a soft spot on a log. The dark-haired man cleared his throat a few times.

"This is a wonderful spot you've got here," he eventually said. Then, "My name is Drew, by the way. I'm really glad to meet you."

Brayden nodded, unsure what to say, how to carry on a conversation with a stranger. It had been easy with Dix. Brayden had remembered him from the class. He saw right away that he and Dix had things in common. This other guy was different. Good haircut. Cleaner, newer clothes. Things bought for the weekend, not for everyday work. He could not imagine why he was here. Or why he'd be with Dix. He seemed someone from a city. Someone from far away. This scared Brayden.

Dix reached into his pack. He released a large plastic bottle and handed it to Brayden.

"Lemonade," Dix said.

Like that was the most normal thing in the world, to be carrying a big bottle of lemonade in the backwoods of the Adirondacks when you're out there hiking with someone who looks like they belong on a television show.

But Brayden loved lemonade. Dix must have known how good it would taste after all these months of nothing but boiled water. Brayden clutched the bottle, unscrewed the cap, and swallowed deeply. He couldn't help but smile. The other men laughed. Brayden did, too. He couldn't remember the last time he laughed. His cheeks ached with the unfamiliar effort. Conversation came easier after that.

Dix asked him a few things about the food, how the bear ball was working, if his tips for improving the fishing pole he rigged up had worked. The man named Drew asked him where he learned the skills he'd needed to make it out here. Brayden shrugged. His dad, he mumbled. Boy Scouts. Camp. Reading. Dix told some stories of his own camp and scouting experiences. Drew said he grew up in a city. Camp was different for him. He didn't have scouts. He was Italian, raised Catholic, and went to church camp with robed priests instead of scruffy teenagers for counselors.

Brayden felt like they were talking about man stuff. It was comforting. He hadn't had these conversations with his father. He hadn't had many friends. This was nice, just sitting here with these two, chatting, with comfortable stints of silence in between. The conversation drifted from one topic to another, and it wasn't until later, much later, when he was reflecting back upon it, that he saw how Drew and Dix were slowly moving the discussion in a specific direction. They knew why they were here. They knew that Drew had something he wanted to tell him and why. Brayden thought Drew was simply talking about how different things had been for him, growing up down there in New Jersey, just across the Hudson River from New York City, a place Brayden had never been and knew only from television. A place totally different from up here, in the mountains, where Dix and Brayden had spent their lives.

Brayden had listened closely to Drew. He found he liked him, and the differences between them became interesting instead of frightening. He tried imagining the sidewalks and asphalt, the tall buildings right up against one another, the groups of Jews and Irish and Italians, the huge quantity of people living so close together, the somber rituals and grandeur of the high church.

Brayden never saw it coming. Even later, he couldn't figure out the exact moment when the conversation turned, when he realized why Drew was there, what Drew was trying to tell him about himself. About what they had in common.

TWENTY-EIGHT

The house was full the night that Brayden followed Dix and Drew out of the woods. They ate pizza, talking very little, and then Sally showed Brayden to the guest room. Sally and Dix went to bed soon after. Colden, knowing she and Drew would have the next day together, as he had requested, resisted asking questions. The promise of full disclosure kept her comfortable in the quiet. Drew collapsed onto the sofa, and Colden, instead of wandering down to the cottage, curled up on the narrow, slightly stale-smelling mattress in her childhood bedroom. She woke in the predawn gray, tiptoed through the house, nudged Drew, and after the briefest of preparations, they left for their hike before the others had arisen. They picked up coffee and egg sandwiches for breakfast at the local Stewarts, along with subs, drinks, chips, and chocolate chip cookies for lunch—she wanted to give him the full experience of being a local.

As she drove to one of her favorite spots for a peaceful day hike, there was little conversation and even less tension between them. Drew sat in the passenger seat, staring out the window, letting himself be led, apparently content to follow wherever Colden wanted to take him. The road she drove dipped and turned, a black ribbon twisting through the dense trees.

Colden parked her truck at an unmarked pull-off spot on the road. She and Drew stepped away from the clear, bright, squint-inducing sunshine of the early-September day and into the heavy shadows and damp air of the woods. Drew had to pause and bow his head a minute to let his eyes adjust. Colden waited for him, a few steps ahead. When he lifted his face, he stared and smiled at her, as if she were a bright beacon in a dark place. She smiled back, reflexively, and then turned away, flushed with some emotion she could not name.

They walked on, side by side when the trail allowed, him a few paces behind when it narrowed. It had rained in the night, and the low, wet spots left a layer of thick, dark mud on their boots. The rocks and roots rubbed raw by countless summer footsteps were slippery, the going slow and unhurried. The trail was relatively flat and the trees spaced wide enough apart that they could see filtered views of a small lake. They walked quietly for about an hour, crossing two shallow streams over rough plank bridges. Then Colden stopped. Drew caught up. She gestured not forward but instead to her right and stepped directly among the trees. She knew it would take Drew a moment to realize she had turned onto a narrow, almost invisible trail, and she was pleased that he might think she was taking him somewhere secret. She led the way up, up, up, along and above a stream, through young birches and beeches. The trail inclined steeply and was hemmed in by gray boulders as large as elephants, towering on either side of them. They climbed for about an hour, through a few sections that required them to scramble with their hands as well as feet; then the trail made a hard turn into a cluster of evergreens. Suddenly, they were out of the mud and in a grove with a soft blanket of dead needles under their feet.

Colden knew what was just ahead. She looked forward to seeing Drew's face when he saw what was already so familiar to her. She stepped through a break in the trees onto a flat boulder about ten feet across, at the edge of a rock cliff, with a view of the green, undulating valley and the lake they'd passed far below them. Drew came to her side. She watched his eyes widen and his face relax as he took in the scene.

"Wow," he said. Then, "Thank you."

Colden lowered her pack and herself to the ground. She unlaced her boots and removed them, along with her socks, which she then spread out on the rock to dry. Possessed by some mischievous spark, she surprised herself by pulling her shirt off, as well—this was something she often did when alone, but not with others around. Then she laid back in her sports bra and shorts, her head against her pack, closed her eyes, extended her arms, and sighed in the sunshine.

"Need to soak this up while we can," she said.

Drew followed her lead, freeing his feet from the confines of boots and socks and pulling his sweat-soaked shirt over his head. Colden felt him lie down beside her. She listened to the slowing of their breaths. She wanted to ask him what he had to tell her, what had happened out there that caused Brayden, who she hoped was still asleep in their guest room, to come in from the woods. But even more, she didn't want to ask him. She wanted him to tell her on his own. She waited. He waited. She felt the sweat dry on her skin, leaving behind a sticky, salty residue. A breeze flitted by. Goose bumps rose and subsided on her arms. Her stomach growled loudly. Drew giggled at the sound and sat up. Colden did as well. He handed her a water bottle. She took several long swallows and handed it back. Drew took a swig, then drew up his knees, wrapped them in his arms, and looked out over the sea of trees that spread all the way to the horizon.

"You're probably wondering what the hell happened out there with Brayden," he said.

"Little bit," Colden replied.

"It's complicated."

"Is it?"

"Well, no, not complicated. Actually, far too fucking common."

Colden felt her stomach tighten. She'd never heard this tone from him before.

"It's just really hard to talk about," he went on, more quietly.

The feeling of airy happiness that had surrounded Colden all day darkened, a cloud foretelling storms. She wondered what was coming. She wondered if she should touch him. Instead, she just mirrored his posture. They were like two gargoyles sitting sentinel on the rock.

"When you guys started talking about Brayden," Drew finally said, taking up his story, "I had some suspicions about what might have driven him out there. I know Sally and Dix; they don't like to speculate. They don't want to condemn anyone without evidence. But I think they, well, Sally at least, given the work she does, had similar thoughts to mine. There had to be abuse in that family. Not just physical abuse. That, that manifests—well, there are no rules, of course, in any of this—but there was something about his retreat, his running away, that made me think he'd been sexually abused."

Colden breathed shallowly. This was not the conversation she expected to have. In fact, this was no conversation because she had nothing to contribute. Drew clearly didn't need or want her to say anything; he wanted to tell her something, not just about Brayden, but about himself.

"Do you remember, I said that I thought I could help him?" Drew asked. "That I wanted him to know that I could help him?"

Colden nodded.

"It's not just because I'm a lawyer," he said. "It's because I've done a lot of work with sexual abuse victims."

"You mentioned that," Colden said cautiously. "Your pro bono work."

"Right," Drew said. "It's not something I talk about much. I should, more, well maybe, but anyway, I don't."

"It sounds like work you should be proud of."

"I am," Drew said unconvincingly. He swallowed. "Colden, I work specifically with people who survived abuse by priests."

"OK."

"We've brought lawsuits against the abusers but also against the church for the cover-ups. As bad as the abuse itself is, well, the deceit is a whole new injury."

"I can't imagine," she whispered.

Drew lifted his face and looked at her.

"I used to think of you as someone who had the perfect, comfy little life," he said. "I'm sorry about that."

Colden flinched. This thing again. She wondered why he had changed the subject. Perhaps just not ready to continue with his own story.

"It wasn't fair of me to do that to you. To make those assumptions," he said.

"I have had it pretty good," Colden said.

"Your dad told me a little bit about your mom."

That surprised Colden, this sudden introduction of Miranda into the conversation. That her father would discuss Miranda with Drew. Maybe Drew asked him. He was like that, questioning things, always questioning.

"That can't be easy," Drew said.

Colden thought for a moment.

"Honestly, Drew, and this is difficult to say, but it's true. I don't really know if it's hard. I never knew her. I don't know what I'm missing."

"You must feel some gap somewhere, some curiosity."

"I guess I do. I feel things and notice things about myself and wonder where they came from. There's a certain restlessness. Maybe frustration or dissatisfaction. I don't like it in myself very much, honestly. I guess I'm just starting to realize that I have three parents. Three very different parents."

Colden didn't want to talk about Miranda. But Drew seemed ready to make himself vulnerable. She would do the same.

"So yeah, there are moments where I wonder what if, what might have been. Especially as I get older. It's so hard to know, to imagine who we might be if we'd had different experiences."

"If we'd had different experiences," Drew echoed her words wistfully. "Don't I know that feeling."

A crow riding a fitful thermal up the cliff face appeared in front of them. It bounced a few times on the warm air, then flapped and flew off.

"How did you get involved in the work?" Colden asked. "Representing the abuse victims?"

"Survivors," he corrected her.

"Sorry. Survivors."

"Damaged. All damaged. But all survivors," he added.

Colden bobbed her head in agreement.

"I'm Italian, Colden."

She nodded once, unsure what he was driving at.

"I was raised Catholic. My mother went to mass every day, every damn day, and my family every Sunday," he went on.

Colden waited for him to connect the dots he was laying out for her. She could not.

"I went to Catholic school, Catholic camp, Catholic everything. I was a choir boy."

Colden looked at Drew and saw that his eyes were full of held-back feeling. He was waiting for her to figure out what he was driving at. She wasn't getting it. Maybe she didn't want to. Finally, he gave in.

"I represented them because I was one of them, Colden," Drew said.

Colden inhaled sharply and brought her hand to her mouth. Flashes of imagined scenes flitted at high speed through her mind: a young Drew, a gothic church, the scared face of a child, weighted down by a wizened, doughy old man in a white robe.

"I'm sorry, Colden," Drew said sadly.

"Sorry? No, no, no. Don't you be sorry," she insisted. "There's nothing for you to be sorry about.

"It's just that every time you share this with another person, you feel like you are bringing the pollution of your experience to their world. I don't want to do that. Especially since you inhabit such an amazing, pristine, beautiful place."

Colden was awed that he could be so generous in this moment. Here he was sharing the very worst moments of his life, and he was concerned about how it was impacting her.

"I can't begin to imagine how hard, how horrible . . ."

Drew gave her a pained smile.

"And now, you've not only recovered, but you are helping others do the same," she added.

Drew pressed his lips together.

"Honestly, Colden, I'm not recovered. Kinda like what they say about addiction; it's really more about being in recovery. For the rest of your life. You find ways to live with it. You can't get over it."

Colden wondered how one would learn to live with something so horrific. Then hurting, and yet helping. She thought about asking how he did it. Not now. Not yet. Leave the man alone. He'd done enough for one day.

"Thank you for telling me," Colden said. "I'm very touched that you shared all this with me. That you trusted me."

"It is hard," Drew said. "Sharing does make you reexperience it, to a degree. But it also seemed unfair to keep it from you. We're friends. Not telling you was getting in the way of being better friends."

Colden reached out to him, ran her fingers over his forearm, squeezed his hand. He did not respond.

"And then there's Brayden," Drew said.

"Did you tell him?" Colden asked. "Is that why he came in?"

"I made some suggestions. Talked around it a bit. I didn't want to make any presumptions. Especially on first meeting. I just wanted to open the door and see if he walked through. He did. He was ready. He didn't exactly say what had or had not happened to him. That wasn't necessary or expected. I could tell. The way he looked at me. He got it. He knew I got it."

"That was kind and generous and wise and amazing of you," Colden said.

"Not really. Those of us who've been through this kind of thing often recognize each other. Like dogs of the same breed. There's just something there."

Just like him to deflect a compliment, Colden thought. She used to be annoyed by what she saw as an irritating flippancy on his part; now, she recognized it as a touching self-effacement. Colden sensed Drew had relaxed a bit. The secret was out. He was unburdened before her. He had even unwrapped his arms from his knees and was leaning back on his hands, his legs outstretched in front of him. He seemed to be back in the present.

"So, what happens next?" Colden asked, thinking about Brayden.

"Next?" Drew asked, grinning, his expression restored to his other, less wounded self. "How about some lunch?"

They ate and talked of other, less consequential things. Colden told him about the habits and life cycles of beaver and moose. They compared notes on music and movies they liked. They sat quietly and looked at the view. They laid back on the sun-warmed rocks and let the breezes tickle their skin. After a couple of hours of resting, it was time to hike out. Drew had to return to Albany that evening. She drove back to the house, and they parted in the driveway with a new lightness and ease between them. A hug, a wave, and a smile.

The house was strangely quiet. She found Sally sitting in the living room, staring out the window. Colden sat next to her. Their hands found each other's. They stayed like that, not moving, each occupied with her own thoughts, as the sun dropped out of sight. Then Sally turned to Colden and told her about Brayden.

He'd slept in very late. Not unexpected, given the circumstances, Sally noted. When he arose, he'd seemed sheepish, confused, unsure of himself. Also not unexpected. Dix made him a big breakfast—eggs, bacon, fried potatoes. He dug in enthusiastically but only ate a portion of it. Of course, his body was not used to such rich food; his mouth craved what his stomach couldn't handle. Sally hadn't expected him to say much, but he did start talking. He seemed to want not only to unburden himself but also to explain himself to them. Like telling them his story was some sort of compensation for the food and shelter they were offering.

Brayden told them his father was "doing things he shouldn't have." He thought it would stop when he got older, when he grew bigger and taller than his dad. And it had. Then he realized that his father had started abusing his sister instead. He had moved from one kid to the other. Maybe he'd been abusing her all along. Brayden took his own abuse, but he couldn't accept that he'd not been able to stop what his father had done to his sister. He was mad that he hadn't even suspected it. Then, his sister ran away. His parents didn't do anything. Brayden, who had bottled up so much, got more mad. He argued with his father. His mother did nothing, as was usual for her. His father told him to shut up, that it was none of his business. Then he called his sister a "bad name." That's when Brayden lost it. He hit his father with a chair and fled.

He didn't think he'd killed the old man, but he was sure the old man would try to kill him if he found him. He stayed with friends after the fight, but no one wanted him in their house for long because they were afraid of his father. So, he ran to the only place he could. The woods.

"Do you know anything about his father?" Colden asked. "How he is now?"

"The reason I knew about Brayden, recognized him, is that after the father came out of the hospital, they did file missing-person reports for both kids. They met with police and social workers. The father came out of the hospital sort of a changed guy. Contrite. Apologetic. Didn't admit anything specific but said he'd been a bad father and wanted to make amends."

"Do you think the dad will bring assault charges? Or will Brayden want to prosecute for the abuse?"

"I don't think his dad will do that. He's a shrunken, diminished man these days. As for Brayden, who knows. He's still pretty shut down by it all."

"Do we have to tell anyone he's here?" Colden asked.

"Who's here?" Sally asked in mock stealth. "We don't have any house guests, do we?"

Colden smiled.

"Our only job right now is to keep Brayden feeling safe enough that he won't run again. And help him find his sister."

"All in a day's work for you," Colden said quietly, appreciatively.

"Unfortunately, yes," Sally concurred. "I keep hoping that someday I'll be fired for lack of clients, but sadly, that doesn't seem likely."

"How will you find out where his sister is?"

"Talk to cops, hospital admins, runaway outreach folks, other kids who have been in and out of the system. The usual."

"Oh, Sally. How do you keep this up day after day, year after year?" Colden whined.

As if in answer, the door opened, and Dix walked in. Colden watched a smile spread over Sally's face, saw her shoulders relax.

"You look like you've been rode hard and put up wet," Sally said as Dix lowered himself to a chair.

Sally disentangled herself from Colden, leaving her marooned on the sofa, and went to her husband. She set her petite form onto his lap, and he wrapped his long arms around her. They bent their foreheads together. Colden flushed at the intimacy that blossomed around them. She looked away.

"Hey, where's Brayden?" Sally asked Dix.

"He wanted to stay there. Seemed like a good idea."

"That is a great idea!" Sally replied enthusiastically.

"Stay where?" Colden asked.

Dix explained that he'd taken Brayden with him over to the farm. Brayden loved animals, especially dogs, but had never been allowed to have one. Or any pets at all. Dix said he'd been a natural with all the animals and clearly hadn't wanted to leave. He discussed it with the caretaker, Janet. She was a middle-aged woman who had had sons. One was in jail. Another had died of a drug overdose. Her ex-husband was who knows where. She was happy to have a gentle, polite, wounded young man around.

"Did he meet Daisy?" Colden asked.

Dix nodded.

"And?"

"It was love at first sight," Dix said. "She wouldn't leave his side."

TWENTY-NINE

It took Sally two and a half weeks. In the meantime, she didn't share anything she might have been discovering, and neither Colden nor Dix asked her questions. They knew she was not one to dribble information. She would wait until she had all relevant information collected and consolidated. In the meantime, everyone stayed busy and subdued. Brayden was at the farm. Janet told Dix that he was quiet, rarely talked or smiled, but was a hard, diligent worker. He cooked for himself, cleaned up, watched dog-training videos on the computer, was reading all the animal care books on the shelves, and had started teaching Daisy tricks. He'd asked if Daisy could stay with him in his room. Janet had, of course, said yes.

Two broken creatures, she'd called them, healing each other.

Finally, Sally called a meeting. Everyone, including Drew, gathered on the well-worn and fur-covered sofas in the room that had once been a den. The wood floors were covered in scratches from dog nails. Half-chewed rawhides, gnawed bones, and rope toys littered the floor. A couple of cats perched on the backs of chairs, leisurely grooming themselves. Dix and Janet stood, conferring about various animals and their health and behavior issues. Daisy was asleep at Brayden's side with her chin on his thigh. She lifted her head and thumped her tail when Colden entered the room.

What a joy it must be, Colden thought, *to be a creature uninterested in assigning blame or holding grudges.*

The animal-care discussion died down, and all eyes turned to Sally. She cleared her throat.

"OK," she said, looking at Brayden and only at Brayden. "Are you ready?"

He nodded.

"First off, I have not told anyone where you are. I have not spoken to your father or mother. I have gathered information that I believe to be reliable from other people who are familiar with what's going on. Of course, things can change. But this seems to be where the situation stands right now."

Brayden watched her speak, his face as blank as an empty cookie sheet.

"I asked you before if you wanted me to tell you this in private or with all of us around to support you, right?"

Brayden nodded.

"You still want us here?"

Again, he nodded.

"OK. You gave your old man quite a crack on the noggin. However, he has recovered, and it seems you may have knocked some sense into him. He does not want to press assault charges. Being in a coma for a few days, lying in the hospital, all that, I guess, made him reevaluate. He walks with a limp now but is basically OK. His wife stayed by him. Nursed him along. He has not confessed to anyone in law enforcement, of course, because that could send him to jail. However, he has become an ardent churchgoer. So hopefully, he's confessed to the big, bearded guy upstairs and got himself right with eternity. He's stopped drinking and goes to recovery meetings, too."

A few tears found their way out of Brayden's eyes and down his cheeks. Colden watched a droplet fall on Daisy's big, square head. She opened her eyes and began licking his face.

"You ready for more?" Sally asked him.

Brayden settled Daisy, wiped his cheeks with the back of his hand, and nodded.

"It seems the old man wants to see you. And your sister. He has no idea where you are, but he wants to make amends, I guess. We have no idea what that means. Maybe he just wants to apologize. Maybe he wants to try and rebuild the family. Who knows. The point is, it seems you don't have anything to fear from him. Or the law. And because you are eighteen, you don't have to do anything you don't want to."

Brayden methodically stroked Daisy's head.

"I am not in any way, shape, or form making any suggestion or recommendation about what you should do, Brayden. I'm just telling you what I learned. Do you understand that?"

He mumbled something. Sally asked him to repeat himself.

"I don't want his apology," he said. "It will just make him feel better and do nothing for me."

Drew blew air from his cheeks and nodded. Then he leaned forward to speak.

"Brayden, you also need to decide if you want to press charges against him. There are a couple of things to consider. One is, do you want to go through the legal process? I'm not going to lie—it takes a long time, is very complicated, and you'll have to testify, which means telling all the things that happened to you in a room full of strangers and to a lawyer who is going to try and trip you up and make it seem like you're lying. If we win, your dad will go to jail for a long time. However, you need to know that we may not win.

Or the judge may decide he's no danger anymore and let him off. It's up to you if you want him to face punishment for what he did."

Brayden mumbled something again. Everyone waited. He didn't repeat himself.

"I'm sorry, Brayden, what did you say?" Sally asked.

"He won't do it again," Brayden said, without lifting his head. "It was just me and my sister. He won't do it to anyone else. It was just because we were there. Because we weren't really his."

Everyone in the room stiffened as Brayden spoke. Then Sally let out a long-held breath. Dix rubbed his forehead. Colden fought back tears. Drew chewed the inside of his cheek. Janet stared off into the distance outside the window.

"I don't want revenge," Brayden said, his voice gaining strength. "I don't want punishment. I don't want to speak in court. I don't want to talk about this stuff. I don't want to see him. I don't want his apology. Maybe my sister would feel different. I don't know."

"Well," Sally said, drawing out the word. "Speaking of your sister . . ."

Brayden's head popped up, his eyes finally eager for news.

"She has been looking for you."

Tears began their slow travel down his face, again.

"Apparently, she did get to Canada. Not for a boyfriend. She was looking for a distant relative. Someone she found on social media. She's living there now. She gave one of her friend's contact information. I have that for you."

"Does my father know?"

Sally shook her head.

"I can call her? I can see her?"

Sally nodded.

"If I go to Canada, can I come back? I mean, do I have to live there, too?"

"Only if you want to," Sally said.

"You can stay here as long as you want," Dix said.

"I like it here," Brayden whispered.

"We like having you here," Dix said.

"We sure do," Janet said. "And so do the animals."

Brayden's eyes got soft even as the muscles in his face tightened. Colden saw his lip begin to quiver. She noticed that his fingers, where they rested on the dog, were trembling. Daisy began to lick his hands.

"I like it here," he said again, fear rising into his voice.

"She can come here," Sally assured him. "You don't have to leave here. Not until you are ready. We'll have her come right here. She'll visit you here."

Brayden nodded, slowly. Daisy stared up at him.

"OK," he whispered. "I just . . . I don't want to go outside the fence. I like the fence. The gate. I just don't want to have to go outside the gate."

Janet sniffed and wiped her nose on a crumpled tissue she pulled from her sleeve.

"You won't," Sally assured him. "You stay right here, right inside the fence."

Dix stood. Sally, Colden, and Drew did, too. They all tiptoed out of the room. Sally wrote a phone number and a name on a piece of paper and left it under a magnet on the refrigerator, alongside several pictures of smiling people squatting next to newly adopted pets. She and Dix looked at each other significantly, he wrapped an arm around her shoulder, and they left together. Colden motioned to Drew, and he followed her outdoors. She wandered over to one of the pastures and leaned against the fencing.

"That poor kid," Colden said. "He's in shell shock."

"He'll recover," Drew said. "We'll get him some therapy when he's ready. There are new techniques they're using to effectively address trauma. He's bruised but not broken."

A horse limped over to them. Colden plucked some strands of long grass and held them out. The horse's thick lips tickled her fingers, and his bittersweet smell wafted to her nose.

"So, tell me about this place," Drew said. "I think your dad said something about it once belonging to your mother's family?"

Where to begin? Colden wondered, silently. *So much to say.*

"Yes, it was my mother's family's summer home," she confirmed.

Then she kept talking, and talking, and talking. Colden had never told this story to anyone, and until she did, she hadn't realized how much she actually knew, how many details she had accumulated over the years. She'd thought that her sparse knowledge added up to no more than a rough sketch. And yet, as she spoke, she created a full picture for Drew about Miranda's life as a restless and directionless young woman after college: the death of her brother and his friend in a car accident after drinking at a concert; her father's death in a thunderstorm when he insisted on standing beneath a groaning tree, and a huge branch split off and killed him instantly; her mother's slow decline into depression and alcoholism and the series of strokes that disabled and eventually killed her.

Colden told Drew how Dix and Miranda's romance had started and ended. She described Darius, the preppy boy turned self-styled, back-to-nature guru who enticed lost women to his commune in a beat-up farmhouse in a damp, overgrown, godforsaken hollow, which was once owned by Sally's grandmother. She told him how Miranda was, unknown to Dix, pregnant; how she tried to hide her condition from Dix; and how, when he found out, he'd assumed Darius was the father. How Miranda had undergone some strange cleansing ritual that involved lots of cold water, outdoors, in the middle of winter, and gone into premature labor and died a few days after giving birth to Colden. Then, the final chapter, when Sally found Dix and helped him get custody.

It felt good to tell it. All of it. It felt like she was telling herself, even more than Drew, the whole story. They stood in the silence left behind when she stopped talking. She listened to the horse's teeth grinding up grass.

"Wow," Drew eventually whispered. "That's some, um, origin story."

"I've never talked about it much before. Didn't think it mattered. I have Dix and Sally. I didn't think I even needed to know about all that other stuff."

"Is the commune, the Source, place still there?" Drew asked.

"I guess so. I mean, the commune is closed. He was sent back to Jersey or Connecticut, I guess, to his parents and his life. I think he eventually went to law school. Made a mint on Wall Street. Ran for office as some hard-core right-winger all reformed from his previously errant ways."

"Of course," Drew said.

"But the old farmstead is still there. Sally never sold it. Haunted. Cursed. Who'd buy it? They left it to rot back into the ground, I guess. So many bad memories. Once in a while, she gets a call from the cops when they have to run off squatters."

"You ever been out there? Ever gone looking for ghosts?"

Colden shook her head. Drew looked at her, incredulous.

It did seem strange, all of a sudden, that she'd never been. It was only a few miles away. She'd driven past it, seen the rusted gate and listing mailbox. She had never felt compelled to turn up the drive and make her way past the copious "No Trespassing" signs, which were the only part of the property Dix maintained, and that was simply to protect against liability.

"Yeah, never wanted to go, I guess. Didn't seem important to me. Didn't want to bring up painful memories for my parents."

"Do you think they'd really care?"

Colden thought for a minute.

"No, they'd probably be happy. Well, not happy, but relieved. I think they find my lack of curiosity about my birth mother a little weird."

"Well, we have to go," Drew said. "I'll come with you. I'll hold your hand."

Colden stiffened. This was not on her agenda. For today or any day.

"How about now?" Drew asked.

"Now? Like now, now?" Colden asked, alarmed.

"It's a beautiful day. I have nowhere I need to be. Do you?"

Colden was swamped with dread and foreboding. Drew was asking her to go to a graveyard. More than that, to a battlefield for a conflict she had somehow caused, yet not participated in. All the combatants were injured, dispersed, or dead, and she hadn't gotten so much as a scratch. That's what she'd always thought, anyway. The war had ended just as she arrived. She'd seemed immune to its ill effects. She was only now starting to consider the idea that there were likely latent scars within her—small, internal, invisible. And yet.

"I don't know," she murmured.

The donkey in the next pasture brayed as if to protest her cowardice.

"My apologies," Drew relented. "I'm being too aggressive on this. Not my business to push you."

Colden felt a surge of disappointment that he'd given up. Which made her realize that she did want to go. She'd always wanted to go. She just didn't want to go alone, and she didn't want to ask either of her parents to take her. Drew was here. He understood what it was to return to the scene of a crime. He'd offered his hand. She reached forward and took it.

"No, you're right," she said. "I want to go. I've just been too scared. If you're game, if you're sure, let's go. Let's go looking for ghosts."

The day was perversely lovely.

Nature was accustomed to trauma, Colden thought.

Crisp sunshine and cool breezes flowed in through the open truck windows as she and Drew wended their way down increasingly narrow roads. Trees were dressed in the hot colors that foretold the coming cold season. Myth and memory combined to lead Colden directly to the driveway that took her to the house where she was born. The gate, askew on broken hinges, was almost completely hidden by undernourished and stunted scrub. Drew got out of the truck and yanked the recalcitrant metal contraption open. He got back in, slammed the door, and looked at her.

"Ready?"

She nodded, took a deep breath, and drove slowly up the weed-choked gravel until it petered out in front of a small farmhouse, brown from age and long-peeled paint, tilting severely to one side like an elderly person in need of a cane. They sat in the idling vehicle, unwilling to leave the confines of the truck, not ready to commit to the experience. A small movement caught Colden's eye—the tip of a dark tail disappeared under the listing front porch. She swiveled her head to look around. The barn ridge and walls were still square, but the half-open door was askew on decayed rollers. A mold-and-moss-covered trailer, surrounded by several insistent maple and birch saplings, stood off to the side, seemingly being reabsorbed by nature. A muddy patch of ground held the skeleton of several hoop houses. A rusted children's bicycle was abandoned in the muck. Drew's face came into view, full of concern and sadness.

"Do you want to get out?" he asked.

"Yes," Colden said quietly. "No."

A faded scrap of yellow police tape flapped and waved at them from one of the porch posts, a dubious invitation. It was the type of thing her father would normally have come out and cleaned up.

But not here. Not this place. The whole place was one large, sad memento mori to her mother.

Colden turned the key, and the truck quieted. She opened her door, and Drew followed, both stepping softly, as if they were entering a room where a person slept. They left the doors open so as not to disturb the quiet. Or maybe in case they felt the need for a quick escape. Colden approached the barn first and peered into the dim doorway. The smells she was expecting, the treacle of grain and the sting of fuels, the tang of manure and the sweetness of hay, were absent, chased away by many seasons of harsh weather and long disuse. All she saw were dusty cobwebs and broken machinery. She looked toward the trailer. Its steps were now a pile of old lumber, fallen in on themselves in a heap. A sheet, once put up as a curtain, the faded images of some childhood cartoon characters still barely visible, blew slowly in and out of a window, its trailing edge tattered and torn by the sharp edges of the remaining shards of glass. Colden took a few tentative steps toward the farmhouse.

"Careful," Drew said, pointing his chin at the cupped and popped stair treads.

She stopped at the foot of the steps. The dim interior, the bright sunshine, and the web-covered glass made it impossible to see through the windows. She noticed a dark, spreading stain on the porch floorboards, as if someone had spilled a pot of something murky and viscous.

A disturbing memory, long buried, came back to her. Something she was reminded of almost every day, yet the connection between the present and the past had been severed somehow.

"What?" Drew asked. "What is it?"

How did he know that something new, something more, was wrong with her? She was touched by his attention, his sensitivity.

"My dad. His bad arm," Colden said. "You've noticed the stiffness, no doubt. It's subtle, but it's there."

Drew nodded.

"It's an old injury. Somehow, I see it every day and still have forgotten, or don't want to think about, the cause. Honestly, I'm not even sure how I know this story. I can't remember if Sally told me or my dad told me."

Colden let herself ramble. It was a strange sensation; she always tried for precision in communication, the scientist in her intolerant of vagaries and digressions. But it was also a relief.

"Anyway. That guy. The guru guy. No one pressed any charges. No one had the stomach for a legal battle, and it wasn't clear what exactly they could charge him with, there being no evidence of wrongdoing, no one who would say anything, who would testify against him. Him having rich parents. They'd just say Miranda died soon after childbirth. So, he leaves. Everyone leaves. The place reverts to Sally. She and my dad come out here to check on things. I was just a baby. In foster care. Strange to say that. I forget I was in foster care at all. Me? Foster care? Anyway, turns out the guru guy wasn't gone. He came out of the house. Dad and Sally tried to talk to him, but he was ranting and raving. And then he pulled out a gun."

"On your dad?" Drew asked, incredulous. "He shot your father?"

"No, no. Not that. Not on my dad," Colden insisted. "On himself. He was going to kill himself. He pointed the gun at himself. My dad tried to stop him. Ran and tackled him. The bullet hit his arm instead."

Drew seemed stunned into silence.

"That stain there," Colden said. "I think . . . I think . . . Well, it must be. My father's blood. This is where it all happened."

"Your dad saved the life of the man who basically killed your mother."

"I've never thought about it like that, but yes. I guess that's true."

"And got wounded in the process."

"Another wound, I guess. A physical one. The others were emotional."

Drew whistled low and soft through his teeth.

"Well, at least he has you," he said. "That's pretty major compensation."

"Sometimes I'm not so sure about that," Colden countered. "Sometimes I think I'm a reminder of the worst part of his life."

Drew shook his head.

"You're a great thing to come from a bad thing. That's rare and wonderful."

A breeze gusted by, twisting something invisible until it caught the light and Colden's attention. A wisp, a spiderweb. No, it was several strands of hair, twisted over and over by the winds onto the porch support. She reached up and rubbed the strands between her fingers. So familiar in color and texture. She knew hair took a long time to decompose. Here, under the porch overhang, protected from the weather, it could easily last twenty-five years. More. Colden thought of curls of baby hair kept in lockets for generations.

She remembered her father telling her that the worst thing Miranda had done to him was cut her hair off. Colden knew that this was her mother's hair. She recognized it at a primal level. Maybe this is where the cutting off happened. Maybe the hair got out here some other way. She thought of the many strands that had undoubtedly been taken away by birds and woven into nests over these past years.

Her mother's hair, nurturing baby birds. It was a small, comforting raft of a thought in this turbulent sea of sadness.

Colden tugged on the hair, releasing a few pieces and watching them float away on the wind. She pulled at a few more, twisted them together, and wrapped them around one of her fingers. She'd find a locket. Or at least an envelope. It wasn't much. But it was something. It completed something.

She felt a clutch of emotions shake free and drift away on the breeze, just as the strands of hair had done.

"I had no idea it, all of this . . . would be so . . ." She searched for the right word. "Pathetic."

"Yeah," Drew concurred. "But maybe it wasn't so bad back then."

"I think it was pretty horrible even then. Sally had been trying to sell it for years. He was her only option. My dad told me they were supposed to be taking care of runaways. Who'd want to run away to here?"

They both looked around. They both knew as forlorn as this place was, it was still better than what many endured at home.

"What did she see out here?" Colden asked.

"Hope?" Drew suggested.

"Hard to believe someone would give up my dad, my home, for this."

"I guess, for some people, having it all is a burden, not a gift," Drew mused. "They need to go find a mess to clean up to give their life purpose."

"Nature is slowly cleaning up this mess," Colden said. "We so often think she needs our help. Ha. Hardly. She just needs us to leave her alone."

Colden lifted her head. The house was in a damp bowl of a valley. Steep hills rose up around them. The maples flared red, the birches yellow, the evergreens a dark counterpoint. A raven flapped overhead. Every living thing in these stark and weather-beaten mountains eked out its own life. In their search for survival, creatures often raised, more often lost, and sometimes abandoned babies. Siblings fought and pushed their brothers and sisters out of the nest to die slowly and painfully, before becoming food for insects and other minuscule creatures. Animals hurt each other. They didn't mean to; they were just trying to get by in the best way they could. There was little meaning and even less fault in most of it.

Acts of selflessness were unusual and fragile, yet they did hap-pen. Humpback whales were known to save other species from orca attacks. In turn, orcas were known to help drowning dogs get back to shore. Animals took in orphans. They cared for the sick members of their family or troupe. This commonness of evil and rarity of goodness was not a cause for despair—Colden felt this with a sudden shiver of awareness. It was simply a reason to seek out and nurture those better, kinder qualities in the self and others. For both the self and others. It was all so messy, inefficient, brutal, gorgeous, and glorious. So massively mysterious. Colden realized for the first time in her life and in all her years of scientific inquiry that she could seek to understand it, without solving it.

She turned and looked at Drew. He met her eyes and waited for whatever it was she was about to say.

"Drew."

"Yes?"

"Stay with me tonight."

His face tightened, and he glanced away.

"Colden," he said cautiously, facing her again. "Sometimes. Certain things." He paused and then went on in a rush. "Colden. You're a beautiful, smart, sexy woman. But for me, sexually, I mean, well, things can be difficult. Sometimes impossible."

He is so brave, Colden thought.

"I'm not asking for any of that," she said. "I'm just asking you to stay with me."

Drew looked at her carefully, cautiously. She responded silently, by creating a picture in her mind of them both lying atop the sheets, huddled under a blanket, fully clothed, curled in on each other like puppies, foreheads touching, legs entwined, holding hands, eyes closed, his long, dark eyelashes resting against the high bones of his cheeks.

"I've wanted that for a long time," Drew finally said, his voice a whisper. "To stay. With you."

Colden released a breath it seemed she'd been holding on to for years.

THIRTY

Brayden didn't understand why these people were all being so nice to him. He simply followed the crumbs of kindness they dropped.

He had spent the bulk of his years storing emotions, as his life had no room or space for the luxury of feelings. He was not able or ready to feel "good," but he was no longer feeling quite so "bad." The boxes of painful memories and experiences were still there, the contents would need to be sorted out someday, but no one was adding to them. The tape that sealed them shut was holding.

His sentiments did flow freely for the three-legged dog, Daisy. She reminded him of the dog he'd seen that day in the woods with Colden. But of course, he reminded himself, that dog had not been injured. Daisy gave him his first experience of abundant, amusing, unconditional love. Of course, he loved his sister, but love in a war zone is both desperate and thwarted by the constant threat of danger and harm. Daisy was an exuberant, happy creature, her face filled with straightforward joy at his presence and a constant readiness to connect. He was sad for the loss of her leg. No one would tell him what had happened, just that it had been an accident. Daisy didn't seem to care or miss her leg, so he wouldn't, either.

Every day, he stared at the piece of paper Sally had left for him on the refrigerator. It took three before he was ready to close the door to the study, pick up the phone, and dial the numbers. Silent tears slipped from his eyes when he heard her voice. She said hello several times before he was able to respond. There were no exclamations of joy at reuniting, just the quiet relief of finding something important, familiar, cherished, and long lost.

She told him how extensive hunting on social media had led her to a distant relative. Yes, they were orphans, but their mother had people up in Canada. There were aunts and uncles and some cousins who had watched their birth mother fall apart to the rot of drugs and addiction and then follow their father south into the United States, where they'd lost track of her. Belinda assured him they were happy to have her among them. They were not wealthy, like their adoptive parents; they worked in factories and cafeterias, had at-home day cares, and fixed cars out back. They worked with their hands and on their feet. They were really, really nice, she said.

They wished to meet him, this couple she was living with, this distant aunt and uncle who had opened their home to her. There was an extra bed in her room. She told him she had found out that they had Native blood. Enough to get some benefits. College was a lot less expensive, much more accessible. She was getting counseling. He could, too.

"Does he know?" Brayden eventually asked. "Did you tell them where you are?"

"I wrote them not too long ago," Belinda said. "Told them I was fine and that I wanted to contact you. I gave them a PO box, nothing else. I didn't want to write to them, but I wanted to find you. He sent a note saying he was sorry. That you'd run away and that they didn't know where you'd gone. He wrote over and over that he was sorry."

"Sorry," Brayden repeated, the word empty of everything but a hollow sound.

He'd said that to Brayden before. He'd said it every time he'd come into his room and again when he left. That's why Brayden would never give him the chance to say it to him again.

"Where have you been?" Belinda finally asked him.

"In the woods."

"This whole time?"

"Yeah. Until these people found me a few weeks ago."

"Where are you now?"

"They have an animal shelter. I'm here. There are dogs and cats. A couple of horses and a donkey. Lots of chickens and ducks and stuff."

"Are you OK?"

Brayden shrugged. Of course, Belinda couldn't see that. He didn't know what to say.

"Yeah," was all he could muster.

He realized that during those years with his adoptive father, he could neither fight nor take flight, so he had frozen. He'd learned in his recent reading that these were the only three options available to animals under attack. Then he did fight, he did flee, and over the months out there in the woods, he had started to thaw.

"Come up here, Brayden," Belinda said. "Come live with me, with us. Come, and we'll make our own home."

Another faint trail of crumbs had been laid out for him. This one led to his sister.

"OK," he said. "OK. I will. There's just one thing."

He asked; she told him to hang on, came back to the phone, and said yes.

THIRTY-ONE

It had been a long time since Colden had seen Gene. As she drove up to his house, fallen leaves swirling beneath her truck tires, she feared for his health, hoped he hadn't worsened. If something truly bad had happened to him, she would have heard. He had friends. He had people he supplied with "medicinal herb," as he called it. However, these people would likely not notice a change in his limp, swelling at his ankles, or weight loss in him or his dogs.

She parked the truck, got out, and slammed the door. That was the equivalent of ringing a doorbell, here. She held her breath in the almost-cold air and listened. Dogs were barking in both protection and anticipation. The door opened; a flurry of fur and legs emerged and rushed toward her. She squatted and let her hands run over ears and ribs and muzzles. The dogs' happiness seemed to wick upward, through her fingers, into her body. Then came the clump, clump of Gene's cane and footfalls. She looked up and saw, instantly, that he was healthy. At least as healthy as she'd ever seen him, if not even better than usual. His color was good, he'd put on weight, he was less stooped. Colden retrieved something from the passenger seat of her truck and then pushed carefully through the dogs.

"Been a while," Gene said.

"Yeah. Bit busy," Colden replied. Then added, "Sorry."

"What's that?"

He nodded his head toward what she was carrying.

"A pie."

"A pie? From your dad?"

"From me, actually. Well, both. He's been teaching me. But this one I made all myself. Apple. Spiced apple. Even the crust is from scratch."

She set it down on a small table on the porch. Gene settled into his rocker, smiling. It was his way of accepting the gift. She listened as the chair legs creaked back and forth. She lowered herself to the step.

"Where's your three-legged dog?" Gene asked her.

"She got adopted. Moved to Canada. Helping heal a young man who needs it. Great match."

"You still out chasing moose?"

"Yep."

"Learning anything?"

"Not much. Not as much as I'd like. Not yet, anyway."

"Nice to know some things manage to remain mysterious and refuse to be understood."

"Kind of like you, Gene."

"Find your gas can?"

"Nope, no luck that way, either."

"Come across any Sasquatch?"

"Actually, I did! Turned out to be a bit of a poser, though. Not the real deal."

The dogs were settling in the yard. The ground was dry, with a smattering of red, yellow, brown, and orange leaves decorating the desiccated grass, like leftover confetti.

"How about you?" Colden asked. "Find your thief?"

"Well, I didn't, but the sheriff did."

"Really?"

"Yup. The usual. Few meth heads cooking in some old deer camp. Stealing shit here and there."

"Huh. Surprised I didn't run into them out in the woods."

"Maybe you did. Maybe they took your gas," Gene said.

"Were they the ones who did the damage to the logging machinery out by your property line?"

Gene didn't answer right away. Colden looked up at him. She noticed for the first time that he was wearing a pair of almost invisible, rimless eyeglasses.

"You got new specs!"

Gene smiled widely now. Colden's eyes shot open in surprise.

"Wow. And new teeth, too!"

No wonder he looked so good. He was undoubtedly eating more and better.

"Where did all these new goodies come from?" Colden asked.

Again, Gene didn't answer. He was considering something.

"Get a sudden windfall?" she teased. "A fresh crop of your 'medicinal' plants?"

Gene stared out into the yard. Colden was waiting for him to tease her back. He looked strangely serious.

"You still hanging out with that guy, Drew?" Gene asked her, seemingly uncomfortable, changing the subject.

"Yeah," Colden answered, wary of this new line of questioning. "Why do you ask?"

"He's a good man, Colden," Gene said, sincere and grave. "A fair man."

Colden had that rush of discomfort again, the peevish heat of feeling left out. She'd almost forgotten that Gene and Drew had become buddies behind her back. That they had been involved in solving the mystery of the equipment vandalism and had kept the resolution from her. Her annoyance expanded, and as it did, it gathered up the disparate bits and pieces of this conversation and several prior ones. The evidence arranged itself in her mind. Then, suddenly, all the parts snapped together. It took her several minutes of silent contemplation to believe what had become very clear. Her irritation vanished. She started to laugh.

"Gene," she said, drawing out the word.

He would not meet her eyes.

"Gene, Gene, Gene. You old devil."

"What?"

"So. It was you. You are the vandal. You ornery old bastard. It was you Drew negotiated a settlement with?"

Gene said nothing. Which was confirmation.

"What was that all about, Gene?" Colden pressed.

"They were using my right-of-way," Gene said imperiously. "They were trespassing."

"You could have gone to jail," Colden scolded him.

"I was angry. I was stupid. I admit it." He shifted in his seat. "I might have had one too many. Or three too many."

"Who would have cared for your dogs if you went and got yourself in trouble?"

"You would have."

Colden sighed.

"Why didn't you tell me? When I was asking you about the situation?"

"Well, Colden, let's just say I didn't consider it my finest hour."

"No, I suppose not," she concurred. "But Gene, that's what friends and family are for. To be there for one another when we're not at our best."

"I maybe don't have as much experience of that as you do," he said quietly.

Colden nodded. She'd recently had plenty of proof of that.

"He's a good man, that guy, Drew," Gene continued. "Never met a lawyer like him. You know how I feel about lawyers."

"Yes, if Drew hadn't been accompanied by my dad when he came out here, I'm quite sure he would have run the risk of getting shot at."

"Truer words were never spoken," Gene said.

"Well, it looks like everyone got what they needed in the end," Colden said. "I'm glad the settlement got you new eyes and new chompers."

"Rarely works that way. But yes, indeed."

Colden turned her face toward the late-fall sun. Her nose was filled with the sharp smell of fresh decay. A chill breeze came up, carrying the portent of the season to come. There was work ahead of her. Back to Albany. Back into the woods. Back to studying moose and beaver. They were lining up the helicopter surveys again. They were going to use a different outfit for the piloting and capture this time. Maybe she'd try again with the coywolves. She felt sure they were out there. She just needed to keep at it. Keep putting herself in the way of whatever there was to discover.

Gene stopped his slow and methodical rocking. He cleared his throat.

"Colden, I don't often give advice."

"No, you don't."

"Not much to go on, here," he said. "Not anyone to give it to, really. And I'm not much of an example to follow."

"Maybe that is the best reason to give advice," she said.

"Well, I'm giving you some now."

"OK."

"Hold on to that guy. That Drew. He's a keeper."

Colden smiled. Not just at Gene, but at the day, at the revelation, at the work ahead. And at the man who was not there, who was waiting for her in Albany, where she was headed, whom she was going to see in just a few hours. She had another pie in the truck, the same kind, that she was bringing to him. They'd cut into it after dinner. He was cooking, traditional Italian, his grandmother's recipe, in his home, still all-plywood floors and dust, raw electric service, and heat in only some rooms but with a functional kitchen and a bedroom that he'd just upgraded from a bare mattress on the floor with a sleeping bag to a real bed with sheets and pillows. Where she would be spending this night, and the next, and the next. They would be returning to the mountains the following weekend. She was taking him on a real hike. A long one. They were going to climb Mount Colden, the long way, through Misery Mile and Avalanche Pass, past the False Summit. They'd camp at Lake Colden. He had asked her for this, for her to show him the place she was named for.

"Yes, Gene," Colden said. "Drew is a real keeper. That he is."

"And Colden?"

"Yes, Gene?"

"So are you."

The End

ACKNOWLEDGEMENTS

Thank you, Amazon Publishing, for offering writers so many different ways to get their work out into the world.

Thank you, Danielle and Meghan, for going above and beyond with sharing your assistance, talent, and encouragement.

And thank you, each and every reader, for spending your time with my words.

ABOUT THE AUTHOR

Laurel Saville is the author of a memoir about her mother's life, *Unraveling Anne*, and two novels, *Henry and Rachel* and *North of Here*, as well as many essays and short stories. She holds an MFA in Creative Writing and Literature from Bennington College.

www.LaurelSaville.com